Through the Green Valley

Barbara Gowdy

PIATKUS

To my husband, Mark Howell

Acknowledgements

Written with the financial assistance of the Explorations Program
of The Canada Council.

Author's photograph by Jim Ingram, Toronto

First published in Great Britain in 1988 by
Judy Piatkus (Publishers) Ltd of
5 Windmill Street, London W1

British Library Cataloguing in Publications Data

Gowdy, Barbara
  Through the green valley.
  I. Title
  813'.54(F)

  ISBN 0-86188-736-0

Phototypset in 11/12pt Compugraphic Times by
Action Typesetting, Gloucester
Printed and bound in Great Britain by
Billing & Sons, Worcester

What thou lovest well remains, the rest is dross
What thou lovest well shall not be left from thee
What thou lovest well is thy true heritage

Ezra Pound
The Pisan Cantos (81)

PROLOGUE

Pembrokeshire, Wales 1797

Michael's foot ached and there was a pulsing in his head as if his heart had gone up there. Light flickered behind his eyes. He heard things. Whispering, murmuring, sea gulls. He smelled apples. Now and then he smelled lavender. And tobacco. He smelled the sea.

Sometimes, when he smelled lavender, his head was lifted and cradled and his mouth was coaxed open. Liquid would pour down his throat, straight down, it felt like, uninterrupted by swallowing. It was a thick, warm, smooth liquid, and he imagined it was the milk that had spilled miraculously from his sister's breasts.

He was bathed sometimes. A moist soft cloth wiped him gently all over. He imagined then that clouds were colliding with his body. But one time a rough hand stroked him, quickly, gripping him here and there. That time he smelled tobacco.

Of course, he might have been dreaming everything. He dreamed of Etain constantly.

Chapter 1

Tyrone, Ireland 1783

He was five years old, coming back from town with his mother, whose name was Kathleen and who was beautiful and very tall, a head taller than his father. Kathleen had mauve-blue eyes the colour of butterwort and she had yellow waist-long hair, so it was easy to find her among the other mothers on a fair day for she hardly ever covered her head with a shawl.

Because it was a fine morning, they were taking the long way home, by way of Bridun Road. But nobody ever called the road that, just as nobody ever said 'Bridun Castle', and nobody called Bridun Castle's lord 'Lord Morrery'. People said, instead, 'The Big Road' and 'The Big House' and 'The Big Lord'. It was an ancient road, winding haphazardly, treacherous to horses where the ruts deepened into fissures. Michael stuck his bare feet down the fissures for the thrill of disturbing any fairies who might be using the holes as doorways. Kathleen kept to the grassy strip down the centre. In town she had sold her eggs and yarn, and now the basket that she had carried full on her head was slung on her back, tied with hay ropes around her shoulders. While she walked she knitted a grey stocking and sang a song about a lass that none could surpass from Kerry to Kildare. Her voice was high and wavery when she sang but low and even when she talked.

At the end of the song she said, 'Would it please you to have a new baby brother or sister?'

'No,' Michael said, since he had three sisters already, and there wasn't room for another brother on the floor behind the dresser, on the mattress that he shared with Neal.

1

Kathleen stopped and so did Michael. They had just turned a bend. A big whitethorn stuck out of the ditch on to the road, framing Kathleen in blossom as in a picture that Michael had once seen of a foreign lady. His mother thought that his saying 'No' was funny. He could tell by her eyes, even though her lips were pursing.

She didn't hear the horse. She said so afterwards in agony, over and over, as if not hearing the horse was the most grievous part. Michael heard. There was suddenly the sound of thunder beyond the bend, and then the belly of a rearing horse between her and the blossoms, and above her the horse's hoofs pawing the air. He cried, 'Mama!'

She whirled around. The hoofs came down and kicked her in the stomach. She screamed and fell, and Michael screamed and fell, too, in terror.

The rider was half out of his saddle. 'Damnation!' he shouted in English. He had a long black braided whip in his right hand.

Kathleen crawled to Michael. The basket had been thrown over her head and it was like a giant's hat covering her. She dropped on top of him. Four times the rider whipped her and with each lashing she flinched but Michael could not tell if she screamed again or if all the screaming was his own.

When the horse galloped away she did not move. Michael pulled himself out from under her and crouched by her side, shaking her and calling to her. He thought that she was dead.

That night she gave birth to a basin full of blood. She never conceived again. It was surely the horse's kick that damaged her womb, yet Michael's father, Hugh, blamed the thrashing, which left a scar in the shape of a large crow's foot across her shoulders. Telling the story, he would say that The Big Lord had whipped the knack out of her, and people would sigh and say thank God that The Big Lord had not run her down altogether. Forgive and forget, they counselled. Even Kathleen counselled forgetting. What else was there to do? The Big Road belonged to the The Big Lord. He had the right to do whatever he pleased on it. And besides which, it was hardly the first time in the world that a big lord had whipped anyone.

Chapter 2

Wales

One day Michael awoke. He saw a young woman's face. Blue astonished eyes. She gasped and said words in a foreign language, then said in English, 'Can you hear me?'

He nodded.

'Do you know where you are?'

'Wales,' he said.

She smiled. 'That's right. At Pencaer. By Fishguard.' One of her arms was behind his neck to support his head. Her other arm went around him and she pressed his face into the rough cloth of her jacket. 'There is glad I am,' she said. 'We feared that your brain would be turned.'

She dropped her arm suddenly, clicking her tongue. 'Your poor head,' she said. 'And I am squeezing the life out of it.' She touched his temple. 'Is it hurting with you?'

'No.' His temple was throbbing but it didn't hurt.

'Your foot?' She leaned forward to touch his right ankle, but he didn't feel her fingers. A tightness was there, together with the ache, and he realized that he had a wound that had been bandaged.

'A bit of pain, not much,' he said, looking past her at a low wall and the sacks slumped against it. Onions were hanging in nets from the rafters. He must be in a loft.

'Well, good,' she said. She smiled. He thought of his sister, Rose — fair-haired, blue-eyed, plump. This same child's smile.

'What is your name?' the woman asked.

'Michael. Michael Malone.'

3

'Michael Malone,' she repeated slowly, raising the second syllables so that each name sounded like a question. And as if there were nothing further either of them needed to know, she commenced gently rocking him.

She had rocked him before, in his sleep. He had a memory of it. He had dreamed then that he was lulling in his cot on the *Vengeance,* untroubled, possessed of a secret knowledge that the invasion was just a joke.

No doubt he had dreamed that because for most of the legion the invasion really had been a kind of joke. During the landing one of the barrels of gunpowder rolled down the cliff and smashed, and the French laughed and then deliberately let a second barrel fall.

They laughed at this woman, the two grenadiers did. She was the woman that the grenadier with the warts went after. Michael didn't know the man's name, though he was in charge of him and the other grenadier. The three of them came here — this must be the same house — to get food and wagons, and the grenadier with warts covering every inch of his body except for his palms and the bottoms of his feet pushed her against a cupboard and lifted her skirt with his bayonet. She screamed and that caused both grenadiers to laugh and slap each other's backs.

'What happened?' Michael asked her now.

She stopped her rocking. 'To what, my little one?'

'To the Frenchmen.'

To the two grenadiers, he meant, but she answered, 'All herded up within the day,' and that sounded as if she were speaking of the entire force.

'All of them?' he asked, thinking it couldn't be.

'They got into the wine that everyone hereabouts had from a wreck, so they were dropping with drink.'

'But *all* of them captured within the day? All fourteen hundred?'

'All but for you. There was a sight, Rosser says. I did not go. I stayed with you. Everyone else for miles around did go to watch.'

'To watch the capture?' He tried to sit up, he was so flabbergasted.

She wouldn't let him. She pushed against his chest, lightly,

4

but that was enough to keep him down. 'No, no, the surrender,' she said. 'On Goodwick Sands. The French marching down the hill, beating drums. They laid all their muskets and arms on the sands, then they were taken to Haverfordwest, close by here. But the general and the three Irishmen, they were taken to Carmarthen, which is farther away. That is where you would have gone to: Carmarthen. You are Irish, am I right?'

'Aye,' Michael said in a breath. All at once he felt barely alive.

'Rosser said that you were. By your English, he could tell. He said that the Irish hate the English and go to France to join a brigade there.'

Michael closed his eyes.

'Duw,' she said. 'Too much talking.' Her arm slipped out from behind his neck and she lowered his head. The mattress rose as she stood. She pulled up the quilt and tucked it in at the sides, her hair brushing his face.

'Are you asleep?' she whispered.

He opened his eyes, too weak to answer.

'Only telling you that I will be down below if you need me for anything. I am putting the spoon on this stool by here, by your head. You bang the stool and I will hear you. You mustn't call out. Rosser said if you did wake I was to tell you this, not to call out. We are hiding you, see.'

Chapter 3

Ireland

The doctor who swabbed and bandaged Kathleen after her whipping, and who was with her when she miscarried, and who had the decency to take the basin to the dung heap and empty it there rather than fling the blood outside the cabin door where the pigs would have lapped it up, was a Protestant named Rennie. It was said of him that he had not seen a sober day in ten years — people said 'ten years' year after year — though he did not show the signs of being a hard drinker; his hands, for instance, did not shake threading a needle to stitch. Hugh said the reason for his reputation was that he let the Irish pay him in poteen and that he was the only doctor in the valley who would have anything to do with the Irish in the first place. Kathleen he tended for two bottles of poteen. He told her to keep to her bed for a week.

She kept to it for a night and a day. Hour after hour she heard Mary spinning in the big room, and finally she got up, shooed her daughter aside and sat at the wheel herself. Mary was a good spinster but Kathleen was better, and ten pounds of coarse flax had to be spun every week or there wouldn't be enough money on gale day to pay the rental. Then John Logan would take the cow and pig and evict the family. It happened to a neighbour. John Logan threw that family out and a day later another family moved in that had sons who earned men's wages and a mother who had two fat hens, ceaseless layers of eggs that brought in a steady stream of cash. So Kathleen got out of bed in spite of what Doctor Rennie ordered.

It was only a day or two later that Rose began collecting

her, steering clear of the dung heap,
ıids grew a little beyond the green sink
case he saw one of the baby's eyes there.
second eldest sister. There was Mary
k-haired like Michael, Rose who was
:d like Kathleen, and Judy who was
: than Michael and brown-haired like
,d like Grandfather Malone, who died
ars before. Just as the sisters' ages
did their heights: Mary the tallest, Rose
:, Judy exactly a head shorter again. To
:e fairy-tale sisters, not only because of
:ted in these precise steps but also because
ent they were from each other. Whereas
1 beautiful, the good sister, Rose was fat
ister suffering under a curse. Judy, the
ıin and mean. When Kathleen was vexed
1 call her Weasel.
the flower collecting as well, because Rose
rom heaven had commanded her the night
ıssoms for the house, so that the baby's soul
ty in a flowery scent, and to find a boy child
anu ₅.. lp in the work.

They picked wild thyme from the rocks, and honeysuckle
from along the roadside. In armfuls they brought the flowers
to the cabin. Nobody was inside. Kathleen and Mary were
washing the bloody bedclothes in the river and Hugh and Neal
were out somewhere together, off the property.

The biggest bouquet of honeysuckle Rose put in the pitcher
in the middle of the dresser. She laid bunches of thyme in the
potato pot and in the bowls and mugs, and placed blossoms
from both flowers around the feet of the stools. Judy and
Michael watched, Judy issuing instructions as to other spots
where the flowers should go. By the time Kathleen and Mary
came back the cabin looked as though all the flowers gathered
on May Eve had been brought to this one house. The smell was
as strong as a new-mown meadow but as sweet as the
honeysuckle itself after rain.

'The Lord preserve us,' Kathleen said at the threshold,
'what have you three been up to?'

7

'Are you mad at us?' Judy asked.

Kathleen stooped to enter. She gazed all around. Behind her Mary said, ''Tis like a dream.'

'Rose did it, Rose did it,' Judy said.

Rose was standing on the churn. She had been about to stick some honeysuckle in the thatch. ''Tis for the baby's soul,' she said.

Kathleen nodded slowly, as if she had heard about the angel's command. She knelt at the creel, took out a sod and put it on the embers. ''Tis lovely,' she said, but she wasn't looking at the place.

After that morning, at least once a week and sometimes daily, Rose brought in flowers for the pitcher and mugs. Hyacinths, lilies, bog violets, buttercups and daisies. Berries and rushes and sprays of wintergreen in the cold months. The beggars and travelling men who ate at the cabin would say, 'Ah, a wedding was here,' or 'Ah, a christening,' since the bouquets took over the entire top of the dresser. Rose would glow from those tributes for days. She thought that she was born to strew flowers, given her name.

Chapter 4

Wales

A rod of dusty light tipped against the window to Michael's right. The loft had two windows, that one, and one across from it, on the same wall that his bed stood against. Both windows had glass in them. At his home his father had gouged out a window, but he had cut a sheepskin to cover the hole. Glass would have been lavish.

Michael had to urinate. Without raising his head from the pillow he looked around the loft. He couldn't see a vessel. Apart from the sacks, which he thought must contain apples, and apart from the onions in nets and the stool and spoon, there were only some firkins and a pair of black boots, standing heels together. An orange cat sat beside the boots, washing itself.

There was a corner of the loft that Michael couldn't see, though. It was behind a curtain that hung along a rope from the middle of the wall behind him to the middle of the loft. At the end of the curtain was a hole in the floor. The stairway down. Michael suddenly knew that a bed and a table were on the other side of the curtain, and a basin on the table. Why he should know that he couldn't remember.

He began to sit up. But he scarcely had the strength to lift his head, and then the pulsing in his temple became hammering. He dropped back to the pillow.

When the hammering died down he touched the tender place. It was a low bump, sticky because of some ointment that had been smeared on it. Only if he pressed it did it hurt. But the continual pulsing and the hammering meant that the bump was just the top of the injury.

9

He wondered about his other injuries. His right ankle was the bandaged one. He started to point it, and the ache howled through his instep. What had happened there? The bump on his head, he recalled getting that. In fact, the sight of the musket butt swinging around, filling the place before his eyes, was his last conscious recollection. But he had no memory of having hurt his foot. The rest of him? He twisted and pointed and flexed his left foot. Shook that leg. He tapped his stomach and chest. He pushed up the sleeves of the flannel nightshirt he was wearing and examined his arms. No more cuts or marks. No other sore spots. So if he could get himself sitting, he should be able to stand on his good foot and hop to the curtain to get the basin.

He used his arms to pull himself up, gripping one side of the bedstead. His head nodded from the pounding in it. But once he was up the pounding softened. He waited a moment, touching his palm to the bump, feeling the heat and pulse. Pounding was going on down in the house as well. The woman was pounding something. Dough. He smelled bread.

The smell seemed to make his need worse. He threw off the quilt and started to slide his legs to the floor. His right ankle struck the bedstead. 'Jesus!' he said. He fell back on the mattress, kindled with pain.

He would have to summon the woman. He hated that, even though it must have been her who had been attending him all along, and done a lot more than simply hand him a vessel. Which was what he hated, the ministrations she had already performed, having to call them to her mind.

The orange cat swivelled an ear at the banging of the spoon. Below, the pounding stopped. Silence, then quick steps crossing to and fro, approaching, coming up the stairs.

Her face was alight, as if she had been hoping he would summon her. In one hand she held a basin with a cloth draped over it. In the other a flask of green glass. She had guessed. Blessed woman. He sank into the mattress.

She stood high over him, like a shadow thrown on a wall. She had to cock her head to keep it clear of the roof. He pointed the spoon at the stool. 'If you would be leaving it all here,' he said.

She used her foot to pull the stool midway down the side of

10

the bed and then she sat on it heavily. 'Oosh,' she said. She put the basin and flask in her lap and fanned herself with both hands. Her jacket was unbuttoned at the neck. No shift showed underneath. The skin there was pink and sparkly with sweat.

'There is warm it is up in here,' she said with a little laugh. 'Who would suppose it is not midsummer?' She leaned towards him. 'You are not so pale with you. You are feeling better, is it?'

'The flask is all I am needing now,' he said.

'So it would be, indeed, after the *cawl*. Now then.' She lifted his shirt and took hold of him between his legs. He gasped. He scissored his legs, hitting one ankle against the other, and gasped again from the pain of that.

'Now then, now then,' she said. She was smiling down at the flask and himself, awaiting the event. Never would he be able to do it.

But she began to hum, and somehow it was like a sign. His gut eased. He heard the flask filling. 'That's the way. Very good,' she praised.

When she was finished she dabbed him once with the cloth and pulled his shirt back down. 'Do you want this on you?' She patted the quilt.

He shook his head, hardly a movement at all for he was wary of starting up the pounding. She picked up the flask and basin. 'Leave that, if you would,' he murmured, looking at the basin.

'Do you think you can do it yourself?' she asked.

'I can.'

She put the basin on the stool. Then she stood there looking at him. Her eyes were blue and happy. Nothing in them except happiness. He could trust her.

Chapter 5

Ireland

On Michael's seventh birthday a pedlar happened to be staying with the family overnight. He gave Michael two new pencils. Michael sharpened them to deadly points and put them in his brass box, which had been bequeathed to him by Grandfather Malone. It contained all his treasure: a stone that was as round as a marble, a shard of blue-green glass, a patch of blue silk, a red feather, one half of a silver buckle, and a bit of delicate fur that he found on a rock and thought was a caterpillar until he showed it to the pedlar who said it was a lady's false eyelash.

Sometimes Michael would pretend to write. He would draw loops on the daub floor, actually just above the floor so as not to dull the pencil's point. One day, after witnessing him doing this, Hugh rode to the huckster's shop in town, bought twenty small sheets of paper and had Kathleen cut and sew the sheets together to make a little book. He presented it to Michael as if it were on a salver, holding it on his opened hands. It was time Michael's castles in the air landed on paper, he said.

Michael touched the cloth cover with the tips of his fingers. He asked, 'Should I draw in it?'

'Write in it,' Hugh said. 'Learn to write.'

Michael moved his fingers to feel the ridges of paper down the book's side. What he thought was that writing must be a thing you could learn in the doing, like walking and talking. You wrote lines and circles and one day you found yourself forming letters.

Hugh sat on his stool. He bent towards the fire and ignited a match for his pipe. The fire was only a crib resting on stones

12

then. A proper fireplace was years down the road. So there was no hob, and the best place to be was with your back to the door, out of the draught. That is where Hugh's and Kathleen's stools were, Kathleen's in front of her wheel. Michael and his brother and sisters sat round the fire on the ground. But Michael sat on his mother's stool now.

Hugh said, 'I have been thinking that you might make use of the green book.' He looked from Michael to Kathleen.

Since she already had the thread and needle handy from stitching the papers together, Kathleen was sewing a tear in Judy's petticoat while Judy was wearing it. 'If his hands are clean,' she said.

Hugh said to Michael, 'Did you hear that?'

'Make use of it for what?' Michael asked. It seemed that his father wanted to bestow books on him. He saw his arms being filled with books, although the green-covered book, an English book that Grandfather Malone had bought at a fair — for an unknown reason, since he hadn't known how to read — was the only other book in the house.

'Here is the plan,' Hugh said. 'Take the green book and copy out a letter at a time into this book here until you can draw the lot of them. When this book is full, I will consult with Father Lynn, and if he tells me that the letters are as fine and straight as any boy's in the parish, you may go to the hedge school after corn harvest.'

It was a miracle. Not one he had prayed for — it had never occurred to Michael to pray to go to school — but a miracle like the day he met The Big House cook on the River Road and she put a section of orange on his tongue, and he loved the taste as though he had always loved it, loved it more when the cook said that likely he was the only Irish boy to eat orange that day, if not that year, if not ever. His father's plan was such a miracle. Upon hearing it Michael was in an instant rapture to be a student, yet the rapture felt years old. Nobody he knew went to the hedge school, none of his friends, no member of his family had ever gone. In the valley there was only the one place where you could learn reading and writing if you were Irish, and it cost money.

Kathleen broke the thread with her teeth and came to her feet. 'This is news,' she said.

13

'The idea only struck me as you were sewing the book,' Hugh said.

'Neal is the oldest,' she said.

'Neal will be a farmer.'

Judy said, 'Dada, I want to go to the hedge school.'

'No, you don't,' Kathleen said.

'Well, I do so.'

Kathleen went to the dresser, opened the money jar and poured the coins on to the ledge. 'One pound six,' she announced.

'After harvest there will be enough.' Hugh gave Michael a nod not to worry.

Judy had picked up a sally rod from the bunch in the corner and was hitting the churn with it. 'I want to go to the hedge school,' she said.

'Counting chickens,' Kathleen warned Hugh.

Judy hit the churn harder. 'I want to go to the hedge school.' One of the dogs woke up and barked at her.

'For the love of heaven, girl,' Kathleen said, going to her and taking away the rod.

Judy ran to the door and outside. In the yard the hens clucked to be aroused.

Judy broke a straight branch off a blackthorn tree and stripped it of bark and twigs and, for all that the family could tell, used it to threaten her friends with. At night she kept it alongside the tester bed that she shared with Rose and Mary in one of the outshots, and there were orders to everyone not to touch it, as if anyone cared to.

During that time markings began to appear in the muddy places outside. Parallel lines a foot long, loops and crosses. 'Fairy writing,' Kathleen diagnosed. She had seen such writing before: it presaged mischief. She buried the butter in the bog so that the fairies couldn't steal it, after which she tied four of her best ribbons on the bush by the door. They were yellow with green velvet stripes down the middle. The fairies were partial to pretty ribbons, and they might take them and go away, forget about stealing the butter and committing worse transgressions.

It was the curate who noticed that the writing was really in

14

English. He was riding down the River Road one Saturday afternoon, and it seemed he glanced into the yard and saw the words "Rest" and "Oliver". The next day, on the chapel green, he asked Hugh what the message "Rest Oliver" meant precisely. Hugh only stared at the curate, as if staring through and beyond him, down the hills to the mystery in his yard.

At dinner Hugh peeled a potato in one long peel but returned it to the basket uneaten and looked at it appraisingly. 'Now then, Judy,' he said, 'what did you happen to be up to in the Protestant churchyard?'

'When?' Judy said, not raising her eyes to him.

'Yesterday. Neal and myself, we saw you there.'

'Oh, yesterday you mean.' Judy dabbed her potato with salt. 'I was playing a game.'

'A game, is it?' Hugh nodded. 'Then what was it you were up to when I came round the back of the byre the other morning and you were running round the side, and there on the ground between ourselves was a new batch of the letters?'

'I suppose I was running round the byre,' she answered, all innocence, meeting her father's eyes now. Michael marvelled at her, knowing she was in some kind of trouble, shivering for her, but she was like a creature too savage to apprehend its fate.

Kathleen perceived where Hugh was leading. 'No, man, how could she at all? Anyhow, haven't the ribbons all been taken off the bush?'

'Not by any fairy, I promise you that. You heard yourself Father Brady saying what the words were. English words. Oliver Rest. Now where would a body be going to find words like that? I'll tell you where. In the Protestant churchyard. *Oliver* Somebody-or-other, may he *rest* in peace.'

He told Judy to put her potato back in the basket. She obeyed, though with a grand gesture, letting it be understood that she was indulging him.

'Now,' he said. 'You will get the ribbons from wherever it is you hid them and you will return them to your mother.'

'I don't have them.'

'You will get the ribbons.' Each word distinct.

Judy deliberated. She twisted her mouth and took dirt out from between her toes. She glanced up at her father, sighed,

15

then stood. Her stick, which had been tucked in her petticoat, rolled across the floor. She went into the smaller outshot and they heard the bedding rustle. When she came out she was clutching the ribbons like seaweed. Rose crossed herself.

'Give them to your mother,' Hugh said.

Judy dropped the ribbons into Kathleen's lap. Kathleen didn't look at them. She looked at Judy, and before Judy could turn away she took ahold of her hands. '*Stealing*, Judy,' she said, as if Judy might grasp her sin by the sound of it.

'And lying. And frightening your mother with the letters,' Hugh said.

Judy pulled her hands free. ''Twas herself that said they were fairy letters,' she cried. 'I never said so.' Tears stood in her eyes. But there was no pitying her, since the tears were wrung out of rage. She backed against the wall. 'I learned the letters fine and straight. Father Brady read them. You have to send me to the hedge school.'

'Why did you not tell us that it was yourself?' Kathleen asked.

'Wasn't I about to? But then you said fairy writing, then . . .' Her breath snagged.

'Then your mother tied the ribbons on the bush, and since you knew no fairy was at work you were free to steal them,' Hugh finished. 'But you weren't using your head, were you, because you cannot be taking credit for the writing and then go stealing the ribbons at the same time.'

Judy pointed at Michael. A thin whiplash of an arm. 'Michael didn't even know that they were English words at all,' she cried. 'He has been writing in his book weeks and weeks and he didn't even know what kind of words they were.'

Michael yelled that their father had told him not to trouble himself with understanding. Judy cried that she was the clever one, she was the one that ought to be going to the school. Kathleen shouted, 'No shouting in the house.' Hugh ordered Judy back to the fire to finish her meal. Michael said that he could have understood the letters if he had a mind to. Judy said that she wouldn't eat, she would wither to a thread, then they'd be sorry, but Hugh got up, pulled her back over, held a potato at her mouth and made her bite into it, so she snatched it to eat it herself. She huddled at the grate like an intruder in the house.

She whispered in Michael's ear that one day he would be drowning in a bog hole, begging for her to give him her hand, and she would saunter on by.

Chapter 6

Wales

After the woman left with the flask, Michael dreamed that Etain was with him on the *Vengeance*, the two of them lying together on his cot, and he was kissing her up and down her arms and legs. He awoke thinking that they were still there because the loft was in gloom, as his berth on the frigate had always been in gloom. He even turned his head to look at her.

It was like those first mornings of waking up after Neal died. Opening his eyes, still half in a dream, then remembering, and then that awful, awful soreness in his heart, such a crippling hurt that for a while he had thought that he must have a real affliction there.

His head throbbed. He mustn't think. Everything was blasted. But thoughts flew at him, like pieces of glass. 'I have come to fight for the liberty, equality and fraternity of mankind.' That's what he said, in French, to the captain at Brest. The captain said, in English, 'Only a spy would speak such rubbish,' and imprisoned him in L'Hôpital des Invalides.

Chapter 7

Ireland

What would happen was something only wise men and fairies could know for certain beforehand. Michael realised that until he was wise, he would have to depend, as most of the world did, on signs and portents. These were not in themselves wholly trustworthy, however. You might see a swarm of winged ants in the evening, yet there would be no rain the next day. Michael knew that he had to heed every possible sign, he had to be vigilant.

On the day that he spoke to The Big Lord, there were plenty of signs that it would be an unlucky day, that it would be unsafe even to step outside the door let alone go to The Big House gates, but for some reason Michael didn't immediately take account of these signs, the most dire of which were hearing a cuckoo from inside the house, stepping on a cricket, and putting his shirt on inside out and backwards then changing it the right way round.

He went to The Big House with Rose, just tagging after her. She wanted to see if there were any daisies growing along the path against the limestone wall. But when they got there they found the daisies past their season. Rose pressed her forehead against the iron railings and said that she would give her heart's blood to see the flowers in The Big House garden. Then she said what a treat it would be if his lordship should suddenly appear, if he should walk across the lawns and they should get to his face and all the rest of him. So remote was the likelihood of this happening that although Michael was secretly terrified of The Big Lord, he did not feel any thrill of fear. Lord

Morrery was hardly ever in The Big House. He lived mostly in Dublin or in the big houses that he owned in other countries, and when he did come here it was always in the middle of the night, unannounced, and then he only stayed for a day or two.

Michael looked through the gates with Rose. Had he been by himself he would have climbed up on to the wall, but he couldn't do it with her there because she said it was against the law. Up on the wall you could see the entire lawn, which was as flat as a plate, and you could see the stables and forge and, in the distance, the glimmer of the lake. Since there were no statues blocking your view you could also see the house better. It was vast. It was made of rose-coloured brick and had rows and rows of windows. There was a poem that everybody knew, about an Irish chieftain whose stronghold had stood on the same site until the English pummelled it to dust; from a corner tower the chieftain and his soldiers held off the invaders for two days. Sometimes Michael would be sitting on the wall, looking at The Big House, and he would think of the poem and a lump would come to his throat because the chieftain had been white of whisker, great of girth and dark of eye, like Grandfather Malone. To comfort himself he would sing this song:

Time has overthrown, the wind has blown away
Alexander, Caesar, such great names as they.
See Troy and Tara where in grass they lie —
So even the very English yet might die.

Rose wanted to return home by the wall path instead of through the woods. She still hoped to come across late-flowering daisies. They had gone as far as the first curve in the path, where it departed from the wall, when she stopped. 'Horses,' she said, as he heard them too, on the other side of the wall. Strangely, he felt frightened despite the fact that there were comings and goings from The Big House all the time.

The gatekeeper opened the gates. Two men rode out and turned their horses towards Michael and Rose. 'Mr Logan,' Michael said, identifying the smaller rider. Mr Logan was The Big Lord's agent and also the middleman who held most of the north shore, which is where the Catholics lived. He was the only son of a Catholic who had turned heathen by becoming a Protestant, and he was a scourge.

'Is it The Big Lord himself?' Rose said, squeezing Michael's arm. The man on the larger horse was very tall and he was wearing a gentleman's riding hat. 'Merciful Virgin. Merciful Virgin,' Rose whispered.

Three years ago, when The Big Lord whipped their mother, Michael did not see his face. Yet he knew that face approaching him now. A long white face like a holy man's without a beard. 'Run!' Michael said. But Rose held on to him. She was agog. Michael yanked his arm but she was too strong, and the white face was coming nearer.

Rose dropped to one knee at the side of the path, pulling Michael down with her. The ground was red muck and grey pebbles. Michael said to himself that he and Rose would not be whipped if he did not blink, if he did not let the ground out of his sight for an instant.

The horses were directly in front of them. They were passing. Michael's eyes watered from not blinking. 'One moment, your lordship,' Mr Logan's voice said. The horses stopped.

'The father of these children is more than able to do the job,' Mr Logan said. 'Girl, where is your father?' His voice was huffy, as if their father were something of his.

Rose didn't answer.

'Speak to them in their language,' The Big Lord said. His voice was like bubbles, like when a pipe is sucked hard. Michael raised his eyes. He saw the greased boots and grey trousers and the tail of the riding coat. The frill of the shirt at the wrists. The gloved hands. He saw the whip, short and looped, not a whip at all but a crop. 'We have English, your lordship,' he said.

Never in his life would he understand why he said that, unless it was only because he and Rose did have English, plenty of the Irish did, and he felt that The Big Lord should know that. He looked into The Big Lord's face. The eyes were round, with heavy lids. The lids slowly shut and opened at Michael, and Michael was certain that remembrance of himself and his mother was there.

'Very well,' The Big Lord said. 'Answer Mr Logan.' He

21

shifted in his saddle. His eyes strayed to the woods.

'Well then, boy?' Mr Logan said. He had red hair and whiskers. There was a red spot on his cheek that was growing like a spill.

'Aye, sir?'

'Where is your father?'

'Cutting oats in Colonel Crosbie's big field.'

'Colonel Crosbie, is it? You go straight there and tell your father to be down by the river in front of your place in one hour flat and to wait there until his lordship and myself arrive. Do you understand?'

Michael nodded. The Big Lord started away.

Mr Logan kicked his horse. 'An hour flat,' he said to Michael.

Rose held him down until the clopping of the horses died altogether. 'I could not speak a word to save my soul,' she said, coming to her feet, wiping dust from her knees. 'I thought I'd been struck dead. He is so tall. Like a king, like one of them old gods.'

Michael ran from her. Into the woods. She called after him but he ran harder and her voice wore thin behind the cawing of the rooks. Rose had not lain under their mother's body and felt her breasts shaking with each stroke, and she had not had dreams of babies, like new-born mice, curled up inside the breasts, their hands at their mouths, dying with shudders.

For two hours Hugh waited at the foot of his property. He didn't wait alone. While Michael had been fetching him, Rose had been proclaiming to everyone she saw that The Big Lord himself was going to be visiting her father, so men who were not cutting corn — old men mostly — and women, children, dogs and pigs had ranged themselves along the road and on the carriage bridge. Some of the women had put cn shoes and stockings.

Everyone wondered what The Big Lord wanted. There was no rent owing on the property, it wasn't that. Hugh was distracted with worry that it concerned a goose he had given to John Logan a week ago. Logan was rich because he rented hundreds of acres on a long lease from The Big Lord and sublet those acres at high rentals, but you still had to give him presents of duty fowl and duty eggs from time to time, and even though the other men said it would be a cold day in hell the day that Logan ever parted with a fat goose, Hugh could not get it out of his head that Logan had in turn given the goose to The Big Lord and that the meat had been tough or wormy.

When the children on the bridge spotted the horses, they cried, 'He's coming!' but fell silent as the riders got nearer. The women made low curtsies, the men pulled off their hats and wigs. None of this was for Mr Logan, but he watched it all as if he had medals to hand out afterwards. He spoke for The Big Lord, in English so that The Big Lord would hear his blandishments. He said that the jewel of Tyrone, Bridun Castle, needed a new wall. The four-foot-high wall that ran from the northeast corner of the castle to the rear terraces was to be torn down and rebuilt with flat sides and capping stones. It was an important enough job that his most gracious lordship had set aside affairs of great moment to ensure that the best man to be had was engaged.

Logan looked at Hugh. Hugh looked back at him as if he hadn't understood a word. At last he said, 'Myself?'

'None of the masons is available,' Logan said. He said that he had told his lordship how Hugh had helped with the extension of the limestone wall and that his lordship had been mightily impressed.

Hugh frowned down at his hat, which he was twisting like a wet rag. He nodded.

'Tomorrow morning,' Logan said.

Hugh looked up. 'No, that is not possible.'

'Sure it is, Malone.' Logan's voice cosseted, but his eyes were full of threat.

'No, it is not,' Hugh said. 'I am bound to Colonel Crosbie and I am cutting for Mr Ingram after that. Then don't I have to cut my own corn that is drop ripe. In regard of all that I cannot start for a week anyhow.'

'Listen close, Malone,' Logan said, in Irish.

But The Big Lord spoke. 'It is one of those nuisances,' he said, blinking across the river. 'Lady Morrery is arriving in several days' time. With my son.'

The people in the crowd who could hear him, and who knew English, stirred. Lady Morrery had been to The Big House just twice since her marriage. The son, Master Arthur, had never been.

'My son's doctors have recommended the bracing air here,' Lord Morrery went on. 'And, of course, a tumbling-down wall would be an awful nuisance to Lady Morrery. Dangerous for the boy.'

Hugh ran his fingers through his hair. It stuck straight up and stayed there. He started nodding, and you knew he was nodding at his own thoughts. 'Sure I had better be getting on with the work right away in that case, your lordship,' he said.

Lord Morrery swept his crop at the children who had pressed close around Hugh. 'Perhaps several of your sons here will lend a helping hand,' he said. Then he pointed his crop at Mary, who stood out from the others because she was so tall. 'Your daughter?' he said.

'Thanks be to God, she is,' Hugh said.

'How old is she?'

'Twelve years, your lordship.'

'What is her name?'

'Mary.'

Lord Morrery flicked his reins and he and Logan trotted back down the road and over the bridge. His lordship sat in the saddle with his back so straight it might have been in a brace. You couldn't imagine that back ever bowing, against the rain, for instance, and it began to rain as soon as the horses were out of sight. A misty rain, not hard enough to pit the water, and on the mountains in the north the light was orange. It was from the south that the clouds came. Out of the woods, where his lordship and Logan were headed, smoky clouds rose and galloped over the south-shore meadows.

For the rest of the day it rained softly, starting and stopping. Hugh did not return to Colonel Crosbie's field. He and Kathleen and two of the old men who had waited for The Big Lord went inside the cabin and talked. Hugh and the men smoked their pipes, and Kathleen smoked hers, too, and knitted. In her own place she could never just sit, with her hands doing nothing. She had a saying about why not: "It is better to be putting knots in straw than to be idle."

One of the old men said that Logan was going to keep the entire wage for himself and call the job duty work.

24

'He cannot,' Hugh said. He didn't argue that Logan intended to profit. As his lordship's agent, Logan always endeavoured to employ his own tenants for Big House jobs. That way he could hold on to the wage against any rental owing, or, if there were no arrears, against any duty work owing. But Hugh said that he had done his duty work for the year, so Logan must be planning on keeping only part of the wage.

'So why wouldn't he want a man that owed him days and days or that had arrears, then he might be getting the entire wage?' Kathleen wondered.

'He has to use a man that can work with stone,' the second old man pointed out.

'He'll be keeping the entire wage for himself,' the first old man said again.

The second old man, who was kinder than the first, said, 'Ach, he never cheats a body outright. He is not a fool altogether, now.'

'Whatever the case,' Kathleen said, ''twas in the hands of providence from the start. Sure there is no refusing the job and The Big Lord requesting it himself.'

The first old man spit into the fire. 'And didn't Logan reckon that all out aforehand, by Jesus.'

Michael blamed himself. If he and Rose hadn't been at The Big House gates, Mr Logan might never have thought of using their father to build the wall, and then if he had only gone dumb, as Rose had, Mr Logan wouldn't have been able to order him to fetch his father from Colonel Crosbie's field. No one else blamed him, though. The next morning his father even told him that he was to be his helper, since Neal was to go on cutting corn, as he had been doing all week.

Neal was just thirteen, but he was sturdy and the very spit of Hugh, so people declared, and Colonel Crosbie had hired him imagining that he was years older. As for cutting their own corn, Kathleen said she was going to hire the Quinn twins, whom no big farmer had hired because they were idiots and prone to fits. Hugh said, not on your life, he would cut the oats himself, there'd be no harm in waiting. But Kathleen had her mind made up. She had a soft spot for the twins, there was no telling why, and besides, she wouldn't have to pay out money. The twins would take potatoes in October.

'I will speak to them when I get home,' she said resolutely. Then she and the girls left the house. That day they had a job across the river, binding the oats that had been down for several weeks.

On the way to The Big House, Hugh said that he supposed the idiots could do no real harm. 'Why is it that your mama ever has her will and her way over myself?' he asked.

'She is bigger than you are,' Michael said, and Hugh laughed and said that was it in a nutshell. 'Big woman, big heart,' he said. 'Long limbs, long life.'

When they got to the gates, he turned grave. Walking across the lawn that was springy, like a soft brush, going past the white lady statues, he didn't speak. Neither did the gardener who showed them to the wall, but the gardener had once been a monk and was still often occupied in silent prayer.

Hugh examined the wall up and down its long length, bending here and there to prod the stones. It was a disgrace, he said. You would have thought it was a ditch in a field. Sure enough it would have to be pulled down altogether and newly quarried stones would have to be secured.

During that day and the next he dislodged the stones. Michael's job was to help sort them into piles of like size and shape, except for the large boulders from the bottom, and these Hugh lined up a foot or so away from their original position. On the third day a carter delivered the new stones and the capping stones, and Hugh began the rebuilding. That was the day that Master Arthur came outside.

He and Lady Morrery had arrived in the middle of the previous night, two nights ahead of their anticipated arrival. This Michael and Hugh learned from a housemaid who brought them a drink of sweet milk at mid-morning.

'Will he be coming outside for the air this day?' Michael asked her.

'In such weather?' she said

It was cold and wet. Every once in a while the wind rose and lashed a tail of rain. The rocks slipped in Michael's hands. His job now was to load a little slipe with whatever stones his father wanted, haul them back over to the wall and unload them.

Hugh was working from both ends and from primary pillars in the middle. He would try this stone and that until he got a tight fit, then wedge the stone into place. The stones of one row had to be laid over the clefts in the row beneath to prevent cracks from snaking up the wall. One across two, two across one was the rule.

By noon the rain was falling hard. Hugh and Michael had their dinner — oat cakes and a jug of ale — under an elm. Both of them looked across the lawn at The Big House, at the streaming windows, for a sign of life. And so, what with their looking at the house and with the sizzle of the rain on the stones, they did not hear Master Arthur approaching from the stables. He was almost on top of them before they noticed him. So white and long was his face, so like his father's, that there was no mistaking who he was.

'Up,' Hugh said to Michael, and they jumped up and took off their hats.

Arthur was wearing a black cloak and a broad-brimmed hat tied under his chin. He walked with his head tilted towards his right shoulder. 'Good day,' he said.

'Good day, Master Arthur, God save you,' Hugh said.

The boy blinked slowly, the way his father blinked. The housemaid had said that he was eleven years old but he looked older. He was tall for his age and unearthly thin.

'God save the pair of you,' he said. He laughed. A twittering girl's laugh. 'What are your names?' he asked.

'I am Hugh Malone. This is my son, Michael.'

'Well, Hugh and Michael, I am here to help you.'

'Are you now?' Hugh said, slapping water out of his hat. ''Tis kind of yourself to offer, indeed it is. However, Michael is giving me all the help I am needing.'

Arthur went to the pile that had the biggest rocks, picked one up and staggered with it over to the wall. 'Where shall I drop this?' he gasped.

Hugh could not discourage him. It slowed work down to a crawl because Arthur overloaded the slipe and then it wouldn't budge. Or he loaded it badly and half of the rocks tumbled off before he got to the wall. He wouldn't let Michael help, not even to retrieve the stones that strewed behind.

'You take a rest and watch,' he ordered, racing back to pick up a fallen stone before Michael did.

Within a quarter of an hour he was panting and his face was so pale it looked blue. When he drew his hand across his forehead he left a smear of blood.

Hugh said, 'Sure you have done a grand job of it, Master Arthur. Why don't you take a rest now yourself and Michael will go on with it?'

'No,' Arthur gasped. 'I have to build up muscles. Is that how you got your muscles, Hugh, erecting walls?'

For another quarter of an hour or so he carried on. Then he suddenly slumped down on to his side on the soaking grass and closed his eyes.

'Dada, he's died!' Michael yelled in Irish as Hugh was running over, but he realized right after the words were out that he was wrong, for Arthur was breathing noisily, his mouth hanging open.

Hugh dropped on his knees next to him. 'Master Arthur,' he said. He sounded frightened. He touched the boy's shoulder with the tips of his fingers.

Arthur opened his eyes. 'I am just getting my second wind,' he said weakly.

'We are through for the day ourselves,' Hugh said. 'Why don't you go inside now?'

'Well, I think I shall, if you are quite through.' He came to his feet, pulling on Hugh's arm. He swayed on the spot for a moment, then settled his hat on his head and toddled towards The Big House.

In fact, they weren't through at all. They'd have gone on working until nightfall. But Hugh said that they couldn't keep at it now, so they went home. The next morning there was no sign of the boy. It was dry and mild the whole day and the building went speedily. The wall rose and stretched. Hugh kept casting fretful glances around the grounds but by mid-afternoon he grew easier and said, 'He has learned his lesson.'

He was there the following morning, waiting for them under the elm.

'Ah, Jesus,' Hugh muttered when he saw him.

Since it was another fine day, Arthur was not wearing his cape and hat. He had on yellow breeches, a yellow and blue waistcoat and shoes with silver buckles.

'God save you, Master Arthur,' Hugh said, taking off his hat.

Arthur tapped the tips of his fingers together. There were bandages around both of his hands. 'God save you,' he replied, then laughed as if that were a witticism.

'You are all decked out in your finery, I see,' Hugh said. 'Going off somewhere with your father, is it?'

Arthur blinked. 'No. Father has returned to Dublin. I am here to help you, Hugh.'

'Ach, now I don't think I can allow that,' Hugh said.

'Yes you can.' Arthur's mouth tightened primly. 'You must. My mother said that you must.' He went over to the slipe and picked up the rope. His eyes slid at Michael. 'This is mine,' his eyes said.

Incredibly, he was not nearly so bungling as before. He listened to Hugh attentively. He loaded the slipe properly, putting the largest rocks on the bottom and the smaller ones on top. He didn't lift the stones any higher than he had to. He didn't rush and get flustered. But after an hour or so he started to flag. His mouth opened into a weary little circle, and as he dragged the slipe from the stone piles, Hugh looked at him anxiously. When he halted with the slipe at the wall, Hugh nodded at Michael. 'Time for that lazybones on the grass there to do a hand's turn,' he said. He scooped up a stone to begin the unloading himself.

'I can do it,' Arthur said, pushing Hugh's leg.

'Sure you can,' Hugh said lustily, stepping back. 'And, by God, so can that lazybones there. Michael, get yourself over here.' Michael stood.

'No!' Arthur screamed. He ran over to the pile of capping stones and hoisted one up as far as his waist. Its beaked end was pointed downwards.

'Easy there,' Hugh said, taking a step.

'You see. I can even lift this fellow.' He laughed. 'You see, Hugh! I can!'

He couldn't. It slipped out of his hands. It dropped like a driven bore on to the flashing buckle of his left foot.

He threw himself on the ground. Michael and Hugh raced to him. Screaming, hugging his left knee, he rolled on to his back.

'You're all right,' Hugh said. 'Pipe down.'

Arthur went on screaming. Michael could see down his throat. Over the screams he heard a shout, and glanced

29

around. The coachman and the monk gardener were running across the lawn. The maidservant who had brought out the sweet milk was running from the rear of the house.

'What happened?' the coachman hollered. He had wild white hair and he looked terrified.

The woman sank on the grass beside Arthur. 'Ah, your poor wee knee,' she said, supposing it was his knee since he was hugging it and there was no blood on his foot. Arthur stopped screaming and started whimpering. More servants were hurrying over from The Big House and the outbuildings.

'He dropped a stone on his foot,' Hugh said.

'Christ Almighty,' the gardener said, horrified.

'Has he smashed it entirely?' the coachman asked.

'I don't know.' Hugh touched Arthur's right shoe. 'Master Arthur, might we be taking your shoe off for a look?'

'No!' Arthur screamed.

'Jesus Christ Almighty,' the gardener said.

'Sure we'll be leaving it on then, lad,' Hugh said. 'So then, what we'll do is, I'll carry you to your house and they'll fetch a doctor, is it?' He slipped his arms under Arthur's back. The maidservant reached for one of Arthur's hands, and his white fingers drooped lifelessly out of her plump brown ones.

Chapter 8

Wales

Dogs were barking. Down below, close by the house. A goose was honking madly. Somebody was coming. The woman's husband, Rosser, it would only be Rosser, Michael told himself. Yet his heart drummed.

A man shouted and instantly the dogs and even the goose were silent. The door of the house opened, shut. Two white cats flew into the loft and stopped just inside, twitching their tails. The woman spoke in Welsh. Then the man spoke. Then the woman again, rapidly, her voice cresting every few words. Michael heard his own name, and he let out his breath because it must be Rosser if the woman was giving him his name.

The man had a heavy scuffing tread. He was crossing the room, coming up the stairs. Light wobbled on the top planks of the stairwell. The two white cats dashed to opposite corners of the loft.

He was big, like his wife. He lowered his light to look at Michael's face. He had thick fingers. The hair showing under his hat, falling long over his forehead and the sides of his face, was white. Michael remembered him from the night that he and the grenadiers came here, remembered the oddity of white hair on a man so young.

'Michael Malone,' the man said, in a deep hollow voice.

'I am,' Michael said.

'I am Rosser Griffiths,' the man said in English. 'Olwen's brother.'

'Olwen? She is the woman . . .?'

'The girl below. My sister.' He stood straighter but still had

31

to stoop so as not to hit his head on a rafter. 'How are feeling in yourself?'

'Better, I think.'

'What age are you?'

'Nineteen. Rising nineteen.'

Rosser nodded.

'How long have I been here?'

'Eight days. This is the second of March.'

'The second of March,' Michael said. He could not feel the passage of any time.

'You saved Olwen,' Rosser said. 'From the Frenchman. The one with the mouldy skin.'

'With the warts,' Michael said. That man wouldn't leave her be. He ripped her skirt, rubbed himself on her. Michael kept pulling him off and finally he had to punch him. Then the musket butt swung around.

'You hit him, do you recall?' Rosser said. 'But the other one gave you a blow by here,' he pointed to his own temple,' and you fell. The first one, with the warts, stabbed you in the foot then. You never stirred. That scared them. They must have thought that the blow had killed you. So they fled.'

They disobeyed him, struck him, Michael recalled that. But leaving him to die ... this made him desolate, though it shouldn't have done. They weren't soldiers, he shouldn't think of them as soldiers of the French Republic. They were criminals, convicted murderers for all he knew. Almost the entire force — the *Légion Noire* — were criminals, released for the expedition from the jails of Rochefort, Nantes and Lorient. Michael had been released from the military hospital, and because he could speak English he was made a lieutenant.

Rosser touched the brim of his hat. 'They reported that you had drowned,' he said.

'Who did? The two men who fled?'

'Aye. They said that you got drunk and fell over the cliff and drowned. There was a search. The children are searching still. A boot was found and everyone said it belonged to you. It was sold as a souvenir in Fishguard.'

The girl moved about below, setting down crockery, chopping. Onions were cooking. 'So they are not searching for me alive, they are not searching the houses for me,' Michael said slowly, understanding that he was therefore safer, yet feeling so queer, awash, as if he really were drowning.

Rosser didn't reply. Above the rushlight his face looked diabolical. Michael thought, "I am at his mercy," and a tremor passed through him. 'Are they trying the other three Irishmen for high treason?' he asked.

'The newspaper says that they will. The French will be sent back to France. Traded for English prisoners over there.'

'They will hang, then, the Irishmen.'

'If they are found guilty.' Rosser touched the brim of his hat. It was like a gesture of greeting. 'You will stay with us,' he said. 'Until you are well or until hay harvest, whichever of the two shall come first.' There was no expression in his voice. He spoke as if he were reading aloud. He said that come hay harvest he would be hiring twenty reapers. Before then no one apart from his man and his man's mother would have cause to be near the house and no one at all would have cause to enter it. He lifted his candle to each window and warned Michael against getting out of bed, nevertheless. Tomorrow Olwen would cover the panes with sacking. But even then Michael must never go near them and he must never go downstairs.

'I cannot move my foot at all,' Michael said to reassure him.

'Olwen will be up with your supper,' Rosser said. He turned to go.

'What will I do when I must leave here?' Michael asked, hearing how forlorn that sounded. He could scarcely expect this man, Rosser, to know.

But Rosser did know. He turned back to face Michael. 'We will dress you as a beggar and give you food and a bit of money. You will act dumb with you so that you do not betray yourself as Irish. Hereabouts the Irish are despised and under suspicion for having landed with the French invaders. You will go to London. Plenty of your countrymen are there.'

Michael's head began to pound. He touched the bump. 'Why are you doing this?' he asked.

Rosser was silent.

'You could be hung for high treason yourself,' Michael went on. 'Your sister could be burned at the stake for high treason. You are sheltering an enemy of the English.'

'We have no love for the English,' Rosser said.

Chapter 9

Ireland

When Hugh and Michael came back the next morning to finish The Big House wall, the coachman told them that Master Arthur would be lamed. Her ladyship was fit to be tied, he said, there'd be hell to pay.

'Will you be arrested, Dada?' Michael asked and Hugh said not on your life, it was her ladyship that sent the boy to him in the first place. He said that not an ounce of blame could be attached to him under any law in the land. But Michael knew enough about the law to be mistrustful. He knew that Protestants made the law, that the law was in the Protestant pocket, and he thought, who were the biggest Protestants in the land if not The Big Lord and The Big Lord's wife? All morning he kept an eye out for the gaol cart.

It never came, but a terrible storm did. In the early afternoon the sky blackened and there was thunder, lightning, sheets of rain and gigantic hail stones that knocked hens senseless and flattened the few fields of corn that were still standing. The storm ended near nightfall, too late for Hugh's oats.

He lost his entire crop. The Quinn twins had been incapacitated by fits their first hour in the field and then one of them had sliced off the top of this thumb and they had both quit cutting altogether.

At cockcrow the following morning Hugh went to see John Logan concerning payment for The Big House wall. He was soon back. The labour was being slated as duty work, he said.

'But did you tell him about our loss?' Kathleen cried.

'Sure I did, and that I am out six days harvest wage, and the

34

gobshite says, "I smoothed it over with her ladyship regarding how you lamed the young master." He says, "I did a job for yourself and you did a job for myself and we are square."'

The flax crop would help pay the rental, anyhow, Hugh said. There would be no luxuries, however. No new ribbons, no pennies for the fairs this year. No hedge school.

That night he poured Michael two thumbs of poteen for having taken the disappointment without a word. 'A man's drink for a man.' The truth was, Michael had been silenced by the shock of suddenly being without a plan for his life. He downed the poteen in one gulp, and all the family, apart from Judy, clapped. They made much of him. He fell asleep on the bare floor.

At mass the next morning, kneeling on a truss of straw, he thought out his life all over. His father had said, 'Maybe a year down the road we will get the fee together,' but that had angered his mother who'd said there should not be talk of it until the money was in hand.

If he was not to be a scholar, then he could not become a schoolmaster. Or a poet, like the man from Munster who visited in the summers and recited poems about fallen Irish chieftains and had all the men weeping and swearing eternal love to each other. The two professions — schoolmaster and poet — had been taking turns dangling in the front of Michael's mind ever since the day his father had given him the book. Which was filled, every page covered with fine straight letters, but all for nothing now.

So he would grow up to be a small farmer. Like his father. Like Neal was going to be. He would have a cabin and two fields on his father's land. He would have a cow, a pig, hens and geese, and he would hire himself out to the big farmers. He would have a good and beautiful wife. His father said there were three things that brought a cotter happiness: a garden of white potatoes covered in blossom, a newborn calf and a good and beautiful wife.

The congregation rose, and Michael looked over his shoulder, across to where the women and girls were. Except for his mother and sisters they all appeared forbidding — baleful or homely or dim. But then he saw, near the back of the chapel, a girl who was small and thin, as he himself was. She had thick black eyebrows that curved up in her white forehead. Her hair fell longer than her shawl did, and was buttercup yellow. He had noticed her before at mass, noticed her bright hair, but not her eyebrows. He had thought nothing of her. Now he thought that she was the loveliest girl there could ever be.

As he was studying her, her eyes dipped sideways, straight at him. He spun around to the front. His skin felt as though sharp drops of rain were hitting it. He believed that he had fallen in love at first sight. In his mind he glimpsed her eyebrows again, and they changed into wings, into a lone black bird soaring into a white sky. This image struck him as a heavenly sign because of where he was and because it came to him as the mass server was sprinkling the row he was in with holy water.

After the service he searched for her on the chapel green. He felt changed forever, and dazed, for his love was already profound. He caught sight of her between her mother and father just as they were turning on to the road. Her mother had a violent rocking gait, and he realized that she was the woman from up the hill who had a false leg made of cork.

'Her mother has a cork leg,' he said to himself, testing his love and finding it undiminished.

He wanted to lie on his bed and muse upon her when he got home, but his father had news that distracted him completely.

'We are going to have a station,' his father said.

'A station?' Kathleen said. A station was when the priest heard confession in your cabin. It was an honour.

'Friday morning. With Mannion's father dying, it cannot be held there, so it will be here instead.'

'Mother of God, man, how will I have the place ready by that time? What will I feed His Reverence at all?'

Puffing on his pipe, Hugh looked at Michael through thin eyes. 'When we are all finished doing our duty, Father Lynn will be examining Michael's book.'

'He will?' Kathleen said.

Hugh waved at Michael. 'Over here.'

Michael went to him, and Hugh drew him close. 'Now then, didn't you set yourself bravely to a task that I laid out for you? Eh? Day after day, month after month?' He gave Michael little squeezes that made him feel bound to nod. 'So now, don't you deserve to find out how the book measures up? For its own sake? Sure I will tell you you did a grand job of it, but who am I to judge? It is a man like Father Lynn that can read and write with the best of them that should be doing the judging.'

'But, Dada, I am going to be a farmer.'

'You haven't got the money, have you?' Kathleen asked accusingly, since if Hugh had got it he could only have done so through underhand means.

'Nay, nay, nay. That is not the point of what I am saying. The point is the work itself. The worth of the book itself. After all his work Michael deserves to find out how his letters measure up, and he deserves that whatever might be in store for him down the road...'

What if Father Lynn said that the book was a disgrace? There would be no bearing the shame. Judy would crow. His father would regret having giving him good poteen let alone having bought all those sheets of paper.

Michael fell into a torpor of dread thinking of this. His voice sounded exotic in his ears; he was clumsy. Twice he knocked over the pail of whitewash when he and Neal were painting the outside of the cabin, and finally Neal told him to clear off. So Kathleen gave him the job of going around to all the neighbours to tell them that the station was being held at their place instead of at the Mannions'.

The day before the station he spent binding with his sisters and mother. He worked just ahead of Judy, shaking out the grass and weeds from the straw after which she pulled a handful from the sheaf and twisted and turned it. Her skinny arms moved in jerks, as if she were fighting the sheaf, as if she hated it, and every once in a while she would lift her eyes to his and the black dots in their centres seemed to be aiming at him like the tips of spears. She said, 'The confessional will be in *my* room,' as though that were a victory over him and she didn't share the room with Mary and Rose.

Before it was even light on Friday morning Kathleen had all the food laid out. Hard-boiled eggs, oat cakes, sweet milk and ale arranged on the meal chest and on a bench borrowed from The Bull and Castle tavern. A pot of porridge simmering over the grate. For Father Lynn and Hugh there were eight strips of bacon, also borrowed. There were bouquets of Rose's flowers along the collar beams and plaited in Rose's and Mary's hair. Michael's hair Mary had shorn to within an inch of his scalp. His cut black curls she'd wrapped in a rag to be sewn on to a dolly's head one day.

Outside in the yard people milled about and prayed. A stranger sitting on the stoop smote his chest with great whacks.

'Look at all the sinners,' Judy said. 'We won't be eating for hours and hours.' She spit over the half door at the stranger to make him leave but he didn't budge. He was not in this world.

She was right about eating. Father Lynn spent half the morning hearing confession in the girls' outshot. Then there was holy communion and after that the women filled their vials with holy water, and then there were the leave-takings. Michael was anguished for everybody to be gone and anguished lest they go. And when the last person left and breakfast began he couldn't eat. After a while he moved into a corner away from the fire and sat there breaking a cake into bits, telling himself that if he broke three cakes into bits without being scolded for it, Father Lynn would praise the letters.

As he crumbled he looked at Father Lynn. The priest had watery eyes that drooped at the corners, and round red cheeks and a little mouth like a hook. Between quaffs of ale he wiped his mouth with the back of his hand, and when he had emptied his glass he said, 'Well, now, Hugh.'

Hugh said, 'Michael, go get your book for His Reverence.'

Michael ceased crumbling, then crumbled frantically to finish the third cake, but Kathleen said, 'What in heaven's name are you doing?' so he swung over to the dresser and reached beneath for his book.

It was not there.

'It is not here!' he cried.

'What do you mean it is not there?' Hugh said.

'I put it here but it is not here.'

Hugh came over and got down next to him. He swept his arm along the floor. He stood, went around the dresser and lifted the mattress. Shook the blanket. 'Mother, where would it be?'

'I am sure I have no idea.'

'Maybe a fairy stole it,' Rose said breathlessly. Judy snickered.

'Judy,' Kathleen said. 'Is this one of your capers?'

'What capers?' Judy crossed her arms.

'Where did you hide it?'

'I never hid it!'

'Tell me.'

'I never did!' She made for the door but Hugh caught her by the petticoat. 'Leave me go!' she screamed, kicking out at him.

Gripping her wrists, Hugh shook her. 'Are you pleased with yourself? Are you pleased to be shaming ourselves all out in front of His Reverence here?'

'I wonder why she would be hiding her brother's book?' the priest asked politely, touching a finger to his cheek. He disliked ructions.

'Ach, she's been envying him,' Hugh said, and over him Judy screamed, 'I never have!'

'Maybe a fairy stole it,' Rose said.

Next to Michael, standing at the dresser, Kathleen said, 'Oh, for goodness' sake. For goodness' sake.' She held out her arm. The book was in her hand.

It seemed that during the cleaning she had moved it to the top of the dresser and forgotten about it. She gave it to Father Lynn and knelt beside Judy. 'Wasn't I as wrong as can be?' she said, taking Judy's hands. Judy looked down at the floor and gyrated one foot. As soon as Kathleen let her go she ran to the door and out.

Nobody spoke. Kathleen stayed on her knees. 'Forgive me, Father,' she said.

Father Lynn tucked in his chin as though taken aback at her saying that. Smiling around the room he came to his feet. He stepped to the door, laid the book on the lower half, which was in sunlight, and commenced turning the pages.

Michael planted his eyes on his mother, on her hands. They had bulging blue veins in them. The seconds passed.

Father Lynn closed the book with a slap, and Michael started and saw his mother start simultaneously. 'Hugh,' the priest said, 'tell me. What is the cost of sending a boy to the hedge school for one year?' He returned to his stool and made room for the book on the bench.

'Eleven shillings four pence a quarter for Latin and Greek. Seven shillings a quarter each for reading, writing, arithmetic

39

and spelling. Then you have your books and papers and all of them considerations on top.'

Father Lynn brought the tips of his fingers together at his mouth. 'I haven't had the pleasure of meeting this Master Dolan,' he said. 'As you may know, it was Father Doherty that brought him to the valley. Nevertheless, I hear he is a teacher of the first water.'

'Well, I hear the same,' Hugh said, sighing. 'Crafty as they come, that's well known.'

'Michael,' Father Lynn said, suddenly lively, turning around to look at him. 'You are hardworking, neat, careful and obedient. I perceive these qualities not only from the book but from your behaviour. If I am any judge of a person's character, I believe that you have the makings of a fine scholar in you. I will pay your fee to attend the school.'

Michael burned. Across his mind there flashed a vision of the girl from the chapel.

'Ach, no, Father.' Hugh scraped back his stool. 'That is not why I asked you to look at the book.'

'We cannot be spending your money, Father,' Kathleen said. 'It would not be right at all.'

But Father Lynn said that he had more than enough money for his humble needs, and the decision was not a spur-of-the-moment one. For many years he had been intending to sponsor the studies of some meritorious boy, but with one thing and another he had never set the wheels to his resolution.

'Now,' he said, 'is the accepted time.'

There was a hallowed ring to that, so Hugh slapped his thighs and poured out whiskeys in celebration, and when everyone was merry Kathleen let Father Lynn coax her into singing a bawdy song about another woman named Kathleen, a tainted woman who slept with Conn, slept with Brian, slept with Rory. Sitting at his father's feet, Michael thought of the girl from the chapel, thought of her lovely, taintless face, thought, because he was feeling so happy and vivid and full of promise, that he was worthy of her.

As the new boy Michael would be lambasted by the other scholars his first day at school. All of his friends thought so, having heard rumours. It was recommended that he just keep running, since he was a fast runner, faster than anyone in the parish his own age of eight, and faster than all the nine and ten-year-olds except for a boy who had six webbed toes on each foot, which was thought to lend an unfair advantage. But the eventual view was that running wouldn't save him, that the scholars would take turns chasing him, wear him down like a fox.

Naturally this cast a pall on his horizons. He was going to start attending when the potatoes had been lifted, the day after All Souls'. His father had settled on that day as lucky because the souls of Grandfather and Grandmother Malone would be rising the evening before to be with the family and bless new undertakings. Michael was depending on those blessings. They, and whatever benefit came from his devout prayers, were his only protection. It dashed him to think of a bully knocking out his front teeth, whose evenness had once been likened to the teeth on a comb, or tearing his new jacket. He would be all decked out with a jacket, which his mother had made from his father's old frieze coat and which had six gold-coloured buttons down the breast in double rows, with Neal's old goatskin cap and with a book satchel sewn from the remnants of the coat that fastened at the flap with two more gold-coloured buttons. One thin hope he held on to was that the scholars would be daunted by how respectable he looked.

On the morning of the first day his mother cooked him and Neal a goose egg as a treat. Neal was walking with him to the school, just this one morning, to make sure he went the right way. While they ate Kathleen smoked her pipe and watched them. She and the rest of the family would have breakfast later.

She said to Michael, 'Not all that long ago and you wouldn't be going at all, whether we had the fee or not.'

Michael nodded. She was talking about a penal law that had made it a crime for Catholic children to be taught. He said to himself, "Now she will tell the story about her grandfather."

'When my grandfather, your great-grandfather, was a boy,' she said, 'there was a secret school in a cave up in the hills. The master was a priest. My grandfather went to the school for one day. On the second day the priest hunters came and took the priest away to get thirty pounds for his head, attached to his neck or not. The only thing my grandfather learned was his alphabet, but thereafter and until the day he died he could tear off them letters at the drop of a hat.'

She picked up the empty egg shells for washing out and using again as cups. 'So,' she said, 'you are following in footsteps.'

His father shook his hand when he and Neal were ready to leave. He had never done that before. His mother kissed him and sprinkled him with holy water, then Rose and Mary kissed him. Judy said, 'You look like a dolt in that cap.'

The old widower Mulligan, their nearest neighbour to the west, was at his half door. As they passed he shouted, 'Ask about the isosceles triangle!' to remind them that he was a self-taught man. The next place belonged to Tyrell the Fairy Man, who leased a large holding using money bestowed upon him by the fairies and who was much loved because he let cotters graze their cows on his grass for free. He was at his ditch. He waved Michael over and from behind his ear brought out something small and hard and pressed it into Michael's hand.

'A piece of fox skull,' he said. 'Slip it under your cap and it will fire your brain.'

Michael and Neal ambled along, they had plenty of time. The road followed the course of the river. To the right, cabins and small stone-walled fields lapped up into hills. The blue tops of the hills met the sky in a line like a ragged tear. If you climbed to the tops you saw the far shore of the river in patchwork stripes: meadowland, pine wood and corn fields. South-shore land was lush and mostly occupied by big Protestant farmers and graziers. North-shore land was scrub and rock, more so the higher you climbed, and that's where the Catholics rented. Both shores were known as the valley. Even a person living on the cap of the hill would tell you that his home was in the valley.

Hugh's property was as good as you might get on the Catholic side. It had a byre and a sty and in the cabins it had outshots, two bedrooms that Grandfather Malone had added on after relations who had been evicted from their own cabin moved in. The next winter Grandmother Malone had nightmares that the animals were conspiring to murder her. She shooed them all out into the yard — the cow, the pig, the poultry, the dogs, even a ten-year-old cat that she had doted on and carried wrapped around her neck. Consequently Grandfather Malone built the byre and the sty. His rent eventually went up owing to the improvements, but he managed through penury and hard work (what sobering stories there were of his virtues!) to pay the middleman on the nail, and when he died, Hugh, his only living child, did the same and held on to the place. People said the Malones were charmed.

The further west you went from Hugh's holding the poorer the cabins became until they were little better than stick and sod nests. Squatters lived here. A mile past these places, starting at the Stone Cross, the road and river parted company and the land was boggy and unpeopled altogether. In another mile it hardened once more and began to rise. A sheep track met the road at this point. Michael and Neal turned on to the track and climbed it as far as its intersection with a wider cart path.

'Let's have bit of a rest,' Neal said, heading for a rock at the side of the path. 'We're early yet.' Dropping the turf sods that he had been carrying for the school fire, he sat on the rock and dug into his coat pocket. He took out a quid of tobacco. 'I heard that you are going to get the drubbing of your life today,' he said, twisting off a chew.

'Who told you that?'

'Your friend Rory. He said a cousin of his near Derry had all his teeth knocked out his first day.'

Michael sat. He pulled off his cap and the fox skull fell out. He picked it up and studied it. He hadn't said anything to Neal in case Neal wanted to threaten the scholars or beat them himself, and then he would be called a coward.

But Neal had considered that. He said, 'I cannot go fighting your fights for you but what I can do is to stand in the school yard with my arms crossed like this.' He crossed them up and out from his chest, like a Red Indian. 'The scholars all get an eyeful of me and then I go back home. Are you with me?'

'Aye,' Michael said doubtfully.

'Then, the minute one of them gobshites come up to you later in the day, you say, "Did you happen to catch sight of my brother? There are four more of the same at home".'

'Ach,' Michael said, rejecting that.

Neal's eyes flicked up and down Michael's body. 'They are all bound to be bigger than yourself,' he said. 'Anyhow, you don't say, "He will break your bones" or anything like that. Only, "Did you happen to catch sight of him, there are four more of the same." 'Tis a warning, but not in so many words.'

'Did you happen to catch sight of my brother?' Michael said, to hear how he sounded saying it.

'That's it,' Neal said, scooping up the sods. 'But put a bit more threat into it.'

The school was a long low clay building tucked into a hill. There were two doors across the front, one that would be for the schoolroom and the other for the master's dwelling. On the flat ground that went from the school to the boreen, twenty or so boys were playing hurling. Neal and Michael watched them chase the ball down the field. One boy tripped over the stick of another and howled and several of the players stopped to see if he was hurt.

Neal snorted. 'A bunch of girls,' he said.

Another dozen boys were loitering about the schoolhouse door. None of them, and none of the hurlers, was dressed anywhere as fine as Michael was, which didn't strike him as so desirable a state of affairs now. He looked down at his jacket, with its gold-coloured buttons shining like beacons, and folded his arms over his chest to hide them.

'Right you are,' Neal said, tossing down the sods and folding his own arms.

They stood like that while more scholars arrived, some from the hill path behind the school and some, going around the two of them, from the boreen that they themselves had taken. There were glances, especially at Neal who was glaring at everyone, but there were no challenges. These would come later. Michael had not missed the indications and whispers.

An older boy, sitting on the stoop, rang a bell, and the hurlers ran to the hedge to get their turf sods for the fire. 'This is it,' Neal said. He uncrossed his arms, picked up their sods and handed them to Michael.

'Good-bye,' Michael said. His voice came out shaky.

'Shall I stay until you go inside?'

'No.' That would be giving the game away.

'Well, then, Little Scholar, good luck. Remember the warning.'

Carrying the sods pressed against his jacket to cover the buttons, Michael crossed the yard. The hurlers bounded past him in a herd. The older boy continued ringing the bell with a languid flop of his hand. His eyes were on Michael. When Michael got to the stoop, the bell went still.

'Halt, you,' the boy said, standing.

Michael stopped, one foot on the stoop, one on the ground, and looked up. The boy was narrow-faced and narrow-eyed. The scholars who were not yet inside stopped as well.

'What is your name?' the boy asked. He had a hard adult voice. Michael told him his name.

'Ah, Michael Malone,' the boy said, nodding as if he'd heard of it. 'Well, Michael Malone, you are to bare your head when I address you,' he said. He pulled off Michael's cap and the fox skull fell into the muck.

'Give that back!' Michael said, snatching at his cap.

The boy held it high. 'Give it *back*?' he said. He smiled. The other scholars laughed.

Michael threw ar arm at the boreen. In spite of having told Neal to go, it was a blow of wind through him not to see Neal still there. Stabbing his finger at the very spot where he and Neal had stood, gathering courage from the accuracy, he cried, 'Did you happen to catch sight of my brother that was there? I have four more brothers even bigger than that at home.' He sounded shrill to himself, like Judy.

He turned to face the boy again and heard the silence girdling around himself. The boy was looking at him in a way that Michael could not interpret.

'You wait here,' the boy said. Then he waved the bell at the other scholars and said, 'Inside with the rest of you,' and they went past Michael in single file, taking care not to brush against him.

But one of the scholars, the last one, touched his arm. He glanced up, and there was the girl with the yellow hair from the chapel.

She leaned into him. 'He is the master,' she whispered.

Her name was Etain McCaffery and she was exactly a month

younger than Michael. She was an only child, an older brother and sister having died of influenza three years ago and her baby brother dying just last August of brain fever, taking his last breath in her arms as she sang, 'I'd Rock My Own Sweet Childie in a Cradle of Gold'.

She was the only girl in the school. Her father was sending her to polish her up for a great match with a grazier or a merchant.

'What about a schoolmaster?' Michael asked.

'So long as he has pots of money,' she said, and Michael slipped that ambition into his newest plan for his life.

He was even more captivated by her than he had been at first sight. Up close she was perfect. Her skin had no pits, her arms had fair downy hair on them, her eyelashes were long and dark, like the false lady's eyelash that he had at home in his brass box. That she should be at the school and that she should befriend him straight away was his salvation. Had it not been for that miracle he would never have returned to the school a second day, so great was his mortification.

The master did not flog him. Nothing so outright. Instead he told the scholars a tale about a poor Catholic peasant who was travelling in a strange parish and who met a Protestant and threatened him with dire veiled threats for no other reason than that the peasant was a Protestant. Little did the Catholic peasant know, however, that the Protestant peasant was really his own long lost twin brother who had been stolen at birth by the midwife and sold to a tinker. The Protestant peasant, though, he knew it. But he turned away from his brother in sorrow and the two were never reunited.

During the telling, Master Dolan's eyes were on Michael, making it plain that Michael was the Catholic churl of the story. For the rest of the morning the other scholars avoided looking at him. Whenever the master's back was turned one particular boy folded his arms as Neal had done and all the other boys laughed.

At midday there was dismiss to go outside and eat dinner. Michael retreated to the boreen. None of the boys followed to beat him, which he took to mean that he was too pitiful and despicable even to be tormented. What the girl must think of him he could not bear to imagine.

46

He sat on the ground behind a bush. He had an oatcake and an apple. As he was rubbing the apple on his leg for a shine, the girl all of sudden appeared in front of him.

'Here you are,' she said, smiling. She sat down beside him and hugged her knees. She said that she thought she ought to tell him that everyone made the same mistake about the master, everyone thought he was a scholar, but the truth was he was twenty-five years old. Michael should pay no mind to Tim Gallagher, the boy who kept folding his arms. On Tim's first day his father brought him into the school and asked Master Dolan where the master was, and Master Dolan said, 'Before your eyes,' and Tim's father, disbelieving him, boxed his ears for a rascal.

She laughed with her hand over her mouth. Her fingernails were clean. It was as if she were one of his sisters, she was so easy in his company. She inquired whether she might have a bite of his apple, and with her strong white teeth she bit off a big chunk. She said, 'I will tell you secrets.'

Chapter 10

Wales

When Michael opened his eyes in the morning, Rosser was standing over him, puffing on his pipe. 'You are awake,' Rosser said.

He reported on the invasion aftermath — an item he'd read in the newspaper at the Fishguard post office, gossip he'd heard from his hired man, who seemed to get about and pick up all the news and pass it on to Rosser in innocence of his secret.

Michael hated opening his eyes in the morning. He did not want to think about the invasion. It alarmed him. All news was alarming. One morning Rosser had said that the houses of dissenters were being searched for traitors, for local conspirators who had helped the French, and he added that he was a dissenter, a Baptist, then said, 'But don't worry, they will not search this house. We keep to ourselves, Olwen and me, people pass us over.' Well, why speak of the searches at all if Michael wasn't to worry?

Rosser asked questions, too, more questions every morning, more intimate questions. First he asked, how did Michael get to France, why did he leave when he did? Then he wanted to know if Michael was a United Irishman, had he read Thomas Paine's *Rights of Man*, how could he obey the pope in Rome and yet be a republican? Michael tried to discourage him with short, vague, weary answers, as if talking exhausted him, which, with Rosser, it did, but then he would get an uneasy feeling that he might be offending him — God help him if he offended this man — and he would say too much.

Rosser listened as if for a secret, he nodded and narrowed his eyes. When Michael said anything against the English he grunted. Occasionally he pronounced against them himself, quoting from some pamphlet that he had read:

"The English would have us dissolve unprotesting into their empire . . . speak only the English language, pay tithes to the English church . . . we must smite all empires of the devil."

He spoke much of the devil. He had seen him in a vision, Olwen said. The first morning after Michael came out of his stupor she confided in him that her brother had holy visions two and three times a week and when the visions started, his eyes slipped up into his skull. He was so pious, she said. Out of piety he soaked his body in a tub of water every other day, and on the days that he didn't soak he still washed his feet and hindquarters. And yet he could be brutal, for no good reason. Michael was witness to this aspect of him right away. The same day that Olwen confided in him, he saw Rosser kick the orange cat down the loft stairs, stepping out of his path to do it.

But to Michael, the man was always cordial, even tender. His thick fingers touched the wound on his temple so gently that Michael didn't feel them. He seemed to need his approval — he seemed, really, to have the same fear of offending Michael that Michael had of offending him. After he kicked the cat down the stairs, he immediately said as a kind of apology that cats were worthless creatures, you couldn't sell them nor eat them nor work them, then he stayed looking at Michael until, to stop him looking, Michael said treacherously that it was so. He slapped Olwen hard for slouching once, then said to Michael that a woman would become a slattern in a minute if you didn't keep your eye out, but this time Michael wouldn't agree, and Rosser shuffled and took his hat off and shook his strange white hair out of his eyes, put the hat back on, took it off again, on and off, as if he couldn't get the fit right.

Olwen didn't cry or mope over that slap. When Rosser left at last, Michael asked her, 'Are you all right?' One side of her face flamed from Rosser's hand.

'Right as a line,' she answered, smiling, opening her eyes wider as if to say, 'Why shouldn't I be?'

Michael thought that this was dissembling, for his sake and for the sake of her pride. But as days passed he decided that he was wrong. The truth was, nothing troubled her. He would hear Rosser throw things, bang his fist on the table, and the minute Rosser was out of the door she would be singing.

She sang whenever Rosser was outside. She sang things instead of saying them. In the mornings, after Rosser had gone downstairs, she came up and sang out how long Michael had been there 'Day fourteen!' 'Day eighteen!'

She had his breakfast on a tray. As soon as he was able to raise his head without it pounding he fed himself, and she sat on the stool and watched, hugging the loaf to her breast and holding the knife ready to slice.

Never in his life had he eaten so much. In Ireland, by March, his mother would be starting to deal out the grain with care; it had to last until the new potatoes were ready to lift. And there would be little else besides grain food, besides porridge and cakes. Here, every meal was a banquet. For breakfast he had two eggs, two slices of ham and as much buttered bread as he wanted. Sometimes he had seaweed wrapped in oatmeal. Olwen called this *bara lawr*. He had tea, the first he had ever drunk, with sweet milk and honey. At midday he drank beer that had a heather taste, and he had *cawl*, which was a leek, onion and carrot broth. There was more tea and buttered bread in late afternoon. Once a week there was a slice of pudding. For supper it was *cawl* again, and potatoes. Or salt beef and dumplings, and more beer.

Everyone in Wales ate like this, Olwen said.

After his breakfast Michael had his bath. Olwen went downstairs with the tray and returned with a basin of heated water, soap, a cloth and a towel, and little bottles of salves and herbs in her pockets. She washed his face first, emitting pitying gasps as she dabbed the bump on his temple. Next she washed his hands and arms. Then his feet and legs.

She had removed the dressing from his ankle. He had a wide violet gash there, healing in layers into its centre. He investigated it constantly. It was hard underneath and if he pressed anywhere near it, pain flared up in his foot and calf. Olwen washed around it. She sat on the bed and lifted his legs on to her big soft lap and wiped the cloth downward, in the direction that his hair grew. The morning air was chill but he never was. The stroking warmed him, entranced him a little, which was a state he let himself enjoy since he believed, obscurely, that these baths were vital to his recovery. Sometimes, because he was entranced and because Olwen was fair-haired and as tall as his mother and as fat as Rose, he let himself pretend that it was one or the other of them that was washing him.

Meanwhile Olwen talked about her family. They were a tragic clan, the Griffiths. Once, she said, they had been tolerably wealthy. Her father had owned hundreds of acres and a salmon fishery, her mother had kept two indoor servants, and Rosser and herself had received lessons from an English maiden lady of noble blood ties. But fifteen years ago, when Rosser was fourteen and Olwen eleven, their mother ran away with an English portrait painter and was never heard from again. She had been very lovely. Although it hadn't been her name, people had called her '*Ceimwen*', which means White Beauty. After she ran off, their father drank and gambled and turned slothful. He went into debt. The salmon fishery had to be sold, then the boundary fields, then the fields next to those. The maids left, the lessons ended. The library and the best furniture got carted away by new owners, and the calves and lambs were vended before they were even born. Had their father not fallen and split open his head on a door latch, everything would have gone. But two years after their mother left, he did fall and a day later was dead. By then there were only sixty acres left for Rosser to inherit. Rosser was not even sixteen at the time but he worked the farm with only one other labourer. His ambition was to buy back all the land that had been sold, and until he did he would not call the farm or hear it called by its name, '*Trefawr*' — Great Habitation. He would not tolerate the hypocrisy.

In spite of what it must have meant to her, Olwen smiled as she talked of her mother running off, her father becoming a profligate. She smiled and, unbelievably, sometimes she laughed. Michael asked her what was funny, but the question sent her astray.

'Gracious, *I* don't know,' she said, lifting the washcloth, smiling into his eyes thoughtfully.

After she'd dried him she smeared comfrey ointment on his gash. On his temple, to reduce the bump, she patted a kind of

51

paste that she said was made from mallows, chamomile, chickweed, ground ivy and his own stale urine. Next she rubbed green hazel on his teeth to clean them, and after that she sprinkled fresh rosemary under his pillow to stave off nightmares. Then she took the rocks that she had put in his bed the night before to warm his feet and went downstairs for newly heated ones, which she wrapped in cloths and tucked under the quilt. And then she took him for his walk.

His head no longer pounded but he could get dizzy and nauseous if he sat up or stood too quickly. So he gripped her hands to come to his feet. She was wonderfully strong. She could support his entire weight, and though he was lean he was neverthless a big man.

With his arm around her shoulders and her arm around his back, they moved across the loft. 'That's the way,' she sang, shooing the cats out from underfoot.

These walks were for strengthening his foot. Yet each day it was as feeble as ever. He could put no weight on it. He wondered if the bones were mending properly, if the bandage hadn't been removed too soon, but she said, 'You will be better by and by,' and she sounded so certain and primally wise that he believed her.

They circled the loft until he grew tired and then they went to one of the windows. He held on to a rafter while she parted the sack curtains to reconnoitre. Just as when she talked of her family, she always laughed, either at her daring — she had said that Rosser would have it out of her if he should catch them at this — or at the view of her pleasant yard or simply at some rosy thought. If nobody was in sight she stepped back and said, 'All clear.'

Michael grasped the ledge and bent down to the little pane. The window nearest his bed faced the back of the house, the one on the far wall faced the front. Out of the back window all you could see was a clump of elm and a border of ploughed land. You couldn't see the hills that Olwen said were not far away and where the sheep would soon go to graze. So Michael usually liked to stop at the front window, which showed a tidy yard, pig sties to the right, a peat house and a glimpse of a rick to the left, and down the middle a paved path. The beginning of two fields that lay beyond the yard could also be seen. Bell

Field and Field-in-Front-of-the-Home had just been planted with potatoes.

The pig sties, being corbelled like those in the valley, the potato beds, these should have made him homesick. But they didn't. Standing next to Olwen he was able to regard things the way she seemed to. Without memories or context. "There is a field, it is ploughed, it will be planted," that is all he would think, and he would even feel a frail peace.

Chapter 11

Ireland

The corn harvest at the end of Michael's first year was a good one, and Hugh was able to pay half of the school fee the next year. In Michael's second and third years Hugh paid half again. In his fifth year he paid the full sum. During the spring of that year the widower Mulligan had died and Hugh had won the lease on the property. He planted oats on the new land, and when he sold them and settled the rental there was enough money left over not only to pay Master Dolan's fee but also to keep the mare through the winter instead of selling her, and to risk a rental increase by building a stone hearth against the outshot wall.

Michael was happy. He had two great friends: Corny Devine, who was thin, like himself, though not so tall as Michael had grown, and who wore spectacles. And Etain. Etain was still small and lovely. The other word to describe her was fiery — she was her very name. It so happened that Etain meant 'little fiery one'. One day Master Dolan had gone up and down the rows of scholars, telling all thirty-seven of them what their names meant. Corny, or Cornelius, was Latin for hornlike. Michael was Hebrew for Godlike. To be called Michael was to be orderly and truthful to a sublime degree.

In a back row Michael sat between Corny and Etain, and the three of them shared books and were allowed to talk softly together, provided that the subject was scholarly. They were also allowed, as any student was, to take books from the master's library at the end of the day and read them on the big table in the schoolroom. Master Dolan owned hundreds of volumes, every year acquiring more on his annual buying trip to Dublin. He kept them on oak shelving in the room where he lived. When he showed the library to a new boy, he would sweep out an arm and say, 'That's where all the fee money goes,' and the new boy would gaze obediently, not sure whether it was commendable or not, all the fee money going there.

Most afternoons Michael and Corny stayed on to read, and Etain did too, when she could, so that over five years they each had become acquainted with the entire collection, including the French books. They had read all three volumes of *The Encyclopaedia Britannica*, and Michael and Corny had read both the Old and New Testaments and memorized passages because Master Dolan said that the Irish people's ignorance of the bible kept them too much in thrall of priests. In the quiet schoolroom, in the compatible afternoon light, Michael would feel that he and Corny and Etain were encircled in a flame of happiness.

He knew that he was lucky. Lucky not just to be a scholar but to be a Malone. Blessed to be so, what with the land hunger that was blighting other families. It was a madness, this land hunger. People were suddenly in a frenzy to have property. When the lease on any bit of property expired and the middleman held an auction, the bidding was reckless, hopeless. People who had lived in a place for thirty years lost it because they couldn't, finally, top someone else's lunatic bid. And nobody cared any longer if he lived on the north shore or the south shore, just as long as he had a holding. So poor Protestants who had lost their holdings to the impossible bids of poor Catholics were moving into the hills, and poor Catholics were moving into cabins near town.

For the middlemen it was a heyday. Every patch of land they had, they rented out. Even the waysides, where the squatters built shelters and where the pigs and geese foraged, were enclosed and rented. One day Michael saw John Logan and two other men flatten a whole row of squatters' houses, the people who had lived in the houses watching dumbly from the road, holding their pots and clothing.

And one day he saw a notice plastered to a post. It read:

55

Take warning to quit this land that is rightfully
anothers by the forth of the month or you and yours
will suffer the severest atrocitys that ever were used.

Michael had heard of these threats and of secret societies
forming and of fights and beatings. Near the town a group of
Catholics, armed with rocks, squashed the hands of a
Protestant weaver. The weaver took to begging at Catholic
cabins, dangling his purple deformed hands in the housewives'
faces to reproach them, and they tossed feasts out of their
doors to make him go away.

Beggars were everywhere. Sometimes when Michael came
home from school there would be a strange shabby family on
the floor in front of the hearth. So hungry would they be that
they'd eat potatoes still steaming in their skins. Hugh filled the
men's pipes, and the men sucked hard and asked what did
Hugh suppose the wage in England was for cutting the winter
wheat? They would never go over there, not the older men,
anyway. The asking was only show. Their wives talked to
Kathleen about their babies that had died.

One of the scholars lost his home and had to leave the
school; some of the older scholars left to become labourers.
Etain had to stay away during corn harvest. All of the scholars
stayed away to help pull the flax and gather the potatoes, but
most of them didn't have to help cut or bind the oats. Etain had
to, though, because she had no brothers bringing in a wage and
because her mother had the cork leg and was no use in the
fields. There were other times, as well, that she stayed home,
when her mother took ill. She said that these days out of school
were a torment to her father, who couldn't do without her help
and yet fretted that she would fall behind in her studies and be
expelled.

Michael rejoiced in these opportunities to be her saviour, to
put her father in his debt. When she returned to school after an
absence he would bring her to his cabin and tutor her. Judy
couldn't bear the sight of her. As soon as Etain came through
the door Judy went out of it, or she lay on her bed until it was
time to eat supper. She behaved as if Etain weren't there; she
wouldn't pass her the salt or the potato basket, she wouldn't
answer her. Then she would do the opposite and stare at her

with her eyes like spear heads. Hugh had smacked her for her rudeness, but that didn't stop her. She was wild with envy. She didn't even try to pretend otherwise.

'Why does she get to go to the school and I didn't get to?' she demanded after Etain's first visit.

'Her father had the money to send her,' Kathleen answered. Hugh said that if Judy turned into a sweet girl, maybe he would pay for her to go next year, now that he himself had the money.

Judy looked at him as if his ignorance was appalling. ''Tis too late! I am fourteen years old. I cannot be starting at the beginning with the little children.'

So Hugh suggested that Michael teach her.

'I don't want Michael to teach me. I wanted to go before. To the school itself, and now people would be saying, "Isn't Judy the clever girl," like they are saying about Etain, and she is not near as clever as I am, barring that she has been going to the school.'

After a while, on the evening that Etain visited, Judy left the house for hours, not even coming back to eat her supper. When she did return, late in the night, she claimed that she had only been paying a call on Andy Coogan, she hadn't been out traipsing, what was the worry? 'Andy Coogan is my friend,' she said. 'The same as Etain is Michael's friend.'

'In that case, visit with him under your own roof,' Kathleen said. She didn't want Judy going to the Coogans' house especially at night. The Coogans lived high in the hills and were reported to carry on once the sun went down. People said that they danced in the yard and wrestled with each other and made such a racket that everybody's dogs howled. Kathleen said, 'Visit with him under your own roof, do the decent thing.'

''Tis a more pleasant place than this, the Coogans' is,' Judy said.

Hugh slapped her for such impertinence. She didn't cry out. She just looked at him, inviting more slaps, and he turned away from her and paced. He issued warnings. One more time coming home in the middle of the night and he would lash her to the pot crook, he would break both her legs. But he wouldn't have done these things and she knew it and consequently she went on coming and going as she pleased. It did not concern her that in the dead of night fairies might pull her into a bog hole or capture her in a fairy ring forever. She wouldn't even let Rose put St. John's wort blossoms in her petticoat pocket, as a precaution. It was beyond belief how fearless and brazen she had become.

Judy and Rose were the sisters that Michael had to watch out for. They might do anything — trick him, make demands, blame him for trouble. But Mary left him alone. She therefore seemed to him to be much older than Judy and Rose, although she wasn't. There was just a year between her and Rose and two years between her and Judy.

Another reason Mary seemed to be older was that she was quiet. She was hard to get a rise out of, as if nothing were new to her, nothing a surprise or an outrage. She helped Kathleen in the cabin and hardly ever went out anywhere. She was shy.

She was also beautiful. The family might forget to what degree but other people did not. A week before her eighteenth birthday she was picked to be May Queen of the valley. The women dressed her in a white gown. They adorned her black hair with so many ribbons and flowers that it looked to be in bloom. She was given a holly bush to carry, and at the head of a procession of all the young men and girls she marched beside the May King through the town.

It was generally felt that she was the loveliest May Queen ever, her black eyes and regal height attracting particular praise. A piper from the south told Hugh that she put him in mind of a Spanish princess he had once met, whereupon Hugh bought the man whiskeys and said that, as it turned out, the Malones of Offaly, from which strain he himself was descended, had blue blood in their veins. He looked at Mary with new eyes.

Only days later the tailor's son began to court her. His name was Dominick O'Flynne but he was called Slieve, which means 'Mountain', since he was so huge. At the Midsummer's Eve bonfire Michael saw Mary slip behind a stone wall, and a minute later saw Slieve cast wary looks about himself and go behind the same wall. On Hallowe'en the peel of Mary's apple fell onto the ground in the shape of the letter 'S', a sure sign that her future husband would have an 'S' in his initials.

Mary picked up the peel and pressed it between her hands

and said softly, 'Faith, it seems that I will be marrying Slieve O'Flynne.'

Two nights later Slieve's father came to call. He and Hugh got drunk and thrashed out a deal regarding what Mary and Slieve each would bring into the union. Hugh promised a blanket, a piece of bleached linen, a stool, two noggins, two bowls, a crock, a wooden trencher, a cock, three hens, two ducks, a goat and, 'the corker', an acre and a half in the hills that he had rented and would sublet to Slieve for a song. To match all of that Mr. O'Flynne had to promise his milch cow's newly born calf, plus a four-poster bed with shelves beneath it, an excellent wardrobe for Slieve, a pig, a potato bin and three guineas in gold. Lastly he vowed to make sure the cabin was built in time, which was no strenuous undertaking as the wedding was not to take place until the following August because Slieve's elder brother was coming home from America then and Slieve wanted that brother to be best man.

The dealing was sealed with many toasts, after which Mr O'Flynne recited *The Snoring Bedmate*, breaking wind between verses to betoken the husband's snores.

Master Arthur and Lady Morrery had stayed on at Bridun Castle and, proving all prediction wrong, their residence had scarcely created a ripple over the years. At the outset, waves of change had been forecast. Balls, hunts, a flood of carriages on the roads, decrees, who knew what, given that none of the family had lived in The Big House for two generations. But Master Arthur and Lady Morrery dropped into the place deeply and soundlessly, living in gloomy rooms, hardly ever going outside. There were various stories as to why this should be: Master Arthur was ashamed of his limp; Lady Morrery was ashamed of it; she was fearful that he would get another injury out in the world. The most cherished story was that the two of them were under the spell of an unnatural love for each other and that they feared The Big Lord and discovery. When The Big Lord made one of his infrequent visits, mother and son locked themselves away together in her ladyship's bedchamber.

He came to visit in mid-November, two weeks after Hugh and Mr O'Flynne made their deal, and on the very morning that word of his arrival went out, a gentleman came to the cabin, asking after Mary.

He did not enter past the threshold. He said to Kathleen that he had come on behalf of Bridun Castle and that he had a request to make concerning one of her daughters: Mary, he believed the girl's name was. Did she still live here?

'Indeed she does, you honour,' Kathleen said in her slow English.

The gentleman's eyes picked out who else was in the cabin: Michael, Rose, Mary. He pointed his crop. 'Is that the girl?'

'That is Mary, indeed.'

The gentleman looked hard at Mary. Kathleen asked please might she be told what it was his honour was wanting with the girl.

'If you have no objections,' he said, 'the girl is to present herself at the gates tomorrow evening at precisely seven o'clock. I will be there myself to meet her and escort her inside.'

'Inside The Big House?'

He frowned at the ground, as if the question took consideration. 'I expect,' he said at last, 'that there will be an interview. I expect that there will be a discussion concerning work that the girl might prove fit for.'

'Ah,' Kathleen said.

'Do we have an understanding?'

Kathleen turned round to Mary. 'God save our souls, a job at The Big House.' She spoke in Irish. 'Do you want to go and see about it?'

'Aye. Surely.' She and Kathleen looked at each other, their eyes opened wide.

Kathleen turned to the man and said in English, 'We have an understanding, indeed, your honour.'

Her ladyship had learned of Mary as a consequence of Mary's being crowned May Queen, this is what Kathleen decided. The servants had reported that Mary was tall and strong and honest and well-regarded. No doubt they had not failed to mention the wedding next August, and yet her ladyship was considering hiring Mary anyway, more than considering, she was asking for her especially, so the position must only be for a short while, or maybe it wasn't a position that bound the girl who won it to live at The Big House. A kitchen maid, for instance, might work as an outdoor servant. Another possibility, which occurred to Hugh, was that her ladyship also had a position in mind for Slieve, once Slieve and Mary were man and wife. The Big Lord paid generous wages, you had to give him that much. Hugh knew for a fact that the cowkeeper earned six pounds a year plus his keep. A housemaid likely earned the same, and a kitchen maid a bit less. Working together at such wages, and with no rental to worry about, Mary and Slieve would be in clover. Even if there was a job just for Mary alone, she could still count on adding two or three pounds to her dowry.

A certain harper came to the cabin for a meal the following afternoon, and his turning up was almost a promise that Mary would be hired because he had the power to bestow good fortune. Under his greatcoat, which he kept fastened with skewers, you couldn't see it but he had a belt that contained secret charms from many lands. He had been born blind, but one day an inspiration struck him that he should swallow one of his charms, a magic pebble, and no sooner had he done that than his sight was restored. Touching his stomach to feel the bumps of the charms beneath the coat and belt or touching his throat that had swallowed the pebble was how you brought yourself good luck.

Kathleen led him to the hob and wiped his dripping coat with a cloth. Outside it was raining in sheets. Rose poured him a glass of poteen, then gave his throat a rub. He obligingly stretched his neck for her.

'Mary is going to The Big House tonight for an interview,' she told him.

'Is she now?' he shouted. He couldn't help shouting, a condition he said came from years of having had his throat rubbed.

He pulled over a stool for his feet and drained his glass and held it out to have it refilled. Then he took his harp out of its tarpaulin sack and yelled, 'Peggy Brown!' and proceeded to play and sing that song.

He played and sang and drank glass after glass for the rest of the afternoon. Everyone had to holler to be heard over him. The whish of the rain on the thatch rose like a fresh noise when he stopped to eat supper, which was bacon and eggs cooked in his honour. He ate two full helpings and then Mary's portion, since she couldn't eat a morsel. In Kathleen's shoes she paced. She was also wearing Kathleen's green petticoat and her jacket with the long sleeves. Her hair was gathered at the nape with one of the green and yellow ribbons that Kathleen had tied on the bush to entice the fairies, and Rose had stuck a sprig of berries in the knot.

Neal would walk with her to the gates, that was the plan. But by six o'clock the rain had not died and Hugh said he would take her there himself on the mare and wait for her in the gate lodge to bring her back. Every few minutes he checked his timepiece. At half-past six he went out to the byre. Mary donned her cloak and Kathleen sprinkled her with holy water.

'Beware of The Big Lord,' Judy said drunkenly, in a ghostly voice.

'Quiet with you,' Kathleen said furiously. 'Give over that jug.' Judy was sitting at the harper's feet, sharing the jug with him and smoking Kathleen's pipe.

Kathleen patted Mary's hand. 'You won't even know himself is in the house. Sure hiring a maid is no business of his. Now go rub for luck.'

Mary rubbed both the harper's belly and his throat. Under her fingers his Adam's apple bobbed. He sang, 'Oh, many and many a young girl for me is pining.'

Where Michael usually read was on the floor in front of the fire. But Judy was sleeping there, curled up around the poteen jug, her head on the boots of the harper, who was asleep on the hob. So Michael sat on the little table under the window. The light of his candle whipped like a scarf in the draught.

There was a kick at the door. Kathleen lifted her foot from the treadle of the spinning wheel. Michael jumped up and raised the latch, and Neal came in carrying a load of turf sods. Water streamed down his coat and dripped in lines from the brim of his hat. He looked around the room. 'Are they not back yet?' he asked, surprised. He dropped the sods into the creel.

'Not yet,' Kathleen said. 'How are the roads?'

Neal had walked from The Bull and Castle. He lifted one leg

and it was mucky past the knee. 'Terrible,' he said.

Kathleen bit her lip.

'Well,' he said, taking off his hat and hitting it against the wall to get the water out, 'the River Road is terrible on account of the flooding. The Big Road won't be so bad.' He ran his fingers through his straight brown hair, in a gesture like Hugh's. 'Shall I go and take a look out for them?'

'No need for that, I'm sure,' Kathleen said, not sounding sure in the least. They were all imagining the same thing. The mare had a weak knee, and they were imagining her fallen, and Hugh and Mary lying injured in the downpour.

Neal put his hat back on. 'Maybe I'll go anyhow,' he said. 'God knows I cannot get any wetter.'

Michael went with him. They crossed the bridge, wading calf-deep in the high water at either shore. The rain was teeming down like a waterfall, and though the night wasn't black, nothing was visible beyond a few feet. They kept thinking that they heard a horse but they passed no one, not on the road or in the meadows or in the woods, and so they went on, all the way to the limestone wall and then to the gates.

Hugh wasn't in the gate lodge. He was huddled beside the mare by one of the gateposts. When he saw Michael and Neal he yelled over the rain, 'Is your mother frantic?'

'Why are you not inside?' Neal asked.

'Gatekeeper's not there. The fellow that met Mary says don't wait for her, he'll get her home. But I thought I'd wait anyhow, she wouldn't be long.' He shook his head at how mistaken he'd been.

They stood close together up against the mossy stones. The lights of The Big House were pale and distant-seeming through the rain. There were four lights in all and then, in a short while, there were two more small lights that grew larger. A carriage.

At the gates the coachman pulled up and leaped down to unlock them. Hugh called out, 'Is Mary Malone inside?' The coachman, jangling keys, called back that a girl was inside and for all he knew she might be Mary Malone or she might be the Virgin Mary but he had reason to doubt that the latter was the case.

'Will you ask her?' Hugh said.

The coachman turned round to oblige, then halted because

the carriage door was opening. A woman in a cloak climbed out. She was tall enough that she had to be Mary. She swayed.

'Drunk as The Big Lord himself,' the coachman shouted over his shoulder, going to her.

But she was not drunk. No whiskey or ale smell was on her. She would not tell them what had happened. She would not speak at all. She balked and moaned when Hugh tried to help her back into the carriage so that she would have a dry ride home.

'All right, darling, all right. I'll take you on the mare, whatever you want,' he said. He walked her through the gates. Before he lifted her on to the pillion she opened her right hand, and two pieces of gold shone in the light from the carriage lamps.

'By Jesus, what's she got there?' the coachman said.

Hugh took the guineas from her and held them in his own open palm for a moment.

'A pair of golden boys, what do you know about that?' the coachman said. He slapped Neal on the shoulder. He said that he might as well deliver him and Michael wherever they were headed for, seeing as he was out in this flood anyway and Mary was going on the horse.

He drove like a charioteer, but Hugh still beat them home somehow. The mare, saddled, sides heaving, was left out in the yard. 'I'll deal with her,' Neal said.

Michael ran inside. Rose was standing in the centre of the room, her knuckles at her mouth. From the bigger outshot there was coughing in morbid heaves, which was not coughing, Michael realized in a moment, it was sobbing, Mary sobbing. Kathleen, in there with her, said, ''Tis not the end of the world.'

Rose slid her knuckles down to her chin. 'She wasn't hired,' she whispered.

Michael looked at the outshot, at the mat that covered the doorway. He could see his father's feet. He couldn't see his mother's or Mary's. Mary was saying something. Hugh said, 'What did she say?' then Kathleen said urgently, 'Out of here, Hugh.'

Hugh's feet turned. He strode around the hanging mat, stopped and looked unseeingly at Michael and Rose, then at the door as it opened and Neal came in.

64

'So what's happened?' Neal said.

Hugh held up a hand for silence. Mary was speaking again, but in sobs, and the rain was falling harder and the harper was snoring, so you couldn't hear what she was saying. Kathleen spoke but you couldn't hear her either. Michael watched drops elongate and fall from the brim of his hat.

'Oh, dear God,' Kathleen said. They all heard that.

Hugh rushed back around the mat. 'What is it?' he said, shouting. It sounded as if Mary were screaming from far away, as if she had the blanket in her mouth. Kathleen, answering Hugh, sounded as if she were gasping. Hugh hollered, 'What? What?' then tore the mat from the entrance and roared, 'Get Doctor Rennie!'

'No!' Mary screamed. With the mat gone, Michael could see her lying on her stomach on the bed, and his mother half-lying over her.

Kathleen twisted her head around. Her face was startlingly red. 'There's no need for that,' she said.

'Get him!' Hugh threw a fist from Neal to the door.

'There's nothing he can do,' Kathleen cried.

Hugh went back to the bed. 'But there's the blood,' he said disbelievingly.

Kathleen stood and pushed him out into the room. She picked up the mat and hung it quickly and askew on the nails.

Hugh seemed thunderstuck. He took a step, halted. A slow grimace overtook his face until he looked so wretched and altered that Michael thought that he was dying before their eyes. Then he reeled over to the dresser. He swung his arm along one ledge and all of the bowls and plates and a mug with Rose's flowers flew towards the hearth, smashing inches away from Judy and the harper sleeping there. Neither of them stirred.

'Damn his soul,' Hugh roared. 'Damn his black soul to hell! By God, by God, I'll slash his black throat. I'll stick his gut for a pig. While I live —' He pounded his chest and glared at Michael and Neal. 'Do you hear me? That bastard, I swear ...' He fumbled in his coat pocket, drew out the two guineas and flung them into the fire. He stood there breathing in gusts. Rose began to cry.

'Whist, whist,' Hugh said tiredly, waving his hand in Rose's direction. He sank on to a stool and picked up a piece of broken plate and sat inspecting it, opening and squeezing his fingers around it.

At daybreak Kathleen swept up the pieces of crockery. Michael dreamed that the sound of the besom was waves pitching on a shore, although waves were a sound that he had never heard. He was on the ground between Judy and the dogs. He awoke with no recollection of having lain down there.

He sat up and saw the harper sitting up also, planting confounded blinks around the room. Kathleen, keeping her eyes on her sweeping, told the harper that he should leave now, that Tyrell the Fairy Man would give him breakfast.

The harper frowned at the pile of shattered crockery. 'To tell God's truth,' he shouted, 'I have no memory of the revelry.'

That woke everyone up. Judy held her head and looked groggily at Michael sitting beside her. 'What's going on?' she said.

'Fetch the pail,' Kathleen said to her, and the two of them went out to milk, the harper leaving with them.

Michael took two sods out of the creel and banked them. Under the grate the guineas glimmered. He covered them with embers then blew at the sods until there was a flame.

Turning from the hearth he saw his father watching him. Hugh was across the room, sitting against the churn. Michael picked up the jug, which Judy had held in her sleep all night, and shook it to see if there was any poteen left. There was a bit. 'Do you want a glass?' he asked his father.

Hugh mouthed no.

When Judy came back inside, it was plain from her staggered look that she had been told. Unasked, she went about making the porridge. Then she fried two eggs for Mary, but when Kathleen brought them in to her, Mary began to cry. So Kathleen apportioned them for everyone else.

Rose wondered if Father Lynn should be sent for. Not this morning, Kathleen said.

'What about Slieve?' Rose whispered.

Kathleen closed her eyes. 'Merciful Mother,' she said, as if she'd forgotten all about Slieve.

'Devil a man will have his name on her now,' Neal muttered.

66

'Shut your mouth,' Kathleen said in a savage whisper. She sat down. In the same motion Hugh rose. He came to the hearth and regarded her. The skin around his eyes was puckered and the colour of meal. His hair stood up all over his head from running his fingers through it. 'I should have gone to law after he whipped yourself,' he said.

'Will you have a bite now?' Kathleen said, holding her own bowl out to him.

'In Derry. Or Belfast. I should have gone to the magistrates where he isn't a power.'

Kathleen snapped to her feet and scraped her porridge back into the pot. 'Do you think big lords in them places never raise whips to anybody?' she said harshly.

'It was murder,' Hugh said. 'You were carrying a baby in your belly. It was murder pure and simple.'

''Tis over and done with.'

'Whether he knew it or not, whether you were showing or not, a baby died at his hand. Murder. Pure and simple.'

'Stop saying that.'

'That's right. I will not say it. It scalds my soul to say it. A man whips the babies out of my wife and I don't lift a finger.'

'What *could* you have done, for the love of God?'

'Gone to the magistrates in Derry or Belfast,' he said, as if repeating it for a simpleton. 'Demanded my justice.'

Kathleen flung out the ladle. 'Listen to himself,' she said. '"Demanded my justice", I declare to God.'

Hugh looked at her impassively. 'There are laws in this land. If there is such a law that says a man can take a virgin girl by brute force, have her for a night and throw her away, then I will hear that law from a judge himself.'

'And do you know what any judge will tell you? Your daughter is honoured. That's what he'll tell you. The Big Lord himself chose her. It is an honour.'

'Dada,' Neal said gently, 'even if the judge is fair-minded and all, you have to prove your case. His lordship will deny it out and out.'

'There's Mary's word.'

'Are you mad?' Kathleen said. 'She can hardly lift her eyes to her own mother. Do you think she'll describe to a judge what it is he did to her?'

'Then I will describe it.'

'You will not. We all of us will carry the secret and the shame of this to our graves.'

Hugh leaned into the chimney, bracing himself with his hands. 'Jesus!' he said, and struck his forehead on the stone. 'Would you have me do nothing?' He struck his head again. 'Would you have me doing nothing? Jesus!' He kept striking his head. Kathleen winced but was silent.

He left the house. At midnight a potboy from The Bull and Castle brought him home, and the boy and Neal carried him into the cabin. It was just before supper the next day that Slieve came by. He rode his father's horse. Hugh met him at the foot of the property, and the two of them walked down the river a ways. A little while later, Hugh came into the yard alone. 'He went dumb like,' he said.

Since Mary would not eat, Kathleen fetched Father Lynn the following morning. He returned with her and spent the entire afternoon in the outshot, praying at the bedside. Mary hid under the blanket. Another night and morning passed and she took only water. Hugh said they could thank Him that made them that she was a big girl to start with.

Near midday Slieve turned up again. He asked Kathleen if he might see Mary.

'Do you still want her?' Kathleen said severely.

'Surely,' he said, slighted, not seeming to understand. 'Surely I do.'

Kathleen nodded. 'Come back in two or three days, lad. She will be better by then, knowing you still want her.'

It was true. Mary ate a cake that night. In the morning, when Father Lynn dropped by, she was sitting before the fire, letting Rose comb her hair.

'Ah,' Father Lynn said with a gratified smile, as if his prayers were to be credited. He drew her hands out of her lap and folded them in both of his own. With her arms lifted like that, you could see the rope burns on her wrists.

Chapter 12

Wales

Michael slept after his morning walk. Between all of Olwen's appearances he slept, waking for meals, sleeping, waking, eating. She could not linger in the afternoons or after supper except on Sunday evenings and every second Wednesday evening when Rosser went to his chapel. On those evenings, as soon as Rosser was gone, she came upstairs and chattered while he dozed off and on. Sometimes she sang Welsh love songs with great feeling, clasping her hands before her breast, smacking passionate kisses in the air, trailing her fingers from her eyes to show the route of falling tears.

When he was feeling vigorous enough they played games. Her favourite was thinking up an object and having him guess what it was by asking questions that had to be answered aye or nay. In another game she would suggest a category, insects, for instance, then he would name an insect and she would name another and back and forth until one of them couldn't go on.

Whatever they were up to ended at the sound of footsteps on the cobbles outside. Then she raced downstairs to sit at her spinning wheel or just to sit quietly, if it was Sunday, because Rosser did not abide games and songs and weekday idleness. Before Rosser washed himself and she came up to bed, the two of them said prayers together.

She slept in the loft, behind the curtain on a mattress. She undressed with her rushlight still lit. If Michael was awake he watched her blurry silhouette, seeing her form distinctly only when she came close to the curtain and then only seeing it in parts. But some nights he saw her in the flesh. Some nights she walked naked beyond the curtain to the front window and leaned her hands on the ledge to look out. She had long thick legs and an alarmingly big bottom. Her breasts were shaped like the bowls of spoons and they filled the cupped space made by her body curving.

He would feel desire. But it was not for her. And then he would feel the oppression that escorted any thought of Etain, that was like being in a coffin under the massive weight of earth and his own stagnation.

Chapter 13

Ireland

Kathleen had always said that Judy was going along a slippery slope, but now she said that Judy was going to the devil on a steeplechaser. The turn for the worse was due to the fact that Judy still would not end her association with the Coogans and, indeed, she spent more time with them than ever before, in spite of rumours that the Coogan brothers, under ringleader Andy Coogan, were stealing horses.

Judy said that the rumours were a pack of lies. Kathleen said maybe so, but while the rumours lasted Judy's good name was tottering on the brink. Judy impudently sang back, 'A woman told *me* that a woman told *her* that she saw a woman who saw a woman who made ale of potatoes,' which was what Kathleen herself sometimes said when she was feeling ill-disposed towards idle gossip.

All kinds of gossip constantly flew about regarding the Coogans, and most of it was outlandish and harmless. But horses *were* being stolen and people were seething. A band of graziers had taken to patrolling the highways, and John Logan, who had lost a pair of stud horses to the thieves, was appearing on cabin stoops at all hours to conduct searches. None of this deterred the thieves. They struck at night. They were never spied. The theory was that the horses were being spirited directly to the south, slaughtered, smuggled across to France and sold to feed the soldiers there.

The first north-shore horse to be stolen was Darby Fennel's Grada. As soon as Michael saw Darby walking along the River Road on foot, the morning after Little Chistmas, he knew that

Grada was meat for the French soldiers. Darby never walked if he could ride. He was tiny and shy about it, so he wore a tall hat that had not once been observed off his head except presumably by Norah, his wife, and he rode Grada, a colossal horse, everywhere, even into shops provided that the doorways were high enough.

He had come by to find out if anybody had heard the thieves during the night. Nobody had, though Darby only lived across the bog. 'Ah, they're cute all right,' he said. He was quaking. He confessed that Norah had flogged him for not being vigilant.

'Did she use the pizzle?' Michael had to ask. His mother smacked him.

'Oh, aye,' Darby said equably. The pizzle, the bull's penis, had been bequeathed to Norah by her father, who had reputedly used it to flog Norah's mother.

After Darby left, Hugh said, 'A marriage made in hell.' The pizzle was the least of it. Darby was a Catholic and Norah a Protestant, so the union was cursed from the outset, on top of which Norah was barren as a result of being part man. She had to shave her face, and her hips were as narrow as a boy's.

Three days later another three Catholic horses had been stolen, and Darby returned to deliver the news that Norah had formed a posse. Everybody knew that Andy Coogan was the culprit, he said. Norah was going to haul him over the coals and get a confession out of him. In the posse, besides Norah, there was John Logan and a dozen farmers from across the river. 'They'll be up there about now,' Darby said.

Kathleen exclaimed because Judy wasn't home, which meant she would be at the Coogans'. Hugh asked Darby if there was a magistrate among the men.

'Well, there might be.' Darby scratched the back of his neck. 'Norah didn't specify.'

Hugh said that he didn't like the sound of it. The Coogan place had been searched with a fine-toothed comb and nothing had been found. He wasn't inferring that Andy or his brothers weren't the thieves, only that a confession made under torture wasn't worth a rotten straw.

Darby looked afflicted.

'I'd better be getting Judy from there,' Hugh said, taking his coat off of its peg.

'Neal has the mare,' Kathleen said.

'I'll borrow Tyrell's.'

Darby went out with him. Kathleen, changing her tack, said, 'Heaven help us, what if Andy is innocent after all?'

Michael was wondering the same thing. He saw in his mind John Logan and Norah Fennel snapping whips around Andy's ears, and the farmers in a circle behind, aiming guns, and he thought of Jesus saying unto the disciples, 'Judge not that ye be not judged'. It occurred to him that the proof that people had been waving about all week was scarcely conclusive. The extent of it was, Andy had been caught stealing chickens a year ago and Mr Coogan, who was too addled to earn a wage, had been buying rounds at taverns with coins that he maintained he had just found lying on the dresser in his cabin. The rest of the proof was really slander. The Coogan brothers were 'sneaky' and 'sly'. Andy was a 'criminal mastermind'. And yet a month ago, when the brothers bought a conspicuously ailing sow that died the next day, people had been making remarks such as you couldn't find two brains to rub together in the entire clan.

Michael hated not knowing for sure. It was not so much the risk of injustice being done as the uncertainty itself. He opened a book of poems and read stanzas and lines haphazardly, searching in his chance selections for symbolic messages pointing to Andy's guilt or innocence.

By supper Hugh and Judy weren't back and Neal hadn't returned either. Only Rose had any appetite. Kathleen kept checking Hugh's timepiece on the dresser and announcing the time with rising distress. At ten minutes past seven there was a light tapping on the door. Michael opened it.

'Mrs Coogan,' he said in surprise, and behind him his mother called out in alarm, 'Mrs Coogan!'

'Afore your living eyes,' Mrs Coogan said, stepping inside. 'God bless all here.' She smelled like a yeasting vat. She swayed and Michael caught her arm.

'Good heavens, what has happened?' Kathleen said, taking hold of her other arm.

'The old legs aren't what they were,' Mrs Coogan answered.

Kathleen led her to the hearth. 'Is our Judy safe? Did my husband send you?'

Mrs Coogan dropped on to Hugh's stool and stretched her swaddled legs towards the fire. 'Ah, there's a comfort,' she said. 'Hours and hours have I been on my way down to here. Since midday. But up by the two bogs didn't I fall in a hole and get stuck entirely, and sure to die but for a sup I had tucked away for the rheumatics and that bringed back my strength.' She coughed, a dry cough with no phlegm in it.

Kathleen nodded at Rose to pour a glass. She pulled a stool up in front of Mrs Coogan and sat. 'Mrs Coogan, why have you come? Is it about my daughter?' She spoke in the precise loud voice that she used with idiots.

Tears spilled from Mrs Coogan's eyes. Rose gave her the glass of poteen and she grasped it in both hands and drank it right down, her jaw trembling. Then she said, 'They are gone forever.'

'Who?' Kathleen said. 'Who are gone?'

'Judy, and my Andy.' She threw back her head and started to wail.

Kathleen stood. 'Judy? Andy?' she cried.

Mrs Coogan wailed on, her mouth opened wide as a baby's. You could count the five brown teeth in her head.

'Stop that!' Kathleen commanded. Mrs Coogan's mouth clamped shut. She looked suddenly alert.

'Now, what do you mean, gone forever?' Kathleen said, but the horror of realization was in her voice.

'Run away together,' Mrs Coogan sniffed. 'You know.'

'Eloped.'

'That's it.'

'When?'

'This very morning. On a horse that my Andy won gaming.'

Kathleen closed her eyes. 'Mother of Heaven,' she said. She stood up. 'Did Judy leave any word?' she asked.

Mrs Coogan nodded broadly. 'Indeed. She says to tell you that I am to have her green stockings and my Sally is to have her new petticoat, the one that was to be for Mary's wedding.' She coughed. 'So,' she said, 'I could be taking them things now and saving a trip.'

Kathleen said, 'Leave my house.' It came out muffled

74

because she had covered her mouth with her hands.

'What?' Mrs Coogan asked pleasantly.

Kathleen grabbed Mrs Coogan by the shoulder to bring her to her feet but got only a handful of her frayed shawl and yanked it so hard that she tore off a whole corner. Mrs Coogan looked scandalized.

'Out of here!' Kathleen cried, whipping the piece of shawl at her.

Mrs Coogan rose, backing away. Still holding the glass she waddled as quickly as she could to the door. Michael shut it after her.

'May she die in a bog pool,' Kathleen said, 'the foolish foolish woman.' She fell on to a stool. She appealed to the Blessed Virgin and all the saints. 'A horse thief, what was my sin?' She began rocking herself. She lamented motherhood. She wished Judy under the sod rather than this. She said the family name was besmirched entirely.

Mary burst into tears at that. Nobody would come to her wedding, she cried. The dogs got skittery and barked to be let outside. Michael put on his hat to go out with them, but then the door opened and his father came in. Hugh surveyed the scene and said, 'So you know.'

'Will she hang?' Kathleen cried.

'She wasn't in on the stealing, Mother, nobody is saying that.'

'But she knew about it, did she not? She knew that her paramour was stealing her neighbour's goods!' She pointed a straight wavering arm in the direction of Darby Fennel's. She was outrage incarnate.

'She may not have,' Hugh said. He said that Andy had bamboozled even his brothers. They, it seemed, thought that all of Andy's newly gained money had been won at gambling, that he had been blessed with the most amazing streak of luck. They never saw any horses, but they did see the men who were probably Andy's confederates — a pair of strangers professing to be operators of a gaming house. As for Andy running off, his brothers claimed it was in order to marry Judy and for no other reason. You had to believe that the brothers were innocent themselves, Hugh said, since they hadn't run off and since they were daft enough to produce, as evidence of Andy's good character, a purse full of gold that he had left behind for the family's needs. Of course, John Logan seized the purse.

Kathleen came to her feet. 'Our new in-laws,' she said sarcastically. She began pacing about the room, attacking spiders on the clay walls with the piece of Mrs Coogan's shawl. She asked if Judy and Andy would be caught.

'No, no, I don't think that they will be,' Hugh said. He told how he had gone with the posse to the lodgings of the strangers, but naturally they were also long gone. 'A wild goose chase,' he said. 'They had six hours on ourselves, them and Andy. They're well on their way south somewhere, to wherever it was they were sending the horses. There will be warrants and more searching and all, but ...' He blew out a breath, shook his head.

'Grand. Grand,' Kathleen said, lashing high up at spiders that weren't there. She was tall enough to reach the rafters. 'Let them get clean away, please God. That girl has no home here.' So incensed was she that when Mary fell into another fit of weeping and said again that nobody would come to her wedding, she said, 'Likely not.'

'I hate her, I hate her,' Mary wept.

Michael left the house. The noise from inside, though less loud, sounded more uproarious in the yard, sounded like revelry within the vaster sounds of the night, the wind wailing, the leaves swishing. He would go to The Bull and Castle, he decided when he got to the road. Neal would be there. He would break the news to Neal, unless it had already been broken. Bad news has good legs.

In the moonlight everything far away was a chorus of shadows. There was no complete blackness. The wind swirled leaves and raised fins of dust on the dry parts of the road. Michael said, 'God speed ye,' to the dust in case it was fairies out on a journey. He thought of Judy galloping through this squally night on somebody's stolen horse. Realizing that he might never see her again, he tried to picture her face. He couldn't. He stopped walking and shut his eyes. Still he couldn't. All he could see was a shaft of bright ragged light, like lightning.

76

Chapter 14

Wales

Not the light itself but the light moving awoke him. He stiffened to see the wavering flame so near his eyes.

'What?' he said.

Then he saw the line of the face and a beam of white hair. He rose to his elbows, completely alert now. He felt as if his body were shooting antennae into the fraught night. He thought he heard riders.

'What is it?' he whispered, realizing as he spoke that Rosser was naked, realizing the strangeness of that and yet still fearing capture, instantly coming to mad doomy understanding — they must strip, hide the clothing, foil the soldiers.

Rosser did not answer. His arm began to tremble then wave convulsively. Candle grease flew. Michael grabbed the arm to steady it, and at his touch it immediately went still. He took the light out of Rosser's hand.

'Jesus, man, what is it?' he said, holding the light up to Rosser's face.

Rosser's head was thrown back, his mouth agape, his eyes all white.

'God Almighty,' Michael whispered. He called softly, 'Olwen.' She had said that she never woke Rosser from a vision because it might stop his heart.

Across the room Olwen snored. Michael put the light on the stool and called to her as loudly as he dared. She slept on. Rosser made a gurgling sound in his throat, like the death rattle, and Michael thought maybe it was best just to stay quiet and wait for the vision to end.

Rosser swayed and gurgled. What anguishing sight was he perceiving? The crucifixion? He leaned forward, his hands before him, and Michael raised his own hands, ready to catch him if he should fall, but Rosser caught himself by gripping the edge of the bed. He dropped to his knees.

His hands slipped under the quilt. They swam over the mattress. They halted, lifted together, and came down gently on Michael's thigh.

Michael jerked his leg away. It was reflex. Rosser blinked. Michael thought, frightened, "If he wakes up and dies, he's killed his bloody self."

He did wake up. Or appear to. His pupils came back to the whites and stared straight into Michael's eyes.

'Rosser?' Michael said.

Rosser turned his head and looked at the stool. Little flames from the rushlight were in each of his eyes. He picked up the light, stood and walked, with a graceful smooth step that he never had normally, to the stairwell.

Chapter 15

Ireland

Early in March the Coogans left the valley. John Logan had evicted them after Andy left and for a time they'd lived in a cavern behind their old property, but with no one giving them work or food they hadn't been able to stay once they'd used up their store of potatoes. They went to Wexford, Neal heard.

People stopped talking about them, and about Judy. For one thing, better gossip came along. A woman gave birth to twins that were joined head to head and that lived for three weeks even though the mother wouldn't nurse them. A curate went demented with grief over his sister's death and moped about the town dressed in her clothing.

For another thing, winter was over and people's minds were on ploughing and sowing and paring and burning and making the lazy beds and hauling and spreading manure. Kathleen still detected aspersions in certain individuals' remarks, but Hugh said that she was listening for it, hearing the worst, that there were two edges to any knife and one edge cut and one didn't. Which didn't deny the fact of the knife itself, Kathleen said.

She believed that the family name held a stigma and she spoke of mortifying herself — fasting and cutting her hair to her shoulders. In the the first weeks after Judy ran off she went through a dangerous spell of largess during which she brought home all the beggars she passed on the road and baked them gigantic cakes and gave them the blankets to keep. Everybody she talked to, even perfect strangers, she invited to Mary's wedding. It was going to be a feast, she said, the biggest let-out

79

in years. She told people, making no bones about it, that she felt that the family had an obligation.

By the way Mr McCaffery squired her into the yard for the bride's breakfast, holding her elbow, nodding at everyone, you'd have thought Etain was the one getting married that day. He was showing off her new green gown. A draper's wife had made it for the price of three geese, a preposterous extravagance. It was a woman's gown, low-necked, tight in the bodice. Etain's mother, swiping dust off the skirt, hobbled behind the pair of them. Etain looked embarrassed. When she saw Michael she reddened and gave him a childish apologetic smile. He turned and went into the cabin.

It was suffocating with so many women inside and all the steaming food. He stood at the door and felt himself perspiring. The naked tops of Etain's breasts still seemed to be before his eyes. He tried to remember exactly how she had looked yesterday at school, in her jacket. Had she had breasts yesterday?

Slieve's mother pushed a trencher of bacon at him. 'Here,' she said. He took it and thought, "They've come too soon," meaning Etain's breasts had. He had not expected them for years yet, not until he was ready to marry her. He felt outsmarted.

'Go on,' Slieve's mother said to him.

A throng was in the yard. Most of them were relations of Slieve's. He had ten aunts on his mother's side alone. The Malones had none, and no uncles either. As for cousins, they were in America or in heaven was what Kathleen told people. The single thing that she could recall about her cousins, whom she met as a young girl before they sailed away, was that they had all been able to bend their thumbs back to their wrists.

Michael put the trencher on the table nearest to the cabin. The tables weren't actually tables, they were the neighbours' unhinged doors mounted on firkins and stools. Two of them were completely covered with food and drink. There was milk, ale and beer, cakes, flummery, two other trenchers of bacon and twelve bowls of eggs, six bowls each of geese and hens' eggs. Michael contemplated the eggs and became serene.

80

Presently, however, his eyes lifted of their own will and looked around the yard.

She and her father and mother had found seats beside an uncle of Slieve's who, being a linen merchant, was probably the richest man present. He was a bachelor. Mr McCaffery was presenting him with Etain's arm and prevailing upon him to examine the cloth of her sleeve. Michael said stonily to himself, "She will marry him." He shrugged, and the shoulders of his new jacket, which was too large for him, fell forwards.

During the breakfast she walked past him once on the far side of his table. She halted as though she wanted to talk to him, but he pretended not to notice her, to be interested in a story that Neal was telling, so she walked on. He only saw her out of the corner of his eye after that. She went to Father Lynn's in a cart with the rest of the girls who weren't in the wedding party. Michael went on foot in the company of six of Slieve's cousins. Like Slieve they were all king-size and freckled. They played a humiliating game with him as they walked, encircling him like a high fence. Even at Father Lynn's, where he should have stood with his family, they kept him corralled until the ceremony ended.

While his family and Slieve's family were kissing each other, Michael slipped outside to be one of the first at the punch. Then he went to the road to watch more guests arrive for the race back to his father's house. He couldn't stop looking around. He kept thinking that he heard her or saw her coming up beside him. He felt that it wasn't that he wanted to see her but that he wanted to see her before she saw him. He was so distracted and wound up that when Neal tapped his shoulder with a crop he spun round and his hat fell off.

'Ho,' Neal said, jerking his right arm back as though he were stopping the horse he was on. On the pillion behind him was Annie Murphy. She was sixteen, a year older than Michael, and the oldest of five girls. Her father owned The Bull and Castle. She was fat and had thick snakey hair like a fury.

'My dada is letting Neal ride our Cyrus in the race,' she said. 'I am riding with him.'

'Good luck to yourselves,' Michael said.

'Why don't you ride behind Darby?' she joked. Darby

Fennel had replaced Grada with a stallion that he'd named Lightning.

'Make believe you're Norah,' Neal said.

'But, Neal, he cannot, he hasn't the whiskers,' Annie cried, laughing.

'Ho, Little Scholar,' Neal said meaninglessly.

Michael looked at him hostilely. "Little Scholar", he was sick of that. Neal was maybe an inch taller than he was, no more. He thought of pointing to Neal's hair, which was sticking out like hay under his hat, and saying, "You look like a lunatic." But something stopped him and then Annie began falling off the pillion and shrieking, so he walked away.

He went to the end of Father Lynn's garden and took off his coat. The day was sweltering. A mile down the hill was the river. He decided to go home along the bank. The others who weren't riding would be taking the road, to see the racers. That he was not racing himself seemed demeaning to him now, yet it hadn't done earlier.

As he got nearer to the river he removed more clothing — his hat and waistcoat, then his shirt. At the shore he laid them on a rock and wet his face and scooped water into his mouth. He fell back on his elbows. Across the river a huddle of black cows stood under an alder, swatting their tails. Everything else — the meadow grasses, the leaves — was still. The river was the motionless world above it, perfectly so only darker. The birds were silent. Everything was silent and still, a picture of itself.

He lay on the long grass and closed his eyes. There were her high little breasts again, trembling before his sight, swelling, being shed, by her hands, of their green bodice. Then the dream changed and her hands, which were now shielding herself, became his hands.

Something startled him, not his conscience but some movement that nevertheless felt like his conscience and made him sit up and idiotically call out 'Aye' as if he had been summoned. It was a pair of ducks down river, entering the water through the rushes. He watched them slice the glassy surface halfway to the far shore then he pulled off his stockings and shoes and his breeches and galloped in after them, sending up fountains of splashing. It was in his mind that if he caught them he would be cleansed of his desire.

For what felt like hours he zigzagged after them up and down the river, finally losing sight of them altogether. He floated on his back. To God Almighty, who was above him, above the pale sky, he prayed for the strength to resist all desires of the flesh, but he knew that he prayed without true penitence. He blamed the heat.

'Ferris won the race!' Rose screamed. She raised Ferris's arm and made him wave at Michael, coming into the yard. Ferris raised his other arm and waved the prize bottle. He was Slieve's brother who had come home from America. Since he was the best man, and Rose was the bridesmaid, the two of them had ridden together to Father Lynn's.

'Congratulations to yourself,' Michael said when he reached them.

'The luck of the beginner,' Ferris said.

'You are no beginner and it wasn't luck at all,' Rose said. 'It was pure skill the way you sailed over the ditch like a bird.' She indicated exactly where at the ditch with Ferris's hand, which she was still holding, then she laid it on her bosom. 'It was like seeing the bird of paradise. I thought I'd died and gone straight to heaven.'

Michael stared at Ferris's hand on his sister's breast. Ferris asked him where he himself had been all this time.

'Swimming,' Michael said, looking up quickly.

Ferris grinned conspiratorially and tugged his hand free. 'Ah, swimming,' he said.

'Swimming is for fish,' Rose said, sniffing. She couldn't swim. She turned her back to Ferris and began to sway her hips to the music. Under her arms there were big circles of sweat. Ferris looked around the yard.

'Rose,' Kathleen's voice called.

Rose sighed. She waved at Ferris with her fingers under her chin. 'Don't budge an inch,' she said and skipped over to the cabin.

The women were bringing dinner outside on to the tables. Eggs, bacon and cakes, the same as at breakfast, and also spiced beef, potatoes, carrots, cabbages, berries and a pudding as big as a sty. After the blessing everyone pushed and grabbed good-naturedly to get at the meat, then found places on the

83

ground because the tables were covered with food. The women spread out shawls. Michael went under the boor trees to eat. He sat there beside the fiddler who was blind and listening to the piper, who was a dwarf, describe the food on his plate.

He knew where Etain was, having seen her before when he came into the yard. She was with a crowd of girls at the hedge, where Tyrrell the Fairy Man had been prophesying future husbands. Who had he prophesied for her? The linen merchant? At this moment her father was actually trying to feed the merchant, offering him slices of meat from his own plate. The merchant, to his credit, was turning away his head. He had his hat off and his hair was almost completely grey. He was far too old for her. Maybe he would die soon.

The prospect enlivened Michael. He cleaned his plate, stood and looked aggressively about the yard. He saw Corny looking around also, probably for him. He didn't feel like talking to Corny, so he strode the other way, to the byre wall where the kegs and hard drinkers were. He decided to get drunk. It was high time, in the day and in his life.

Behind the kegs two of Slieve's friends were posted, filling jars and bottles. Both of them were named Kinnard — Tall Kinnard and Small Kinnard, in spite of which they were the same size. Small Kinnard greeted Michael in the most loving manner and poured him a jar of 'the special stuff'.

'Your health,' Michael saluted him. He drained the jar in five swallows, igniting a line of fire down his throat. 'Another,' he gasped, and he gulped that down. 'Another.'

He didn't drink the whole of the third jar because it slipped out of his fingers. He dropped to his knees to pick it up but forgot about it once he was down. The earth beneath his hands and legs was so cool and firm. He stayed kneeling a long time, until somebody knocked him over. Then he crawled into a space between two kegs and nestled there and watched the shifting forest of legs in front of him, feeling surpassingly fond of them all. He felt that he was glowing and orange-coloured.

Some time later he thought he would have another whiskey, and he stood up. Small Kinnard said that there was going to be a leaping match, and then Michael saw that the tables had been carried to the edge of the yard, and boys were making practice leaps and removing their shirts and shoes and stockings. He

84

stayed where he was, happy to be only a spectator. A lump came to his throat. He could have sobbed in the fullness of his affection and regard for the competitors, for all competitors since the world began.

The victor was Reagan Lunney, the boy who had the emerald eyes that caused the girls to faint. Girls swarmed on him when he made the winning leap.

'Give the girls a kiss,' people shouted.

'Give the girls a kiss,' Michael chorused. He watched as Reagan pulled one of the girls to his naked chest and kissed her on the mouth. The girl had yellow hair and a green dress. The girl was Etain.

Michael pointed at her. 'Murder,' he yelled, and so did the man next to him, just because Michael had. The man smiled and offered Michael his bottle. Michael snatched it and gulped down what whiskey was left. When he looked at the man again he was gone, and through the space where he'd been Corny was approaching.

'Why aren't you in the race?' Corny asked.

'What race?'

'The race to the river.' Corny nodded at the hollow behind the byre. A line of boys was there, taking their marks. 'You could show all those O'Flynnes,' Corny said.

'What race?' Michael said. He swayed. He saw only one boy clearly in the line. That was Reagan, already there. He was tossing his brilliant smile at the bystanders and pawing his feet on the ground.

Michael dropped the bottle. He swept Corny aside. He charged through the crowd.

The race started. The runners passed him going the opposite way as he ran to get to the starting line. Without slowing, he circled beyond the line and crossed it. He flew past the smaller boys, past the pack in front of them. On either side of him people cheered, and bright kerchiefs waved out at him like licks of flame. His legs churned faster and faster, he passed more boys. He was a cart let loose down a hill.

Only two runners were ahead of him now. One was the boy with the six webbed toes, who always won races. The other was Reagan. Michael was convinced that if he didn't win he would die. He exhorted his legs to go faster, faster, and for the first time in any race with the webfooted boy, he hurtled past him.

The green before his eyes became brown. The River Road. At its near side he was behind Reagan's shoulder, close enough to touch him. At its far side he was in front.

Uncertain of the finish line and, in any case, unable to slow his legs, he kept going, over the bank and into the river. It was milk-warm and lapping. Girls cried out his name.

He awoke in darkness, in his own bed. The air was steamy and there was a smell like cloves and old butter. There was singing and hullabaloo coming from outside the cabin.

He was wearing only his breeches. They were wet at the knees and waistband, which made him remember the race. 'Ha!' he said aloud to think of Reagan vanquished. But he couldn't remember what had happened after he'd run into the river. So fairly soon after winning he must have lost consciousness. On what? Three glasses? That was pitiable. It meant that he had a bad head, a woman's head.

His legs were heavy. He moved them and something slid off his knees. Raising himself and reaching to touch the thing, he saw that it was a baby. It began to produce sucking noises. All around him, like bolsters, other babies were slumped.

Without waking any of them he slipped off the top end of the mattress. When he came to his feet the insides of his skull slopped about for a moment. He went around the dresser. A man was snoring on the hob, and a heap of bodies were in front of the fire. In the outshots more babies and children were sleeping. For the sake of quiet, presumably, the door was closed, top and bottom halves. He opened them and his eyes were assulted by the light of a huge bonfire that was blazing in the middle of the yard. People were dancing around it crazily, like fairies. The men dancers were bare-chested. Boys were throwing burning sticks into the air and yelling, 'Shooting star!' The tables were gone, and people were sitting on the firkins and stools. Michael saw Mary and Slieve sitting with old people.

He stepped out, closing the door behind him. A girl came running towards the cabin. She screamed his name, and when she passed into the light he saw that it was Annie Murphy. She was breathless. She took his hand in hers. Her bodice was unfastened almost to her waist, and the skin of her bosom looked slippery.

'They're burning the doors, can you fathom it?' she said fervidly. She swung his hands back and forth. 'Michael Malone,' she said. 'May I never stir but that was the most thrilling race I ever saw in my life.'

He laughed.

'Reagan Lunney saved you from drowning.' She let go of him and acted the incident out. 'Picked you up by the hair just before you went under. Then threw you over his shoulder. Flop. Like you were a fish. Didn't I laugh my head off? Oh, and Michael, your eyes! Opened they were but only the white parts showing.' She shuddered.

What he should do was go back inside and lie down again with the babies. But she took his arm and pulled it. 'Come along to the hollow now,' she said. 'The games are starting.'

'Games?'

She drew herself close to him and he felt the ruffle of her bodice on his chest. 'Kissing games,' she whispered. 'You can kiss me now if you want to.' Her lips touched his ear lobe.

Neal approached from behind him. Consequently Michael didn't see him and he thought, as Annie shoved him from her, that she was offended by something about his ear. She ran to Neal. 'Michael tried to kiss me,' she said in a little girl voice, laying her head on Neal's bare shoulder.

'Out to win the girls as well, eh, Little Scholar? By God, if that race didn't beat all. How's the noddle?' He knocked on his own forehead.

Michael said that it was as good as could be hoped for considering the quantities of whiskey, ale, poteen, beer and punch he had downed. Neal just looked at him without expression, so Michael went on to enumerate pints and glasses. Annie, publican's daughter, said, 'Horseshit. Nobody can drink that much and recall it.'

'Well, now, Annie, darling,' Neal said, smiling, adult-like, and Michael knew that he wasn't fooled either. 'What you have to bear in mind is that Michael is a scholar, and scholars can hold a deal more in their heads than mortals such as ourselves can.' He reached behind his back. 'Speaking of the devil . . .' he said, and extracted a bottle from his belt. He uncorked it with his teeth, spit the cork away and took a swig. He tipped it at Annie's mouth, then at Michael's. Michael seized it and drank it right down to show Annie.

'Ho!' Neal shouted. He squeezed Annie to him and threw an arm around Michael's neck. 'Forward, march!' he shouted, and locked together like that the three of them staggered to the hollow.

They had to pass between two boys who were acting as guards to keep boys and girls under a certain age out of the game. 'Ages?' one of the guards demanded, raising his torch at Michael.

'And ages,' Neal sang, charging through. 'Ages and ages my heart's been a-yearning,' he sang.

The rim of the hollow was ringed with silhouettes. Rush torches were stuck in the ground here and there, and Michael saw faces. Neal's friends, friends of his sisters', relatives and friends of Slieve's. He didn't see anyone his own age. He wiped his hands on his breeches. What if he were called to kiss one of these girls? These girls were older, they knew how to employ their mouths. They were capable of beguiling, having learned from the snake.

He wasn't getting enough air. Neal's face was turned towards him and he was breathing Neal's sour breath. He felt lightheaded. He thought that everyone at the wedding had fallen into carnal delirium, including his own brother, who had dragged him here; including his mother and father, who had allowed the neighbour's doors to be burned for a bonfire and riotous dancing.

And yet when Neal's arm dropped from his neck he didn't run back to the yard. Somewhere in the world there was a perfect line of light. Purity and order. It was not here, though, and not within him. He, too, had descended. At the riverside he had lusted.

A boy, carrying a torch and swinging a stool over his head, passed through the silhouettes on the far side of the ring and ran to the bottom of the hollow. There were hoots and clapping. He placed the stool in the centre of the hollow, then dug a hole with his hands in the soft earth down there and planted the torch. Then he sat on the stool and folded his arms. You could see the white moon of his face but not his features.

Some boys near Michael started the chant:

'Good prince sitting on your throne...'

All the voices carried it on:

'Good prince sitting all alone,
Kissing will dispel your frown.
Milwort, pipewort, ragwort,
Who do you call down?'

It was intoned, not sung or shouted, and therefore it sounded the opposite of how everybody felt. It sounded bloodless, like corpses chanting.

'I call Biddy McGinn,' the boy said.

A girl squealed. Biddy came out of the ring, giggling into her hands. At the bottom of the hill she waved up to the spot where she had emerged from. The boy yanked her to him. They kissed. The watchers were silent, and it was as if the wind had blown out the candles in a darkened room.

The boy and Biddy parted. He ran up the hill to applause, and Biddy sat on the stool. The chant began again with 'Princess' instead of 'Good Prince'.

'I call Neal Malone,' Biddy said.

Clasping his hands over his head Neal trotted down to her. He bent her over his arm and rotated his free hand on her buttocks. Annie gasped. A boy yelled that Biddy's father, who happened to be a thatcher, was spying from the cabin roof.

The girl that Neal called was Annie. She pretended not to hear and he had to say her name twice. Then she made a show of being surprised, then shy, and suffered herself to be pushed forward by the girls around her. She and Neal kissed standing straight, their arms out of sight between their bodies. Michael kept swallowing because he thought that he was going to vomit or weep or explode with laughter or imprecations. During the chant for Annie he squeezed shut his eyes. He was certain that she would summon him and when she didn't, when she said, 'Tall Kinnard,' he wasn't sure how he felt.

Kinnard called down a girl who, after he kissed her, stood on the stool, bent over and flicked her skirt up and down. This produced hilarity, and all the princes and princesses thereafter got up to antics. The girls flared white skin, their legs and the tops of their breasts. A boy put a jar in his breeches to simulate arousal.

Ferris O'Flynne, who was beckoned as 'Slieve's brother from America that won the bottle', went down the hill thrusting his hips in and out in the copulation motion. Immediately at the end of the chant for him and before he could say a name, a girl cried out his name and went on crying it, running down to him. She was fat and fair-haired.

'Oh, Jesus, 'tis Rose!' Annie screamed.

Rose couldn't slow herself down. Arms circling backward she ran into the stool, knocked Ferris off it and fell on top of him. The two of them lay there squirming. Either Ferris was fighting to get out from under her or he was enjoying her. Everybody howled with laughter. Boys shouted lewd suggestions. They shouted the Pretty Peg song:

'Lives 'twixt two legs,
Never been sheared,
Shy Pretty Peg,
Girl with a beard.'

Eventually Rose rolled on to the ground, and just as she did so the torch that was next to the stool burned out. Ferris climbed up the bank in a stagger, but that might have been more capering. He received loud cheers.

Someone ran down with a new torch. Rose flounced on to the stool and swept an arm at the old torch to indicate where the new one should go, which was obvious. The crowd laughed. Rose didn't seem to hear. She must have been drunk, for normally she hated to be laughed at. She rocked and commenced bawling out the verse herself: 'Princess sitting on your throne...'

The boy she chose didn't come forward. There was more laughter, though it was less roisterous. She said his name again and still he didn't emerge. It was possible that he wasn't present — that he had never been there or that he had gone back to the yard. Rose came to her feet. She stood there doughtily with her hands on her hips. She asked for another boy, Mickey McWeir. The name was echoed around the ring and a commotion broke out across the hollow, but

Mickey McWeir didn't come forward either.

It was untoward. You could not conceive of her ever being kissed now. A boy hollered, 'Mickey Mc*Spear* is here.' Annie let out a delighted squeal and Neal told her to shut up. He stepped over the lip of the hill as though he was thinking of going to Rose himself. But somebody else was already striding down. Ferris O'Flynne, striding back down.

'Where is my kiss?' he shouted, marching up to her. 'Where is that kiss you denied me? Ah, 'tis a cruel girl you are.'

He wrapped one arm then the other grandly around her and made a loud grunt of pleasure as they kissed. When he released her she stayed leaning against him and he had to turn her face to the hill. The watchers clapped and cheered. She kept falling in her climb and finally remained on her hands and knees and crawled. At the top she was helped to her feet. She waved sloppily in every direction.

'Good prince sitting on your throne,
Good prince sitting all alone,
Kissing will dispel your frown.
Milkwort, pipewort, ragwort,
Who do you call down?'

'Etain McCaffery.'

A violent hiccough issued from Michael's throat. Neal looked at him and Michael gestured at his chest. ''Tis her gown,' he shouted to explain why Ferris would suppose that Etain was old enough to be in the game. 'The cut of her gown.'

Neal's eyes flickered back to the hollow. Michael shook his head. Everything inside him seemed to bubble with amusement. 'Here we go again,' he shouted because, as had happened with Rose, another name would have to be called.

But halfway around the hollow a small slender girl with hair that was white in the torchlight started down the hill. Michael would have recognized her by the swing of her arms alone. She went up to Ferris. She didn't hurry, she didn't hesitate. How could it be? Where was her father, why was he permitting this ravishment? A child began to cry back

91

at the cabin, a faraway cry that was like the feeling in Michael's chest, and he said to himself, "They cannot kiss. If they kiss I will murder Ferris."

It was the longest kiss in the world. When it was over Ferris returned to the top of the hill twitching his hips. One day he would go to Father Lynn and seek redemption for having walked like that, Michael thought, and Father Lynn would forgive him. There was so much excess, he thought coldly, because there was so much forgiveness.

He did not hear the chant or his name being called.

'Little Scholar,' Neal said, nudging him.

'Wake up, wake up,' Annie sang.

'Michael Malone?' the voice in the hollow said searchingly, on the brink of abandoning that name for another.

He flew down to her. There would have been a second collision except that unlike Rose he had the sense to gallop by the stool and come to a halt behind it.

''Tis not a race,' Etain said as he ran back to her. The watchers above were also laughing, and suddenly he was overcome by the white skin pouring down from her throat, and then by his connection to Rose and her foolishness. He couldn't move. He couldn't even lift his arms.

She, however, had no trouble moving. She rose from the stool and laid her hand on his chest. Her eyes closed slowly, her chin lifted, her lips pursed. She had already acquired method.

Something spasmed in him. He grasped her shoulders, pulling her up on her toes, and pushed his lips against hers. He mashed and pressed, hurting his lips with their teeth. He felt only fury until he drew away and realized that she had not resisted him at all, that she had let him kiss her so brutishly and would let him again — she was limp against his chest.

Then he felt tenderness, in immense billowing waves. He lowered her and loosened his fingers, flinching at the thought that he had bruised her shoulders. She opened her eyes.

'I *hated* kissing Ferris,' she whispered, and turned and ran up the hill.

He called Annie down. Other than Etain's, hers was the only name he could think of, and when they kissed she shoved her tongue between his teeth and churned it in his mouth.

He didn't stay in the game. After running up the hill he kept on running, through the ring, across the field, across the next and next fields and up the hills to Stone Peak where there were ancient graves and a celebrated prospect. He dropped down on his back, bending dewy ferns. There was a hazy half moon directly above him. The stars seemed close and torrid.

She was his, she was his. It was as good as written in the stars that she would marry him and not the linen merchant or Ferris O'Flynne or Reagan Lunney or anyone else. Just as he had always planned. Her yielding to him, and what she said, giving such ardour to 'hate' — that was a vow. So, now they had kissed, the first big step. He supposed that whenever he wanted to he might kiss her again, and maybe he might touch her breasts, which couldn't be a sin between two people who were betrothed. If only he could touch her breasts he promised God that he would not defile her.

Presently he came to his feet. Being upright made his head throb, and he realized that his back and breeches were wet from lying down and that he was chilled and famished. He was a bit unsteady. But at the same time he felt completely awake and bright. He felt unbeatable, graced. He felt, standing on this peak, like the good prince of all those people down there.

They were walking back to the cabin from the hollow. The torches had burned out. In the yard the fire was dying, but there was still dancing going on, in the red ember light. It was almost dawn. The valley was appearing by degrees out of the blackness, the effect being both the same as and the opposite of eyes adjusting to the dark. Soon everyone would leave, women and children to their cabins, men across the river to cart hay or up to the bog to cart turf.

A great encompassing abiding love for them seemed to glow out of him. Even Ferris O'Flynne he loved, even Reagan Lunney, even the terrifying Annie. All those tiny grey figures down there.

Any one of them, from this far away, could have been Etain.

93

Chapter 16

Wales

Since Michael was finding sleep during the day less and less to be had, he left the bed and stood at the window almost every time that Olwen went outside. The treachery of this was just another thing he would not dwell on.

It wasn't so much boredom as the current of his thoughts that drew him to the window. When he lay sleepless on the bed he thought of Etain, of her betrayal, envisioning it as if he had been a witness.

There was so much else he should consider. Such as what he would do when he had to leave this house. But when he thought of that, all he could imagine was skulking and starving in London streets and seeing his name on wanted notices everywhere.

And thinking of going back to France, that was no better. He would rave and get heartsick when he thought of how he had been tricked — the captain at Brest telling him that the squadron was for the West Indies — of how France had no real ambitions for Ireland. And without help from the French there could be no revolution in Ireland, no victory.

It was different looking out of the window, seeing things that invited contemplation of themselves. There was always movement to divert him — dandelions tossing, rain, the hens pecking, geese returning from the commons. He would look at these things and not be savaged by thoughts of Etain.

She was not entirely absent from his mind though, even at those times. In whatever he regarded there was an aspect of her, as if she had been here once. This was nostalgia, he knew

94

that. Sometimes all he wanted was to go home to her.

He had a feeling, awful and soothing, that he would be in this loft forever. Rosser said, the day after having the vision at his bedside, that maybe he would build a hiding place, a false wall at the gable end of the loft for Michael to slip behind when strangers came into the house, and then he might stay through harvest. And Olwen was always saying that with his dizzy spells and lameness there was no question of his going away for months and months.

Chapter 17

Ireland

Rose was in love with Ferris O'Flynne. She believed that her feelings were returned because he came to her unbidden in Good Prince.

Swishing her skirt, standing in front of her mother, she said, 'There might be another wedding down the road before you know it.'

Kathleen went on grating potatoes for boxty. 'Has Ferris spoken of marrying?' she asked.

'Well, he hasn't got down on his knees.'

Kathleen picked up potato slivers that had missed the bowl. She examined them, frowning, before throwing them in. 'Has he told you that he cares for you at all?'

'He told me that I was a cruel girl for not kissing him. Michael and Neal, they heard.' She looked at Michael. 'Did Ferris not say that?'

Michael moved his head vaguely and turned a page of his book.

'Well, *I* heard it,' Rose said. 'And so did fifty others.'

Early in September Ferris called on her at last. She was flustered with surprise despite the fact that ever since Mary's wedding she had been accosting him at hurling games and after mass, giving him little currant and apple cakes (baked at Mary's so that Kathleen wouldn't know about them) to cajole him into visiting her.

He turned up wearing his Sunday coat and a hat from America that had two beaver tails hanging from the brim, one over each ear. In his coat pocket he had a bottle of whiskey to pass around. He presented it as "moonshine", but it was only Bull and Castle brew. Rose gasped at the sight of it anyhow and declared that her mother must have the bottle as a keepsake. She led him to the hob and sat down, patting the place beside her.

"Tis too close to the fire,' he said jovially, going to one of the stools.

He told stories of his American exploits. It seemed that he had fought Red Indians, killed a bear with a club and was notorious from Philadelphia to Charleston for the fortunes he had won and lost at the gambling tables. He addressed Neal and Hugh almost exclusively, turning to Rose only when she questioned him insistently and when she made him a plate of toast. For some reason he called her 'Teapot'. She was flattered. 'Is that American?' she cried, but he was talking to Hugh and Neal again.

After he had gone Rose was in raptures. 'You see? You see?' she said to Kathleen.

'I see that he is a mite shy of yourself,' Kathleen said coolly.

Certainly he was shy in the company of her mother and father, Rose said. What Kathleen didn't know, she said, was that on the stoop he had held her hand and tickled her palm with his finger. She started dancing with a make-believe partner and she said, let Mary have her summer wedding, as far as herself was concerned Shrovetide was the only decent time to wed.

Three days later Ferris left for England to cut the late crops. He went on a whim with a friend. When the harvest was over they would try to find dock work. They wouldn't be home until summer.

Rose learned from Mary that he'd gone. She had walked to Mary and Slieve's cabin to give them a miscaun of butter, and fortunately Slieve was standing right next to her when Mary delivered the news, for she fainted and would have fallen into the fire had he not caught her. He lowered her on to a stool, but she slipped to the floor, whimpering, 'Let me die, let me lie here and die.' So Mary said that she had best be taken home to their mother. As Slieve did not own a horse he heaved her over his shoulder and carried her. She squalled the whole way, and they arrived trailed by children, dogs and the idiot

Quinn twins, who had been attracted by the noise.

'What in God's name?' Kathleen said, striding into the yard.

'She is all right,' Slieve said, meaning it wasn't an injury. He took her inside, and Kathleen shut both halves of the door.

'Ferris has gone to England,' Slieve explained. This brought forth a really distressed cry from Rose, as if she hadn't yet heard.

'Quiet, child, for heaven's sake,' Kathleen said. 'We'll have the entire valley at our door.' She wiped Rose's nose with her apron. 'Didn't I fear this would be the upshot?' she said crossly.

'I will just be laying her down,' Slieve said, scuffing across the floor.

He dropped her on to her bed. She looked disgraceful, with her petticoat thrown up to her thighs, ashes all down the front of her, mucous smeared under her nose. Kathleen sat beside her and drew the petticoat back down.

'He'll be coming home in the summer,' Slieve said, 'Mary told her that.'

'The summer,' Rose said tragically.

'Well, then, he is not gone forever, is he?' Kathleen said.

Rose sniffed. 'Why did he not tell me, Mama?'

'Maybe he didn't want to cause this hurt. To see yourself like this.'

'To see me crying?'

'Aye.'

'Because he could not bear it?'

'That's right.'

Rose chewed her hair. 'And maybe,' she said, 'he feared he would cry himself?'

Kathleen glanced at Slieve, who spread his hands. He had no idea what his brother's sentiments were.

'Maybe,' Rose went on, 'his heart was fair wringing, but he must go over there for the work, and he thinks to himself, if I tell Rose and she cries then I will never go.'

'Goodness only knows what he was thinking,' Kathleen said.

'Poor Ferris,' Rose said.

'Are you done your weeping and wailing now then?'

'Miles from home and all alone,' Rose said, forgetting that his friend was with him.

She got it into her head that he had left to earn a nest egg for their marriage and that the wedding would take place in the summer after all, just as Mary and Slieve's had. Now that she thought about it, she preferred a summer wedding. Kathleen was alarmed. 'You're ahead of yourself,' she said. 'You're selling the butter before you've milked the cow.' Rose rolled her eyes.

There was no telling her that she wasn't betrothed. She would have sent him love letters, Michael doing the writing for her, but as it wasn't known precisely where Ferris was and, no, Michael said, a letter addressed "Ferris O'Flynne, England" wouldn't reach him, she decided instead to make herself a book, a journal, and record her love in that. She entitled it, *Pearls of Adoration*, and had Michael write this on the cloth covers, back and front.

Three or four evenings week he recorded thoughts or 'pearls' that had struck her. To Michael's disappointment Rose never said anything shocking or instructive. All she did was liken her love, her heart and parts of her and Ferris's bodies to things that she had seen during the day. She would say that their love was healthful like manure or that a slaughtered pig was herself should any misfortune befall Ferris, and the pig's blood was the pool of her heart's tears. Her heart could be anything: a lump of fat melting on the griddle, a dead insect, any flower, wilted or in bloom.

'The fuel of false hope,' Kathleen had said when Rose was sewing the book. But it turned out not to be the case. In fact it was just the opposite. As more and more pages were filled, Rose seemed to grow less and less certain that Ferris truly loved her. It was as if her affection and Ferris's were on the pans of a scale, and any weight added to her side made his side lighter. After she was done dictating her thoughts she would ask Michael, had he ever seen Ferris talking to other girls? Did he think it was true, the saying "When the sight leaves the eye, love leaves the heart?" She would ask him to describe the scene in the hollow again, Ferris's kissing her and calling her a cruel girl. She carried a bit of looking glass in her apron pocket and consulted it constantly and with diminishing satisfaction.

When the last page of the journal was filled she spoke of beginning a second one. This time Michael said he wouldn't be her scribe, he had his own writing to do, which he did. He had lessons to prepare because he was a Latin monitor and also he was copying out *The Life of Saint Patrick* with the intention of starting his own library. Rose didn't make much of a protest. Later she said it was just as well, since she was soon going to be up to her ears herself — during Advent she planned on saying four thousand Paters and Aves, she didn't say why, and nobody asked her, being only grateful that her preoccupation with Ferris would be rivalled.

Any day of the week you might be told about a family that had been turfed out of its cabin for rental arrears or for not winning a new lease. You would hear that the family was living in a cave or just wandering and begging, that the babies were ailing. After a while these stories didn't excite your pity. You hardly listened, unless there was some especially deplorable aspect. Such as when John Logan flattened the Jamesons' cabin while Mrs Jameson was alone and in the throes of labour, and she gave birth squatting in the yard, the baby plopping into a sink of urine and faeces because she had only waddled out as far as the dung heap. Or such as when the O'Neills were thrown out of their place on Christmas Eve.

Mr O'Neill wasn't told who the new tenants of his place were. At midnight mass he was meek with shock because although he'd been a year behind in the rental he'd believed himself safe on his remote rocky holding. Who would crave such a place? His wife's suspicion was that the new tenants were scoundrels — thieves or counterfeiters who had offered Logan the earth.

They turned out to be neither of these. They were John Logan's newly widowed sister and her eight sons. As a girl, Logan's sister had eloped to Donegal with a Presbyterian — somebody-or-other-Willis. Her and John's Catholic-born father, having devoted the whole of his adult life to persuading people that he was Church of Ireland Protestant in his heart and blood, disowned her for her treacherous marriage. Twenty years later, she was back, now that her husband and her father were both buried. She arrived in the dead of Christmas night.

100

In the days and weeks that followed, John Logan was twice seen heading towards the cabin, once with a cow and once with crates of poultry and sacks of meal. The Willises themselves were not seen, except at a distance. They kept to their property. Few people ever passed by there but those who did reported that the children all seemed to be very young and that if you waved or shouted a greeting from the road they didn't acknowledge it.

One day in February Rose brought home the news that the oldest boy was actually sixteen years of age, only very small, and that his name was Gil.

'As in the respiratory organ of fishes?' Michael asked, just picturing this runt nephew of John Logan's. 'As in the wattles of fowls?'

'He's a cudgel fighter,' Rose said. 'He has fairy blood in him so he never loses. In Donegal he killed a boy entirely.'

Michael snorted with disbelief.

''Tis true,' Rose said, and maybe it was. Gil Willis, the tiniest sixteen-year-old anyone had ever laid eyes on, was fighting boys and beating them, and every day he was out prowling for more opponents, carrying a pair of shillelaghs with him in case the boy he challenged didn't have his own stick handy. Michael himself saw one of these fights at the market, a week after Rose told him about them, saw this little boy jumping like a flea around a boy twice his size and winning with one blow.

It had to be that he had unearthly tricks up his sleeve. He seemed to fight fair though — he didn't challenge you if he found out you were very much younger than himself, he didn't strike you when you were down. But if you accepted his challenge, all the fairness in the world wasn't going to save you. If you didn't accept it, everyone knew you were a coward because he chose opponents out of groups, probably to thwart refusal. Or maybe he wanted spectators. Yet he didn't appear to fight for the crowd. He didn't draw out a match, and when he swung his stick there was a private cast to his face that was almost unseemly. Afterwards he never said a word. He picked up his second cudgel and walked away, not looking at all pleased with himself but looking like a man who still has a long row to hoe and had better be getting on with it.

In the schoolyard he was all that the scholars talked about.

Michael and Corny and the other four senior students were believed to be sooner or later doomed. It was unlikely that Gil would challenge any of them when Master Dolan was around, but before class Dolan went walking with his dog and locked the schoolhouse door, and then there were all those hours spent away from school, at markets, knocking about the town. Tim Gallagher, a big, strong-armed boy, said he would smash the wee bastard to smithereens, but that was bluster. Tim didn't have eminent skill, he was only mighty, and might apparently did not signify. Michael, Corny and the others had no skill whatsoever, never having acquired it because of studying and reading all the time and because, being scholars, they were respected and had never been bullied.

They all agreed with each other that it wasn't getting hurt that worried them, it was getting injured. If Gil broke your arm or your hand or poked out your eye, your schoolwork would be disrupted and then you might be expelled. A precedent existed. Two years ago a scholar who was hit on the head in a stone-throwing fight assumed a queer condition which was that instead of answering what he was asked, he repeated it authoritatively. Master Dolan knew that the boy couldn't help himself but he lost patience with him anyway, after one day, and sent him packing.

Really there was no hope. But Corny, for one, wouldn't admit it. Every moment he planned his own salvation. He couldn't refuse the challenge — you just did not refuse to fight a Protestant, let alone such a small one — still he wasn't too proud to plot how he might avoid being challenged in the first place. He considered exploiting Gil's sense of fair play by pretending to be lame, and he practised going to and fro across the playground in a good imitation of Etain's mother, which Etain found offensive. He would no longer walk home from school with Michael in case the two of them together constituted a group in Gil's books. He was stealthy in crowds. He concocted ways of murdering Gil and hiding the body to give the impression that Gil had merely gone off somewhere.

Tim Gallagher said, well, shut up and do it.

'If I could be sure that the body would never be found,' Corny said, 'or even if Gil weren't a relation of Logan's, I would. But imagine the vengeance Logan would deal out on the valley if parts of his nephew were unearthed.'

'If the bastard weren't a relation of Logan's, he'd have been murdered long since,' Tim said.

In private, Michael also schemed, or tried to. He wouldn't lower himself to contemplation of Corny's shenanigans, and yet no less shameful ideas came to his mind. It galled him, not being able to reason his way out of this trouble. He was certain that there was a wise decision, an escape, if only he could find it. All he could think of doing was practising with a cudgel so that at least he wouldn't die.

He asked Neal to teach him defence manoeuvres. Neal was a crack fighter. He said that it was lucky for Gil that he was too old for Gil to challenge and that he himself couldn't challenge Gil because of Gil being Logan's nephew. But Michael thought that it was lucky for Neal. He thought that it was true about Gil being invested with preternatural power.

Hanging in the chimney corner Neal had a choice collection of shillelaghs. He had alpeens, which were knobbed at the ends and which were wielded with both hands, and oaken cudgels and blackthorns. The blackthorns had lead in them, for extra weight. As they were what Gil carried, Neal picked out two of them. He struck them on the fireplace to show off their sturdiness. 'Hear that?' he said, smiling at Michael.

Kathleen said not inside so they went to the byre, out of the rain. Michael brought a rushlight and fixed it in the holder on the wall.

'So,' Neal said. He motioned for Michael to stand opposite him. Michael was aware of being the taller one and also of how useless being tall was compared to being wide, to having Neal's arms like flitches. He remembered Neal's arms folded in the schoolyard to warn off the scholars. That was another time when mutilation had been forecast. Wrongly forecast, as it happened. But the evidence then had been only rumours whereas now the evidence was a dozen limping losers, blood on the ground, splintered sticks.

'You are going to be beaten,' Neal said. 'There is no doubt about that. But you don't want to be beaten by his first stroke and look like a fool altogether.'

Michael agreed that he did not. He believed, however, that

103

looking like a fool was inevitable regardless of which stroke beat him. What he really didn't want was death or impairment.

'So,' Neal went on, 'your strategy is, ward off all the strokes you can for as long as you can and take the others in places that won't break. Your joints — your elbows, knees, wrists,' he pointed with his cudgel, 'they will break. Your temple is a bad place as well. But here, here and here,' he hit Michael hard on each shoulder and on the top of the head, and Michael thrust his stick around belatedly to defend himself, 'you can take thumpers in them places and not be the worse for wear.' He pushed up his sleeves. 'Are you ready then?'

Michael nodded.

Neal held his cudgel low, at his thigh, and started to circle. Michael held his cudgel likewise and turned round to keep himself and Neal face to face.

'That's it,' Neal said. 'No, don't be staring at my stick. Stare at my eyeballs. ''Tis them that will tell you what I'm calculating.'

Suddenly his cudgel flew up and seemed about to strike Michael's right temple. But then it swept down and tapped him on the elbow instead. Michael was caught guarding his head.

'If you cannot bring your stick down quick enough, spring away,' Neal said. He leaped deftly to one side. 'See that?'

Neal feinted another strike, to Michael's left temple. Michael jumped backwards into a post, and a peg that was sticking out of it grazed his head. 'Damn,' he said. He touched his head to feel for blood.

Neal said, 'You've got to look where you're leaping, that goes without saying.'

Again and again Neal pretended to deliver strikes and not one of them did Michael successfully check. And if he jumped it was always after Neal had already hit him. Never had he felt so clumsy, so powerless. Finally he was only thrashing his cudgel anywhere like somebody crazed by flies. 'Ach, this is a joke,' he said, and threw himself on the ground.

Neal combed his fingers through his hair. Michael lay on his back and watched a St. Brighid's Day cross twirl gracefully from the rafter.

'Well, Little Scholar,' Neal said. 'Do you want to know the sorry truth?'

'No,' Michael said.

It was like the pauses between a dying person's breaths, waiting for Gil's challenge. When the scholars were out of doors, all of them, even the youngest, stayed close to the schoolhouse. They scanned the hill and hedge and the path and saw small boys in the distance that weren't there. When one of the senior boys arrived in the morning they watched him approach for signs of injury. Tim Gallagher took to carrying his own pair of blackthorns, hiding them in a bush during classes. He said that the bastard could choose one of *his* sticks, and before and after school he practised, swinging both cudgels at once and emitting frightful battle cries.

A week passed. At the end of it the O'Flynne family got a letter from Ferris, written for him by a professor of the learned languages, or so the writer described himself. Ferris, but not the friend he had left Ireland with, would be back before St. Patrick's Day. 'Back with a wee surprise, so start getting the stuff out,' the letter said.

Mr O'Flynne did. Fifteen gallons of poteen he bought for a St. Patrick's homecoming celebration. He said, hang the cost, he'd bet his last farthing that the surprise was a purse full of gambling winnings. You didn't meet that class of company (the professor) in a field.

Rose knelt over the stool and thanked God. She said that, all the same, she had had no thought of reward. She must have meant for her four thousand Paters and Aves.

Then she began to decorate her market basket with ribbons and wool.

Kathleen said, 'What in God's name are you doing?'

'Making a welcome-home gift,' Rose answered. She got a sack from some cranny in her outshot and proceeded to extract things from it and put them in the basket. A tin whistle, a picture of the Virgin, a plug of tobacco, a pair of red garters, a pair of grey stockings and a box wrapped in a faded green kerchief.

Kathleen wanted to know where the whistle and tobacco came from. The stockings and garters Rose had supposedly made in secret. The picture was a bequest from the widow Mulligan.

'I bought them,' Rose said.

'When?'

'St. Brighid's Day fair.'

'Using what money?'

'I had yarn money.'

'Eggs or sweet milk would have done,' Kathleen said.

'Eggs or sweet milk,' Rose said disgustedly. 'All the girls will be giving him that.' She arranged and rearranged everything in the basket many times, then sprinkled dried roses on top and covered it with a white cloth.

Early the following morning she heated a pot of water and washed her hair and herself. Kathleen said, ''Tis unlikely that he'll be showing up this very day.'

'I know it.'

'Are you planning on sitting on his stoop 'til he does?'

'No,' Rose said, insulted.

'Well?'

'I am only going to deliver the basket so it is there when he does show up.'

'And you're risking catching your death for that?' Kathleen dropped a towel on Rose's head and began vigorously drying her hair.

'I want to look agreeable, is all. I want to look agreeable going into his house.'

When her hair was dry she curled it with a hot knife, after which she donned her best gown, the yellow bridesmaid's gown. Already she had grown too fat for it, she could hardly lift her arms. She leaned out of the half door for the light and studied herself in her looking glass, pulling back her lips to inspect her teeth, then picking at the wart on the side of her nose and getting a smack from Kathleen for that because you could give yourself the pox that way, picking at warts.

At the beginning of the next week Master Dolan said that a celebrated colleague of his from Munster would be visiting in a month's time to examine the senior scholars. Only those scholars who displayed brilliance would be allowed to stay on at the school. He said that beyond the age of fifteen the scholar's life was a dispensation that must be earned.

The six senior boys and Etain met behind the schoolhouse after dismiss that day. There was a downpour, so they stood in

106

a line under the eaves. Michael said that they were lined up for the firing squad. They couldn't imagine appearing brilliant to a celebrated teacher from Munster, it being the place where the most brilliant minds in the country congregated.

None of them heard Gil's approach. Suddenly he was in front of them, out of the mist. He had a dark face and black eyes. He was smaller even than Etain. Corny didn't notice him and kept on talking for an impossibly long time until Tim told him to shut up for Christ's sake, and then, seeing Gil at last, Corny affected lameness, collapsing his left leg and falling back against the wall.

'Can ye see out of them things?' Gil asked in a low man's voice. He pointed one of his cudgels at Corny's spectacles.

Corny did not even hesitate. 'No.'

Gil spat out of the side of his mouth. 'Where is the boy that has the hare-skin cap?'

He didn't ask anybody in particular, but Corny answered. 'Gone home.'

'What age is he?'

'Twelve, thirteen.'

'The rest of ye then, barring ye with the specs and the girl, I'll fight ye one a day.'

No one spoke. Tim shifted from foot to foot and breathed hard.

Gil said, 'Starting tomorrow, this time of day. In the clearing on the hill.' He pointed at Tim. 'Tomorrow.' He moved his cudgel along the line. 'Wednesday. Thursday. Friday. Saturday.'

Michael was Saturday. When Gil pointed at him, Etain, standing beside him, squeezed his fingers. At the other end of the line Tim sniffed and rocked. He muttered, 'Bloody coward.'

Gil had started walking away but he stopped and turned around. 'What was that?' he said.

'Ha!' Tim said. He wiped his nose with his sleeve. 'You heard it,' he said.

Gil only looked at him. Tim looked at the others. He nodded at Michael and spoke as if to him. 'You know bloody well that if one of ourselves so much as scratches you, let alone breaks your bones, your uncle John will have it out of our fathers.'

107

'My uncle has nothing to do with this.'

'Ha! Do you mean to say that he'll be letting it go if I bash your head in? No bloody fear.'

Gil tucked one of his cudgels under his arm, which made Tim recoil. Gil smirked. With his free hand he fished in his jacket pocket. He drew out a guinea and flicked it off his thumb on to the ground. 'Pick it up,' he said to Tim.

Tim just stared at it. They all did.

'Pick it up or are ye afraid to?'

Tim grunted and scooped it up.

'That's right. Put it in your pocket and hold it there 'til tomorrow. Now, here is how it'll go. If your stick touches me, only touches me, mind, the guinea is yours to keep and the match ends at that. But if your stick doesn't touch me before you're beat, then I take the guinea back.'

Tim shrugged.

'Is that a bargin?'

Tim shrugged and looked around the yard.

'One last thing,' Gil said. 'If the guinea is not in your pocket there when I've beat ye body and staves, I will kill ye dead.'

He walked away towards the hill, bouncing on his toes which made him seem taller than he was. When he had climbed into the mist, Tim smashed his fist against the schoolhouse. 'We'll be seeing who kills who dead, the little shite,' he said.

Etain was still squeezing Michael's fingers. He had lost sensation in them. 'You don't have to fight,' she said.

Corny took off his spectacles and wiped them dry with the tail of his shirt. 'These were honourable men in their generation,' he quoted.

'Jesus, you give me the puke,' Tim said.

'I'm off home,' Michael said to Etain.

She let go of him. 'You are all children,' she said wrathfully.

He went round to the front, but instead of going straight on, he ran to the far side of the schoolhouse, stopped and looked up at the hill. He waited for Gil to pass into view, then decided it wasn't necessary and crossed Dolan's potato field to the hedge and crawled through a gap. In a crouch, so that Etain and the others wouldn't see him, he ran along the hedge to the hill path. There was only the one path that Gil could have taken.

108

He had no plan. While Gil had been walking away he had imagined the pleasure of chasing him off with stones, then he had imagined simply following him, and had thought, "I could really do that." So he did. It was doing something at least, it was counteraction.

On the hilltop he could see through the rain to the vale below. Gil was already down there, walking in the direction of the river. Michael raced down the muddy path, seizing branches to keep from falling, and when he got to the bottom, the distance between him and Gil was only a hundred yards or so. He went off the path and dashed from bush to bush.

Eventually the vale opened up and the path widened into a crooked road. Gil left it and kept going in a beeline, vaulting banks. He went right into people's yards, over their gardens. Nobody hailed him, nobody was outside on account of the downpour. Michael went back to the road. He trotted, stooping, pacing himself to remain a little behind Gil and ready to drop if Gil should turn around. He was drenched, but the wetness felt hot, like sweat.

The road ended at the river, at the spot where Gil appeared to be headed. Except for a small stony point, the shore was swampy there, so Gil would either have to halt or go back.

He went into the water. Michael knelt behind a hawthorn hedge and watched him. Gil waded until he was in the current up to his thighs, then stood still, head bent, arms hanging in front of himself. Minutes passed. The rain pocked the water. Michael thought that he must be performing a ritual. He had heard of the Baptists, but Gil was supposed to be a Presbyterian. Maybe, Michael thought, thrilling, this was a ritual that had to do with his special fighting powers.

A dog ran up to Michael and barked, and in the same moment one of Gil's hands shot into the air with a trout hooked on the fingers. The dog, distracted by the noise of Gil wading ashore, went silent. Gil stunned the trout on a rock, tucked it into his jacket, picked up his cudgels and started running. The dog pursued him.

When Michael could no longer hear barking, he stood. Gil was a blue speck in the distance, and it was getting dark.

What he had thought, seeing the fish at the end of Gil's fingers, was that he would report Gil to The Big Lord's water bailiffs and Gil would be thrown in gaol for poaching, and the scholars and himself would be saved because nobody, not even John Logan, had fishing access to the river, and the water bailiffs were pitiless and undiscriminating. But then he had thought that it would be his word against the word of John Logan's nephew, and he watched the speck that was Gil disappear and was aware of being cold and wet. And yet, he had no idea why, he was inspirited, as if he had irrefutable proof, or as if he knew that all would turn out well in the end. The shivering in his limbs felt like suppressed laughter.

All the way back he felt like that. He shook and laughed out loud. At home Kathleen laid her hand on his forehead and pronounced it hot. She made him a drink of elderflower tea and ordered him to strip and go to bed. After drinking the tea he fell right to sleep. He was awakened in the middle of the night by Neal's boots dropping on the floor. He told Neal about the challenges.

'God Almighty, what are you going to do?' Neal said poignantly. He was drunk.

'What can I do?' Michael said, hopeless again. 'I'll fight him.'

Neal got under the blanket. 'Ah, Christ. Well, see that you guard your noggin, that's all I can tell you. Better that he breaks your knees or someplace like that.'

'How will I go to school if he breaks my knees?'

'I will carry you.' He belched and hugged Michael around the head. 'Has he ever done that before?' he asked, leaving his hand across Michael's neck.

'Done what?'

'Challenged every lad in a group. One by one like that?'

'Not that I've heard of.'

'You know why he's doing it with yourselves? You know what it is, don't you?'

'What?'

'Envy. You're scholars and he's not.'

In the morning Kathleen felt Michael's forehead again and said that he would have to stay indoors for the day. Michael got frantic. It was inconceivable that he should miss Tim's match with Gil. It would seem duplicitous of him. It would seem cowardly and faithless. He told his mother that there was a

Latin examination and if he wasn't there to take it Master Dolan would expel him. She spread a blanket on the hob for him to lie there and said that she would speak to Master Dolan herself if it came to that. So he decided that he would stay home until early afternoon and then run out and pay the price later, disobedience being the lesser of two evils.

He tried to read. But the sequence of words was mystifying, and every now and then a shudder would ripple through him. The shudder was not fever, though. He knew that it was his insides auguring events.

He watched his mother and Rose work. His mother swept the floor, ground oats in the quern, made cakes, then settled down to her spinning. Rose went in and out to feed the hens and turkeys and collect eggs, and in between coming and going she pampered him. She made him a mug of warm milk and honey, she rolled up a towel and placed it under his head. Mid-morning she carried the trough and beetle and a sack of gorse in from the byre and sat down with them in front of the fire to pound the gorse for the mare, doing it there to keep him company, she said. She rolled up her sleeves. She had muscular arms that he was envious of.

When all the gorse was pounded she announced that she was going to Mary's to bring her the skeins for knitting. Almost every day now she visited Mary on some pretext or other. This was because, to get there, she had to pass by Ferris's house. She didn't say so but obviously she hoped that she would happen to be strolling by at precisely the moment when his coach pulled up. (It was assumed that he would arrive in style.) Always for these journeys she wore her bridesmaid's gown, the skirt of which had become brown and stiff with road muck, and she stuffed into her bodice a bunch of whatever flowers she had gathered the day before, on the way back. Today they were anemones.

She didn't return at midday. Neither did Hugh and Neal, who were ploughing for Mr Thomas across the river and would take their meal in the kitchen of his house. But right after Michael and Kathleen had eaten, Neal appeared. He was holding a ploughshare. Michael and Kathleen looked at it.

'Ach, I had to get a new one,' he said, frowning around the room.

'Where is Rose?'

'At Mary's,' Kathleen said. 'What is it?' Her voice was braced.

'Ferris is back. This morning.'

She nodded.

'With a wife.'

She went on nodding while Neal spoke. She had envisioned this or something like it. Or she was thinking herself a fool for not having done.

'That was the surprise,' Neal said. 'Not money. Only the girl, the wife. It turns out that she is the daughter of the fellow that wrote the letter. They were married in Liverpool. By a couple beggar there.'

'Have you seen Slieve?' Michael asked.

'I've seen themselves. Ferris and the girl. Isn't he parading her up and down the road on a horse, stopping one and all to show her off?'

'Jesus,' Michael said.

Neal turned the blade over in his hands. 'I'd have knocked his pretty teeth down his throat but the girl was there,' he said. 'A wee girl she is.' He touched his toe to the beetle that Rose had left on the hearthstone. 'A waist on her like that. Black hair.'

Kathleen came to her feet. She went over to the pegs by the door and lifted off her cloak. 'You'd best be getting back to your father with that.' She nodded at the ploughshare.

'Where are you off to?' Neal asked.

'To fetch Rose. Sure she'll be having another fit on Mary's floor.'

'You're taking the cart then?'

'I'd better be.' She tied the neck strings of her cloak into tight knots.

'I'll hitch up for you,' Neal said.

'That hat Ferris wore here,' Kathleen said bitterly. 'With them beaver tails. That scoundrel's hat.'

Michael listened to their voices in the byre, then listened to the clacking of the cartwheels, then to the silence. He wondered if Rose had met Ferris and his bride on the road, as Neal had done, and he winced, unable to bring his mind as far as what would have followed. Her journal had ended with this poem:

112

'Ferris O'Flynne,
Heart of my life,
End of my strife,
I'll be your wife.'

It was some minutes before he realized that he was free to go.
He kicked off the blanket. He felt his forehead but couldn't
determine if he still had a fever or not. He ran most of the way
to school and when he got there stood at the edge of the
playground, unsure whether to go inside — he hadn't brought
his slate — or to wait for dismiss. He decided to wait. In case Gil
should turn up early and prowl, he hid in the hedge.

The fight was calamitous. A stranger watching it would have
been on the side of Gil, the tiny, assured, divinely protected
David figure. Tim in comparison was ogreish in his rage, the
Philistine.

After a while the scholars gave over cheering, since every
time that Tim went to strike Gil he missed. It was no match, Gil,
dancing around Tim's stick, wasn't even trying to strike, which
made Tim more and more livid and lumbering. 'Stay put, you
little shite,' he shouted, barging after him. He abandoned all
rules. He swung his fist, hurled stones and handfuls of mud.

'For God's sake, Gil, put him of out of his misery!' Corny
yelled.

Gil didn't seem to hear that but Tim stopped and stood
panting, swinging his head like a bull. He stumbled over to
where Corny was. 'I'll lambaste you, anyhow,' he growled.

Gil hit him at last. He ran up behind him and smashed him on
the elbow. Tim's hand opened and his blackthorn dropped.
Immediately Gil struck again, making an extraordinarily high
leap to whack Tim on the temple. And even as Tim fell Gil was
bending over him and his hand was in Tim's pocket. He flicked
the guinea in the air and caught it neatly in his fist. Without a
word, without looking back, he walked off. Tim lay silent and
still. For all Gil could know he was dead.

He wasn't. In a moment he opened his eyes, howled and
gripped his upper arm, and Michael and another boy got him to
his feet and walked with him to Doctor Rennie's across the
river. Doctor Rennie said the elbow was damaged but it would

113

heal. He bandaged it and hung it in a sling. 'Do not take this off for a month,' he ordered.

'A month!' Tim said, aghast. 'How will I write at all?'

Doctor Rennie tapped Tim's left hand. He told him to bring by a bottle of poteen within a week.

On the way home Michael invented a story to tell his mother about Tim showing up at the cabin badly injured and having to be taken to the doctor's. But when he got there his mother scarcely glanced at him as she handed him a bowl of stirabout, covered with a praskeen to keep it warm. Michael sat on the hob next to Neal. 'Is Rose at Mary's?' he asked quietly.

'She's lying down,' Neal said, nodding at her outshot. 'Mama found her on the road, walking back. Not in a fit, not wailing or anything.'

'But she knew about Ferris?'

'Oh aye. She's seen him and the girl. She just came home and went straight to her bed. Wouldn't even eat.'

Neal and Hugh left for The Bull and Castle after supper. Michael lay on the hearthstone and copied out *The Life of Saint Patrick*. Kathleen spun. They didn't talk to each other because Rose was sleeping. Kathleen seemed to have forgotten about his fever.

An hour or so passed. Kathleen rose from her wheel and said she had better be shutting up that pig that had rooted under Norah Fennel's door last night or Norah would kill it. When she was outside Michael stood and looked around the hanging mat into the outshot. Rose was lying on her back. 'Are you sleeping?' he whispered.

She turned her head toward him. He went into the room and sat on the bed. A single anemone was still in her bodice. It was white and so were her teeth, the two top-row teeth that protruded over her bottom lip. He held her hand. It was damp and cold, which put him in mind of Gil's trout. 'I am that sorry,' he said.

'I gave him the journal,' she said.

'Ferris?'

'In the basket.'

'Ah, Rose.'

'I wrapped it in my green kerchief.' Her voice was sickly.

He let go of her hand. 'You shouldn't have done that,' he

114

said. He thought of the ridiculous title: *Pearls of Adoration*, of that ridiculous poem on the last page.

'She'll have seen it,' Rose said. 'He'll have shown it to her.'

'I'll ask for it back. Tomorrow before school, I'll go up there.'

'No.'

'Rose, they shouldn't have it.'

She shook her head as if in delirium. She picked at the blanket. He knew a word — it was in one of Master Dolan's medical books — for when a person picked deliriously at bedclothes: "carphology".

''Tis too late,' she said.

He stood up, suddenly furious. Furious with her for being so stupid and hopeless and with himself for having abetted her by doing the writing. He wanted to deliver some sharp sarcastic retort. He wanted to punish and rouse her. But he heard Kathleen at the door, so he said nothing and went back around the mat. He did not tell Kathleen about the journal.

For breakfast Kathleen boiled Rose a goose egg, even though it was Lent. She called, 'A goose egg is out here for you, Rose,' to make her rise from bed, which Rose did, she could not resist eggs. Coming into the room she resembled a gaol bird, with her dirty dress, her cloudy look, blinking at the light.

That day Tim stayed at home. A boy who usually walked with him to school said he was practising writing with his left hand and wouldn't be coming to classes until he was adept enough not to annoy Master Dolan. Contagious influenza was the story that the boy was to give.

At dismiss Gil was waiting in the clearing for the Wednesday scholar. The match ended after Gil's second strike split the scholar's nose open and the scholar threw his cudgel and himself on to the ground, and there was so much blood that his not getting up and carrying on didn't appear altogether craven.

When Gil left, Michael stalked him. Just as before, Gil headed in a beeline for the river and waded into it and tickled a fish. What else was the same was how exhilarated Michael felt to witness the poaching, to be the secret witness, although why he should feel that way he had no idea.

He was late for supper again. The family was already eating, Rose with them. She had changed into her everyday apparel, and her hair was combed. He asked her how she was feeling but she stared raptly at the fire and didn't answer. When her bowl was empty she helped herself to all that was left in the pot and then scraped bits from the pot's side and ate those. Then she ate the cakes that were meant for the following day. Kathleen let her, saying 'Ah, there you have your appetite back, darling,' and that people who were all skin and bone were an eyesore, which was vilification of Ferris's bride, Michael understood, and did not include himself.

He heard Rose weeping in the night. Muffled weeping. It must have been after midnight because Neal had been in bed for hours. Michael hadn't slept at all. In the night the exhilaration left him and he couldn't imagine having felt it. His saliva tasted like blood and he was unable to swallow and had to spit, and his skin felt sore, his insides ruptured, as if Gil had already been at him. The sound of Rose's weeping seemed to be his own expiring emanation. But as the weeping went on it was only her, very much her alone. He didn't go to her because she was crying into her pillow, crying privately, and because he thought how foolish she had been giving Ferris the journal; thought sourly, "She has only herself to blame," and because he did not yet have experience of grief to know what he was hearing.

Day dawned. Thursday. Never had Michael been more impressed by the passing of time. Walking to school, he was walking towards Saturday. All action, all awareness consumed seconds. For the Thursday scholar, the boy who was going to be beaten that day, the recognition of time running out produced the shakes. Dolan thought that the boy, whose name was Keefe, must have caught Tim's influenza, and he sent him home. But since all the scholars knew better, Keefe waited behind the school for dismiss to take his turn bravely. By then he had the staggers and had to be half carried up to the clearing. Gil handed him one of the blackthorns and sized him up for a moment. Then he snapped his fingers, which was how he started the match, leaped behind him and hit him squarely on the back of the head. He retrieved the blackthorn as Keefe was falling, and when Keefe opened his eyes he was gone. The only injury was a bump. Keefe touched it and said, marvelling, laughing with relief, that it didn't even hurt.

Michael had intended to stalk Gil again, but Etain said

formally that she would like to speak with him, so instead he followed her to Master Dolan's horse shed. She would not stand close to him when they got there. She folded her arms. 'That was luck,' she said.

'Keefe has the luck,' Michael said, disregarding her implication. It was true about Keefe, he was always finding coins and guessing the right answer.

'You could put an end to it,' she said. 'You could refuse to fight, you could stand up to him.'

'Backing down isn't standing up,' he said.

'If yourself or any boy were to say to him, "I won't be bullied, I don't consider a fight with you to be a test of my honour", then the other boys that he challenges after you would be free to say the same.'

'But I do consider it a test of my honour.'

'Why? Why should you at all?'

'Because it is.' He felt himself to be wiser than she was. 'Maybe girls cannot understand,' he said.

'Not understand, is it? Not understand what? Honour? Is it an honourable thing to be thrashed within an inch of your life because *he* wants that? No, what I don't understand at all is why the lot of you allow him to do this, why you leave yourselves no choice.'

'We have a choice.'

She shook her head.

'The choice not to fight him and be dishonoured,' he said, 'or to fight him and be beaten.' In fact, he knew that this was no choice at all. The true choice, the alternative, he had not yet apprehended.

She looked at him, aggrieved. There were tears in her eyes. Then she looked away and began picking splinters off the stall. 'You are willing to risk being so injured that you cannot take the examinations,' she said. 'You are willing to risk being expelled.'

He did not hear the rest of what she said. When she had looked at him he had been struck by an intuition that he might touch her breasts. Her wet eyes, wet for his sake, had seemed to be inviting him. He had never done it, never touched her there, although since Mary's wedding he had kissed her twice, once at a wake, sitting on the corpse's old bedstead, and once at

117

another wedding. Her eyes those times had been wide open, her lips closed, her back rigid against his hand pressing her near, and his intuition had been that he would be sorry for it if he laid his other hand on her front. Now he was certain that she would let him.

He went over to her. His legs felt liquid within but like clay without. He put his hand on her stomach and smiled.

Her eyes flamed at him. But with umbrage. She punched his arm. 'What are you doing?' she cried and ran into the yard. She turned and shouted, 'If you fight Gil, I will never speak to you again.'

He watched her run around the corner of the schoolhouse. What startled him was the fallacy of his intuition. He felt stupid and strange. He dismissed her threat, it meant nothing. Either he would be wounded within an inch of his life, which would soften her, or in the two days before it was his turn to fight he would discover an escape and not have to fight at all.

As he walked home he scanned the waysides for signs of his immediate future. He did this out of habit, for he knew well enough that natural signs, by themselves, were no more reliable than Etain's wet eyes were. He saw a white kitten crossing the road, which was lucky, and a magpie alighting on a whitethorn, which was unlucky. He wondered what omens were strewn along Gil's route home. And wondering that, he quivered because it came to him that luck turned from bad to good and good to bad for everybody, even Gil, and simultaneously he saw in his mind Gil's hand shooting out of the river with the trout, and the quivering he now felt seemed to be remembrance of the exhilaration he had felt then, spying, and he said to himself, "I will spy on his house." He went back to the sheep track that he had just descended and climbed it into the hills. He had no plan aside from going to that isolated cabin and looking at it.

By the time he got there the sun was setting and he thought that if Gil had gone to the river he would likely be back. He stood behind a bush at the foot of the boreen. Both halves of the cabin door were closed, but to the right of the door, bowered by a sapling, there was an uncovered window. Smoke-swirled light and sounds came out of it. Children's voices, a child crying, a spoon banging on a pot.

Michael imagined miracles — Gil leaving the house and leading him to a cavern of illegal whiskey stills, and he stepping out of the shadows and saying, 'My silence has a price'. Pitilessly he imagined the cabin catching fire and all within it perishing. After a while he smelled cooking. He told himself that he should go home to his own supper, it was dark. But he didn't go. And in another moment something happened.

From the cabin he heard a braying, only higher than braying and with a rise at the end that made it sound entreating. He had never heard such a sound before. The other noises within the house seemed to cease. There was only that sound, over and over, but it was not frightening because of the entreaty in it.

He ran on his toes in long strides across the yard. When he got to the cabin he crept along the wall, past the door, sinking to his ankles in the dung on the stoop's far side, then grasping the trunk of the tree and halting under the window. The braying stopped. A child's voice said, 'I want a bit of it', and a woman's voice said, 'No.'

If Gil should catch him, a spy at the window, he would die. Michael was sure of that. He thought, "I cannot possibly look inside." But then the braying started again, and a boy's voice said, so tenderly, 'Now, now,' and Michael wondered, "What boy is that?" and he rose to the sill.

The back of a woman's head, her white cap, was directly at the window. The window was low, and Michael assumed that she was sitting until he saw her move away. She was that short. She went to the open crib fire in the centre of the room and then she did sit, on an overturned firkin. A circle of little children were on the ground there, eating potatoes, and the pig and the dogs were contending for the peelings. Michael rose higher and to the far left of the window so that he might see into the room past the fire. Against the wall he saw a turf with two lighted candles in it. Then, further down the wall, he saw Gil, sitting on the ground, another boy's head in his lap, tilted back, and Gil feeding the boy pieces of fish from a pan, placing a piece on the boy's tongue, tearing another piece off the fish, picking out the bones, placing it on the boy's tongue. The boy's mouth was opened wide as a bird's and his head was tilted so far back that his neck also was like a bird's. His body, lying between Gil's legs, was under a draped coat.

119

It was the boy that made the braying sound.

Gil said, 'There you go,' in the tender voice that had said, 'Now, now.' He gave the boy more fish and put his hand under the boy's head to lift it, to ease the strained neck. Michael saw the boy's face — his eyes flinching open and shut, his mouth chewing slackly. The next piece of fish the boy refused. He thrashed his head.

'He's wanting the coat from him,' the woman said.

'Are you warm, then, Charlie?' Gil asked the boy. He pulled off the coat. The boy had no legs and no arms. All he had was an upper body. It was wrapped in brown cloth.

Michael backed away from the window. He lost his footing and grasped the sapling, which cracked and bent right into the window. He got his balance and ran, slopping through the muck to the road, to the sheep track and down the track until he was sure he wasn't being followed. He dropped on the ground. The boy's swaddled body with the idiot head on top of it seemed to be everywhere he turned his eyes. He gasped with revulsion.

Nobody knew. There were no rumours. John Logan, though, he knew. That was why he evicted the O'Neills on Christmas Eve. He needed a hiding place for the family as soon as it came from Donegal. Because he had a nephew that was an idiot, that had no limbs.

What had happened to the boy? An accident? But what kind of accident could have caused that? And there was the secrecy. No, he must have been born that way. A wonder that Logan hadn't killed him, evidence of bad blood, on Christmas night. More of a wonder that the sister had let him live at all. In Donegal, maybe people didn't know or care that malformed babies were changelings, fairy babies. Maybe the mothers in Donegal nursed any kind of infant. In the valley malformed infants died. The twins who were born joined head to head, they were left to die. At the burying everyone said, 'The will of God.'

Michael recalled Gil's voice. He imitated it aloud, 'Are you warm, then, Charlie?' to persuade himself that Gil could utter words so lovingly. It was too preposterous, too momentous that there was a boy right here in the valley who had no arms or legs and that he was Gil's brother and John Logan's nephew.

Oh, he could blackmail Gil now. Blackmail him, blackmail John Logan. Amass riches. He envisioned it: his mannerly insinuations, Logan's rage and prostration, coin pushed across a table, Logan refusing his father's rental on gale day — 'No, Malone, keep your money. The place is free, don't ask me what for.'

But it was like looking at a sharp knife and saying to yourself, 'I could kill a person with this.' He wouldn't do it. He wouldn't even speak of it, he knew he wouldn't. Already, having done nothing but spy, he felt ashamed, felt drafted into secrecy.

He came to his feet and carried on down the hill. He was almost home before he thought that he would therefore have to fight.

The same day that Michael saw the limbless idiot boy, Rose died. It was the wages of sin, of having beheld that precious hideous sight, he knew. And he knew that one of his family had died before he was told, as soon as he looked up from the River Road and saw that his cabin was aglow. Yet even then, weren't events in his hands? Couldn't he have thought, "There are visitors, it is a *ceilidh*?" It was as if by fearing the worst he willed the worst into full fledging, because he saw the innocent light and thought, "Somebody has died," and then saw that too many horses were under the eaves and that men filled the door, and when he got to the foot of his property, the wailing started.

'Jesus, Jesus,' he said, beginning to run.

One of the men in the door called to somebody within, 'Here is Michael now,' and a man came between them out into the yard.

It was Neal. He clamped Michael's shoulders. 'High and low haven't we been searching for you,' he said. His face was wet and twisted.

'Is it our dada?' Michael said.

'Rose.' Neal dropped his head.

'She is dead?'

He nodded.

'How?'

Neal shook and wept like dry coughing, patting Michael to say that he would speak in a minute. Inside the house the keen died down. At last Neal said, 'She drowned.'

He held Michael there on the path and told him that she went out to pick her flowers, which was a good sign surely, but she must have slipped on the bank, reaching for some water flower maybe, and fallen in. Darby and Norah Fennel found her mid-afternoon at the bend by the forge, caught amongst the reeds, her hair so entangled that Darby had to cut it free.

'Did she say anything before going out?' Michael asked. 'Did she behave queer?' Her poem sang in his head: "Ferris O'Flynne, heart of my life, end of my strife, I'll be your wife."

Neal brought his face close. "Twas *falling* in,' he said intensely. '*Falling* in, see. Don't go asking them things, now.'

The men at the door were Tyrrell the Fairy Man, Slieve's father, one of his uncles and the grandfather. They touched Michael in condolence as he went in. Tyrrell said, 'A terrible loss.' Men and boys lined the walls. Darby, Denis Murphy, who owned The Bull and Castle, Tim and his father and brothers, Slieve's brothers and cousins. The women were on stools or kneeling on the floor in a circle. Seeing Michael, old Sheila Cassidy raised the keen. Neal led him past her, through the circle of keening, clapping women.

Michael's toe touched the mattress. He didn't look down at it. He looked at the tall candles that were in moulded candlesticks on a table at the foot of the mattress. He counted them. Seven.

And then his father was embracing and kissing him and saying fiercely that she was so good, that heaven would receive her, and Michael heard the spheres of his grief: Rose dying, Rose dying without the priest, Rose passing into eternity unpurified. And his father knelt, pulling him down with him. Rose's hands were crossed over her breasts. Her beads were woven through her fingers, which were swollen and clean, which was what being in the water so long would do.

'Queen of Heaven,' his father prayed, 'have mercy on my little girl's tender soul. Suffer her to come unto Jesus.'

Michael looked at her face. It was bloated, like her fingers. The skin was waxy and grey, sloping up to a perfect oval bump over her left eye. Her hair was cropped off on that side. His mother was combing the other, the long side. One corner of his mother's mouth twitched, but her eyes were dry and so were his.

122

All during that night and the following day and night people came and went and the women keened, but Kathleen did not keen or cry. Not until the men were nailing the coffin shut. Then she screamed and clawed at the lid, and the men had to open it again so that she could kiss Rose's bloodless bloated face and hands and arms, take her shoes and stockings off and kiss her legs and feet. Then she just lay crying on Rose's stomach.

Michael still did not cry. He tried to, he pretended to when his mother did and when the sexton was shovelling dirt on the coffin, but he couldn't squeeze the tears out. He felt only an exceptional lucidity that enabled him to see every pore of a person's skin and the detail of things on the horizon, and to hear the air buzzing. He became unnerved by the thought that not crying meant that he had not loved Rose. But the day after the burial, when he and Slieve were loading a cart with stools and empty kegs to bring back to the tavern, Slieve said, 'You are bearing up like a scholar,' and he thought, relieved, "So that's it."

He stayed home from school. He was weighted with a sense of duty towards his family on account of having this strength of intellect over feeling, which they, being uneducated, did not have. They wept and prayed for Rose's soul, day and night, Hugh and Kathleen never leaving the house. It was Slieve who ploughed the oat field. Neal led the team, but he nipped from a jug as he walked and got drunk and kept calling a halt to go inside and see if Hugh wanted anything. Michael did Rose's chores: the milking, feeding the hens, collecting eggs, and he also broke clods in the field once the cross ploughing was done.

On the fifth day of mourning Hugh announced at dawn that Rose was in heaven. The Blessed Virgin had appeared to him in a dream and told him so.

'Are you sure and certain it was the Virgin herself?' Kathleen whispered.

'As sure and certain as I am standing before you. A veil of glory was around her and her voice tinkled like a bell.'

Kathleen breathed, 'No,' as if such a perfect picture couldn't be.

'Our girl is the with angels,' Hugh said. He put his arms

123

around Kathleen's waist and she laid her head on top of his and held his face and cried.

After breakfast she went to inform Father Lynn. Hugh went outside to survey his property and stock. When he came back he praised Neal for the ploughing.

''Twas Slieve,' Neal said. He punched his fist into his palm and said that he was going across the river to see if Colonel Crosbie would hire him. He didn't take the jug.

Hugh looked at Michael. 'Why are you not in school?' he asked. But before Michael could answer, he said, 'As you're here anyhow you can take whatever we have to market.' He hastened about, gathering things for the basket himself.

Michael arrived early enough to get a spot at the end of the inn wall, close to Castle Street. The market was the brown linen market. Once a month it was held on the town green. Drapers and their clerks stood on a platform in the middle of the green, weavers filed past holding up their webs. All other kinds of market-making that day took place along one wall of the inn, where the weavers and drapers were accustomed to retiring once the dealing was over.

Michael had stockings, yarn and eggs, and he laid them out on the kerchief that had covered his basket. The woman next to him knew Kathleen. She asked how his mother was holding up, presuming that he was there because Kathleen was feeling too poorly to come herself. What she had to sell were ginger cakes and soap. She gave him a cake, put it on his kerchief without asking whether or not he wanted it. He ate it looking away from her to discourage talk.

A small boy was approaching down Castle Street. He was wearing a white shirt, which was what caught Michael's eye, the whiteness against the green and brown of everything else. In spite of how far away the boy was Michael believed that he could see a patch on the shirt, see even the stitching, yet he didn't see the features of his face. Inexplicably he didn't look at the boy's face.

In fact the boy was crossing in front of the shop next to the inn before Michael knew who he was. He jumped to his feet. He was suddenly so violently angry that his ears felt plugged up.

'Gil!' he shouted.

Gil kept on walking. Past Michael, past the inn and the saddler's shop. Michael saw the cudgels now. They were twisted in his rope belt, hanging just behind each hand.

'Gil Willis!' he shouted. He started running after him. Gil started running too, through the horses and carts and on to the green, and Michael halted, not understanding why Gil would run. Then Gil disappeared into the crowd, and Michael went after him again. The remarkable clarity of his vision sliced his eyes. The clarity was his fury, and his fury was a volley of knives flying out of his eyes. He felt that he was only an instant away from a week ago, that Rose's death was only a thought he had or a quick deep dream, for though Gil and the limbless boy had come to his mind during the week they had not meant anything to him.

He saw white moving like a patch of sunlight among the men. There was a forest of men between him and the white. He pushed at the men who were in his way, rammed into the webs that they were carrying. One man caught his wrist and growled, 'Hold there,' but Michael cried, 'Let me alone!' with such rabidness that the man did.

When he saw the white once more it was stopped. He charged towards it, then stopped himself, a few feet away. Gil was standing before the platform, cocking his head up at the dealings.

'Willis,' Michael said. Gil didn't turn. Maybe he hadn't heard. On the platform they were calling out prices.

'I'll fight you here, Willis,' Michael said louder. He didn't know why, it wasn't fear, but he was disinclined to go in front of Gil.

Gil started away, down the side of the platform. He patted the cudgels. "Warning me," Michael thought. "Who are you to warn me, who are you to hold my fate?" And he ran to him, grabbed him by one arm and pulled him around.

Gil had man's eyes that seemed to be looking through smoke. He jerked his arm away. 'I am not fighting ye,' he said.

Michael hit him. Not in the face, as he'd intended, but on the shoulder because Gil ducked and turned. Michael swung again. Gil leaped aside. So Michael threw himself at him, he was the bigger one, he would knock this tiny boy down with his body, but all at once Gil wasn't where Michael threw himself, and he thudded into the platform.

He felt Gil behind him. Behind his knees he felt the length of a cudgel. His legs buckled and as they did Gil was before him again, shoving the stick against him, and Michael fell on to his back.

Gil planted one foot on his chest. He touched the cudgel to Michael's groin.

'Give me your other stick,' Michael said, as if that would make any difference.

Gil shook his head. Michael tried to sit up. The cudgel pressed down.

'Don't you know who I am? The scholar that never turned up on Saturday.'

'I know who ye are,' Gil said.

'So fight me, you bastard.' There was a crack in his voice. 'God damn your soul.'

With his man's creased eyes Gil regarded him. Up on the platform, a draper appeared and waved a measure. 'Clear off, lads,' he said.

Gil lifted his foot and the cudgel, and Michael stood. Gil watched him closely. But Michael's fury was gone, Gil meant nothing to him again. There was an ache in his throat. The draper who had told them to leave was shouting at a weaver, 'Thirty-six inches, what did I tell you over and over, Coleraine is thirty-six inches,' and Gil was saying something.

'I heard about that,' was all Michael caught.

'What?' he said.

'Your sister getting drowned,' Gil said, twisting the cudgel into his belt. He gave both cudgels a pat. The gesture seemed now to be only making sure that they were there and secure.

During the scuffling Michael's hat had fallen off. He picked it up out of the puddle where it had landed, slapped it against the platform and put it on, pulling it lower over his eyes. He walked on to the green. Midway across he remembered his eggs and things, and he made for the inn.

'Well, you decided to come back, did you?' the woman who knew his mother called out in a sarcastic voice. A pedlar was in the place where he had been, laying out crockery and knick-knacks.

126

'Where are my things?' Michael asked the pedlar.

The woman came over with his basket and handed it to him. It was empty except for the kerchief, which was folded inside. 'Running off like that,' she scolded. 'Leaving your mother's things for any thief in the world to snatch up. Lucky for yourself I was here and keeping an eye out.' From her apron pocket she took out a handful of coppers. She put them in his palm and closed his fingers around them. 'Now here is your money,' she said. 'Everything was bought up. Tuck this away safe.' He put the coins in his breeches' pocket.

'That's right,' she said. 'Tuck them away. Sure your mother would be wanting you to go straight home with them.' She looked at him mistrustfully, cocking her head to see under the brim of his hat. Then she looked surprised. 'Ah, there's something the matter,' she said. 'Whatever's the matter, *a bhuachaill*?'

'I'm obliged to you,' he murmured, walking away from her.

He walked the wrong way but didn't go back because he would have to pass her, so he went through the town. Smoke rose in wreaths out of the chimneys. The wreaths were blue and the hills behind a darker blue. The tops of the highest hills frayed into mist. Michael began to run, leaving the streets and heading towards the hills. He wanted to climb to Stone Peak and lie there and be blissful, as he had been on the night of Mary's wedding. But first he had to cross the river, and at the river he couldn't find the foot bridge.

'Where is it?' he cried. He ran up the bank some distance, then down it. He slid on the stones and kept stepping into water. When he fell he didn't get up, but rolled on to his back, the stones jabbing him.

He cried until he was not really crying, only doing it for the comfort of it. The sun came out and he stood and watched the water, which was rippled and silver like the back of a fish. There were no reeds here. If Rose had fallen in here she would have floated like a petal downstream, maybe all the way to the sea. She would at least have done that.

Chapter 18

Wales

'You are awake,' Rosser said. He dropped a bundle that opened upon landing on the bed. It was newspapers.

Michael sat up, keeping the quilt around him. With one hand he pulled the top paper over and turned it towards the light from the back window. *The Times,* he read, *Monday, February 27, 1797.* 'The London *Times*?' he said.

'For filling the hours. I can bring you a week's worth once a week.' He pointed his pipe at the pile. 'But they be five, six weeks old. Jones the Post, he holds them until everybody will have the opportunity of reading them.'

Michael opened to the middle of the paper. He read, "The Defendant then spit in the Plaintiff's face. The Plaintiff returned it, and that went on two or three times." For something to say, he read the next sentences aloud: 'The Defendant said, "If you call me a villain again, I will throw you behind the fire." The Plaintiff replied, "If you repeat what you have said, I will call you a villain again and again."'

'I did read that,' Rosser said. 'Fisticuffs in a coffee house.' He nodded and sucked his upper lip.

Michael scanned the column. 'That's right.'

'I told Jones that I wanted the papers for my own studying,' Rosser said.

Michael glanced up at him. Rosser touched the brim of his hat. 'I am grateful,' Michael said. But he wasn't at all. He felt frightened, assailed. Rosser had brought into the loft the outside world.

128

All the same, he read. After Rosser left, and after eating and having his bath, he turned back the first page of the first newspaper, and maybe Rosser had selected the issues deliberately, because what Michael read was this:

Two French frigates, a corvette and lugger, appeared off the coast of Pembrokeshire, Wales, on Feb. 22 and on the evening of that day disembarked troops reported to be fourteen hundred.

On the appearance of the enemy's landing, the country people fled in the utmost consternation. But having recovered from their panic, the whole country around rose in a mass, and without waiting for the regular troops, returned to face the enemy, many of whom were in the act of pillaging the cottages and regaling themselves with wine. In the course of the day, the entire legion was captured. It was soon determined that the legion was comprised of felons from French gaols and galleys.

We cannot positively state what the object of this ridiculous expedition was, although there is every reason to suppose, in view of the composition of the troops, that the intention was to destroy property and generally play the devil. Another, and more menacing, possibility exists that France was testing our coastal defences, in preparation for an invasion of Ireland. It is a sorry truth that a great number of the Irish peasantry would welcome an invasion, in the belief that the French would incur the enormous expense and peril of an expedition for the good of the inhabitants, whilst, obviously, the ambition of the French would be to divide and weaken the British Empire.

If, indeed, invasion is the enemy's desperate design, this foolhardy expedition to our shores has served no other purpose than to give us warning, and, therefore, to ensure the defeat of any future such expedition.

This was terrible and mortifying, but none of it was revelatory. Michael turned the page and read: *Tyrone, Ireland, Feb. 24,* and his heart lurched, but there was no surprise in that story, either. A letter about the Orangemen in the county was all. He turned page after page, he went through all the papers, looking for news of Ireland, of the murder, terrified of seeing his own name and, in fact, seeing it, but it was only a namesake in a list of bankrupts: *Michael Malone, fell-monger.*

Chapter 19

Ireland

Neal married Annie Murphy on his twenty-second birthday — Shrove Tuesday in the year seventeen hundred and ninety-five. They began their life together prosperously, having been given a cow, a horse, a cock and six hens by Denis Murphy, and a pig, two goats, a newly built cabin and three acres by Hugh.

The day after the wedding, Annie's stomach bulged. She said what an easement that she didn't have to bind it anymore. Naturally everyone was taken aback. Annie herself was blithe, smiling at the surprise in people's faces. She told Kathleen not to fret. 'There's a Malone in here,' she said, patting the bulge, 'with his father's round head and his father's hair sticking out all over it. Haven't I seen the creature in a dream?'

Neal at least had the decency to be flustered, but he was also obviously pleased and proud. He led Annie around by the hand, at arm's length, showing her off. In secret he had made a rush rattle, and he talked of making a duck with a beak that opened and shut and a miniature cart.

After taking Annie and Neal to the priest's, Hugh and Kathleen let themselves be pleased and proud, too. They couldn't regret Annie's pregnancy, despite the ill timing; there hadn't been a baby in the family for seventeen years.

'Every blessing comes with its burden,' Hugh said.

Kathleen said that there might be more to this particular blessing than what met the eye. She said that Annie's fruitfulness might well rouse Mary into conceiving. One pregnancy begetting another was commonplace within families, she alleged.

131

Hugh warned her against raising hopes, either hers or Mary's. Reach for a hope and grasp a misery, he said. Kathleen said that if the blade of grass did not hope it would never split the stone. Hugh said and how many blades withered entirely under the strain? Hadn't Mary swallowed every potion and recited every charm known to fairy woman and midwife? Weren't there a dozen corn dollies hanging over her and Slieve's bed? Hadn't she crawled around the holy well until her poor knees were in tatters? 'The girl is barren,' he said.

'Only providence, blessed be his name, can know that,' Kathleen said.

'The father of a girl that was spoiled all out by The Big Lord can know that,' Hugh said, reddening.

'So he can, so he can,' Kathleen agreed to stop him from saying more.

'He killed her inside herself,' Hugh muttered. 'You cannot change that by hoping.'

But Kathleen still tried to. By hoping, praying and scheming. She made her own rounds at the holy well. As often as she could she conspired to bring Mary and Annie together, then to seat them next to each other. You'd have thought that the last thing in the world Mary would have wanted was to be presented almost daily with the spectacle of her sister-in-law's big belly. But it didn't seem to bother her at all. She began to knit the baby a blanket. She called herself, 'Aunt Mary'. 'Let's have a kick for our Aunt Mary,' she said, laying her hands on Annie's stomach.

It was Slieve who was bothered. He could scarcely look at Annie. He kept telling everyone about his great-great-grandmother who didn't bear children until she was married ten years and then bore eleven.

Mary told Kathleen that Slieve wouldn't go to the christenings. Then she said he was drinking all of the time. Then, a week later, she said he had given over the drinking because he had started to fight in wrestling matches. He travelled to several matches outside the valley and returned from them a champion. Considering how huge he was, this was not surprising. Once his prize was a guinea and once it was a coat of many colours like the one Israel made for Joseph. Then, after winning the coat, he gave up wrestling and joined the Defenders.

This was surprising. The captain of the Defenders was a tanner named Devlin, and Slieve had always called him 'Devil' owing to his intemperance. Devlin would set fire to a row of Protestant cabins when setting fire to a single cabin was excessive. On one Defender raid he branded a cross into a Protestant boy's back. Now Slieve called him 'Captain Stout', Devlin's name for himself, and he spoke up for the intemperance. The Peep o' Day Boys had to be shown that they could not go on doing what they'd been doing, he said.

What the Peep o' Day Boys had been doing was turning up at Catholic homes near dawn and terrorizing families into giving up their places. The fight was the old one between Catholics and Presbyterians over leases, especially on coveted places close to town. Mostly Peep o' Day Boys only threatened and wrecked furniture and sometimes beat the men, but there was a rumour from Armagh that a Catholic there had been castrated. So Catholics living near town formed their own secret society: the Defenders. They terrorized Presbyterians as they themselves had been terrorized, only more so. There were battles on the highways and at markets and fairs, there were burnings and beatings, the trouble going on until both sides dreaded each other enough to call a truce. Then Devlin turned to threatening middlemen and small landlords. He had his lieutenants post notices:

Remark the consequences. Any man demanding rent
above four guineas an acre had best prepare his coffin.

The notices meant what they said. One night a magistrate arrested two of Devlin's lieutenants, and the next morning that magistrate was fished out of the river. From then on, no magistrate would lift a finger, and the landlords and middlemen lost courage and lowered rentals. John Logan didn't lower his rentals, but he did hire and arm Peep o' Day Boys to guard his house and fields and to surround him when he was out riding. You could hear him coming from miles away because his guards let out whoops to put the fear of God into any Defender who might have ideas.

133

When Slieve disclosed, one day when he and Mary came by for supper, that he had become a Defender, that he had taken the oath, and that he had sworn to obey 'Captain Stout' unto death, no one spoke for a moment. No one even chewed. Hugh, for no evident reason, went to the dresser, picked up his timepiece and announced, 'Half-six.' He looked at Kathleen and said, 'I thought that only journeyman living round the town were taking the oath.'

'Men everywhere are taking it,' Slieve said. 'Them bloody Peep o' Day Boys have got to be shown that they cannot go on doing what they've been doing.'

'Your Captain Stout has shown them that plain enough,' Hugh said.

'Now it is rentals,' Slieve said. 'Rentals are too high.'

'Indeed they are, but not in your case.' Hugh sublet Slieve his land.

Slieve flushed. 'There are other grievances. Taxes. Tithes.'

'Let me ask you this, Slieve, lad,' Hugh said. 'For how long do you suppose the magistrates are going to suffer Defender threats?'

'For as long as they will not do what's right.'

'They'll be bringing back the penal laws.'

'Then they'll be bringing back civil war,' Slieve said, his eyes leaping to Hugh's.

'Nay. Do not wish for that, lad. Your Captain Stouts on one side and the English Army on the other.'

'We should be setting off,' Mary said, patting Slieve's arm.

Michael had been wanting to speak, and now, before Slieve left, he did. 'The Anglo-English landlords, men like Lord Morrery, they are the villains,' he said. 'Instead of poor Catholics and poor Protestants fighting each other, they should join together and fight to purify the corrupt Irish parliament. Then they could change all the land laws.'

Hugh blew out a breath. 'Catholics and Protestants joining together,' he said dismissively.

''Tis what Master Dolan says,' Michael said back, but even as he'd spoken he'd thought how impossible it sounded. When Master Dolan had said it in the schoolroom it had sounded like the long sought-after answer.

Annie came to her feet, pushing her fists into the small of her

134

back. She went to the dresser for the poteen bottle, drank what was left and then held it at her groin, the mouth end pointed at Slieve. 'All I advise, Slieve,' she said, 'is mind your private parts. Remember the lad in Armagh.' She winked at Mary.

Slieve saw the wink, and glanced at Mary and back at Annie and shouted, 'What are the two of you laughing at?' although Annie was just smiling and Mary looking bewildered.

'Christ's sake, Slieve,' Annie said. 'What ails you?' Her face emptied. 'Oh, Jesus,' she said, bringing her hands to her stomach. 'The brute's kicking like a mule. Who wants to feel?'

Chapter 20

Wales

The days were longer and warmer. Every morning Rosser was coming up to the loft a little earlier. One morning his news was that no treason charges were being preferred against the three Irish officers from the *Légion Noire*. They were going to be returned to France, in exchange for English prisoners.

'So,' he finished, looking straight at Michael. He had light blue eyes, the same colour as Olwen's, but hers were big and happy and his were small, deep and evinced nothing. Sometimes, the queerest thing, they quivered in their sockets.

'You did not have to hide me,' Michael said for him. 'I would have lived after all.'

'Ah, well, there is a question about that,' Rosser said, brushing a strand of white hair out of his eyes. 'You are not well with you. The prison ships have vermin and only ballast for sleeping on.'

'I cannot be surrendering now without accounting for my whereabouts all these weeks,' Michael said quietly.

'Indeed. Olwen and I would be arrested.'

'That was not my implication. Sure I would invent a story.'

'There would be investigations of your story. Lying would be harder than you suppose.' He went over to the rear window. 'It is best that you stay on here,' he said. He nodded at the wisdom of his decision.

Chapter 21

Ireland

From the south, from the far side of the river, you could see the hills rising with a regularity that didn't seem to be of God's making, and wasn't. Tyrrell the Fairy Man said that hundreds of years before St. Patrick, when giants were in the land, there was a great battle between two rival giant factions after which the bones of the defeated were hurled throughout Ireland, and it happened that a spine landed in the valley and became the stairway of hills.

Maybe it was because the hills seemed to start and ascend right at the end of his father's property, but for Michael they were more peculiar even than their legend. They were his own life. When he looked at them he didn't think of a giant's spine, he thought of heights he would reach or had already reached, each hill climbing to the highest hill that would be some glorious event before his death. So far his life had gone up two hills: the day that Father Lynn said he would pay for the hedge school, and the night of Mary's wedding.

The third hill was Pattern Day, in the year that Neal and Annie married. Michael awoke on the morning of that day feeling like light, glimmery and weightless, and also sad, although he was not sad, and this feeling seemed supreme to him — as if he were just for a moment being fixed in the immensity of all time — supreme and auspicious.

He lay there and listened to his mother and father rise and dress, put sods on the fire and go out with the dogs. He didn't get up until he heard his mother milking, then he came out from behind the dresser and went to the door. Such stillness

137

outside. His mother, sitting at the byre door, the black cow, the dark July green hedge were not quite there in the mist, which was not like any mist he'd ever seen before but like wet light, the yellow dulcet light you see in pictures of angels or Jesus, blazing out from their heads.

'Here is the sleeping beauty,' his mother greeted him, and then she pointed at the water and cried, 'Oh, look!'

A big spectral bird, a heron, was flying slowly south over the river.

'There'll be sunshine for the Pattern,' Kathleen said.

And as the heron was a harbinger you could rely on, there was. By midday the mist had burned away and the clouds had withdrawn to the horizon. The sky was so blue you wanted to run your hand over it. Kathleen said that it was the blue of heaven, that on such a day the gates of heaven opened wide and hundreds of poor suffering souls wafted upwards on every breeze and breath. Even though Rose was already in heaven and in some exaltation there, the family offered up the rosary for her before leaving for the Pattern.

It was hot walking. Neal fretted over Annie's health the entire way because her time was upon her. He hadn't wanted her to go at all, but she'd said that she must pray for a safe birth, and she'd promised to take things easy once she'd circled the holy well.

'No, you won't,' Neal had said, and she'd bridled at his distrust. But it turned out to be justified. After the devotions at the well, Michael walked by one of the big tents that had been set up for the day, and there she was inside, leaning over the fiddler, one arm around the man's neck, one arm reeling a pint, wearing Neal's hat and joining in on 'Will you Float in My Boat?' in the loud manly voice she sang with.

Michael didn't go into that tent. He was looking for Etain. He hardly saw her anymore, except at mass. Seven months ago her mother had died of griping of the guts, and she'd left the school to keep house, which was a shame because she was one of the three senior scholars who'd been praised by the celebrated teacher from Munster. The other two were Michael and Corny. The three who weren't praised — Tim was one of them — were barred from coming back.

Since he was tall, Michael could see over the crowd. He

looked for her yellow hair, and in case her hair was covered he also looked at all the small women and girls. He hoped that she had parted company with her father.

He stopped at stalls and jingled his money, dripping the heavy cool coins through his fingers. All of it was his, earned by his own labour, nights and nights writing letters to Cork for the miller's homesick bride. The stall owners heard the jingling and exhorted him to spend. For a penny he bought a gingerbread and then lost another penny to a card trickster. He gave a farthing to a singing blind boy. At a book stall, spending sixpence, he bought a little volume of verse for his library.

She was at the end of the line of tents, with Corny. Her shawl was down around her shoulders, so it was her hair that caught his eye. He hung back for a moment, seeing her and Corny together, standing apart from everyone else like sweethearts. They had their backs to the tents, and she was touching her temples as though thinking hard.

What she was really doing was holding Corny's spectacles on. When Michael came nearer and she turned and saw him, she took them off.

'What do you have those on for?' he asked.

'Only trying them out.'

'Are your eyes going?'

She handed the spectacles to Corny. 'Sometimes they go bleary like,' she said carelessly. She smiled at him. 'Where have you been hiding yourself?'

'I bought you something,' he said suddenly. He took the book out of his coat pocket.

'A book,' she said, surprised.

'Verse,' he said, giving to her.

'Ah.' She opened to the middle.

Corny looked over her shoulder and read, 'Where tender babes suckle . . .'

Michael felt his face redden. 'Come along,' he said, taking Etain's arm. 'We'll have a glass of something.'

'All right.' She closed the book. 'Corny?' she said, turning to him.

Behind her back Michael made a fist, and Corny said, no, no he didn't have a thirst at all.

They passed the first tent. Her father was inside that one, she said. Her father thought that she was with her older cousin, Deirdre, but Deirdre had glided off with some boys the minute Mr McCaffery's back was turned. The next tent had a piper playing at the entrance, and they went into it, into the smoke and gloaming, and found a place to sit on a bench near the back. They had to sit close together. Her hair smelled of oatmeal, so she must have washed it.

He bought a punch for her and a whiskey for himself. She said, 'I had better tuck this away safe,' and she put the book between her thighs.

For some reason that made him laugh. 'Success,' he toasted her, raising his glass. 'Drink up.' He dug coppers out of his pocket and waved them at the potboy.

They got drunk. In their drunkenness and in the smoke and rumble they were cocooned. He said whatever entered his head and she wept with laughter.

'Don't,' she begged.

'Don't what?' he said, laughing at her laughing, gloating upon her transport.

After some time he became aware that the tent was emptying, that the piper had stopped playing and that the music was now fiddle music and being played outside. There was hooting and clapping out there, people were dancing. He wondered if Etain would dance with him. He tried thinking of a clever way to ask her, and was, in fact, opening his mouth to do it when his hat was snatched off. Annie's hand appeared between him and Etain. She was still wearing Neal's hat. 'Lovebirds,' she said accusingly, looking from him to Etain. She leaned over him and hugged him around the neck. 'I've been searching everywhere for you, Michael,' she said. ''Tis desperate I am for a dancing partner.'

'You cannot dance,' he said, meaning with her time so close upon her.

She hit his chest. 'I can dance circles around yourself!' Etain smiled at him sideways.

'Where's Neal?' he said.

Annie kneaded his arms. 'Isn't it you that's grown up all at once,' she whispered. 'So big and strong. Amn't I wishing that I had waited for you to grow up.'

Behind them, Neal's voice said, 'You ran off.'

Annie pulled herself up. 'Michael and myself are going to dance,' she said gaily. 'You can dance with his sweetheart here.'

Neal was holding two tankards. 'I brought you an ale,' he said.

She grabbed the tankards and banged them down on the table. 'I am going to shake a toe,' she said.

'But the baby,' Neal said.

'But the baby, but the baby,' she mimicked. She bent down between Etain and Michael again. 'You two want to dance, don't you?' she said in a little girl voice.

She led them out of the tent and through the crowd to a clearing. 'Dance,' she ordered, pushing Neal at Etain and then starting to heel-toe in front of Michael. Her belly bounced after the rest of her did. 'Lay it on, man!' she cried.

Michael imitated her steps, exaggerated them in tomfoolery because he felt bashful about flinging his limbs around now that he was called upon to do it. But Annie seemed to imagine that this was how he danced, that he was even nimble.

'That's the go!' she shouted, nodding him on, and he kicked higher, sprang up, spun and landed perfectly, clicked his heels together, and it struck him that this *was* how he danced, or how he had somehow come to dance on this numinous day. He glanced at Etain to see if she was watching him, and she was. She laughed to catch his eye. He laughed. They went on glancing at each other and laughing, laughing at Neal who wanted to know what the joke was.

Since one tune flowed into another there was no opportunity to change partners, so Michael stayed with Annie, who didn't flag though sweat flowed down her face. Finally Neal shouted that she'd had enough and he put a hand on her shoulder to steady her.

'Have not!' she cried, swatting him away. She snapped her fingers over her head, throwing the snaps like darts.

Looking undecided, Neal danced with Etain again. But Michael, worried now that it was his fantasitc leaping and twirling that was goading Annie to dangerous extremes, stopped.

Annie seemed to think he stopped because he was wearing down. 'Peel off the trusty!' she cried, grabbing the lapels of his

141

coat and starting to yank it over his shoulders.

What happened next he was not really sure happened at all, not at the time he wasn't. She had the coat off except for one sleeve that was caught, and she was cursing the sleeve and tugging it, all the while still dancing. Her stomach bumped against him. She tugged at the coat with one hand, bumping him and laughing and cursing, and he felt her other hand brush his groin. He felt her cup him there. That's what he thought he felt.

He went still, and she whipped the coat free at last and whirled it in victory. She dropped it to the ground and began to do a jig on it.

'Stay alive!' she cried, snatching his limp hands, pumping them. He looked at her, and there was nothing to see in her red wet exuberant face. He thought, "It must have been the cuff catching. Or my own hand maybe. Or just nothing, nothing at all. See, I had all those whiskeys."

There was a fight. If there hadn't been the day wouldn't have been a summit in Michael's life. Annie would have stayed a bulwark between him and Etain for the whole Pattern. Or Mr McCaffery would have found her and taken her away. Or neither of these would have happened, which still wouldn't have made any difference since it would never have occurred to Michael that he could get Etain to run off with him to the abbey wall. He was out of confidence with her lately because of being able to talk with her only when they met in a crowd and then, more often than not, her father was hovering. He hadn't kissed her since before her mother died.

The fight seemed to be at the far end of the passage. There were roars of 'McIlroy!' and 'McGlinchey!' — the two big rival factions. The fiddler stopped playing and everyone started running down the passage to watch the fight or join in. Men produced cudgels and flaunted them.

'Come along!' Annie screamed.

'The baby!' Neal shouted. But she was already away and carried into the crowd, so he chased after her.

Michael got his coat up before it was trampled in the dirt altogether. He took Etain's hand, just expecting her to run with him after Annie and Neal. He didn't know, maybe he would even fight, he was so wound up.

Etain pulled back. 'I don't want to,' she said.

''Tis a fight,' he said, as if that weren't evident.

'I don't like fighting,' she said.

They looked at each other, and he got an idea. Moving in front of her to be her shield, he pulled her down the passage between the tents, pushing through everyone going the other way. When they came to the end of the tent where they had been drinking, he led her down the side of it. Kegs and benches blocked the way, but they clambered over them to the back of the tent and the open field.

After the shadows of the tents the sun was blinding, it was so white. He wanted her to think that they were going anywhere, just to escape the crowd, while in fact he was heading for the ruined wall of the old abbey. He'd heard that sweethearts slipped away from Patterns to lie at the wall, in the long grass.

They had to climb a hill to get there, and he thought, "This will give the game away," for the ascent was steep, not a course you would choose aimlessly. She was breathing hard, and her hand gripping his was exquisite because in it he would feel when she descried his intention.

But there was no moment of resistance, he didn't even have to pull her. Either she didn't know about the wall or she knew and didn't object. These two possibilities, as he thought about them, put him into a mild panic. He wasn't at all sure that he would be able to lie down. How was he supposed to do that? Lie down first and sweep his arm alongside himself? Kiss her standing and then sink? They had never kissed lying down before.

At the top of the hill he couldn't even look at her. He stepped gingerly, mindful of other lovers in the grass. But they didn't come across any. He wondered, was this the right place, was there another abbey wall somewhere? No, he would have heard of it. His hand in hers was clammy. Did this disgust her?

She was walking beside him now, and she steered him to the wall. It was a triangular swarm of ivy, all that was left of the abbey. Etain let go of his hand and leaned against the wall, pressing the side of her face to the leaves.

'They are cool,' she said. She was flushed.

'Take off your shawl,' he said, innocently enough, yet he burned to hear himself.

143

She sighed. He thought it was disillusionment in him.

But she drew the shawl off her shoulders, dropped it on to the grass, knelt and spread it out, patting the lumps that the bent grass made. She got it all smooth then sat on it, her legs curled behind her, and leaned on one hand. She smiled up at him, or squinted. The sun was in her eyes, so he couldn't tell. And since he couldn't tell and since it behooved him to do something, he threw his coat down.

'Don't sit on that filthy thing,' she said. 'Sit here.' She tossed her hand at the spread of shawl that she wasn't occupying.

He sat on the edge of it with his legs out before him on the grass, which wasn't wet. There was no need to sit on anything. He remembered the time he'd had an intuition that he could touch her breast and she'd punched him.

'Feel the sun,' she said, going back on her elbows and lifting her face.

He considered this, he severed it from his desire, and it seemed to him that it was permission to bask, that he might lie down without scaring her off. Still, he did it by degrees, to forewarn her, shifting his weight, lowering himself to his elbows, staying like that for a minute looking at the sky, then letting his head slowly fall as if gravity were doing it.

She dropped down beside him on her back and said, 'Ah.'

His blood plunged. What did she mean, 'Ah'? Was it only the sun and friendliness? The truth was, she had never kissed him with abandon. There were girls who didn't kiss at all until their wedding day. She at least had shown that she wasn't one of them, or she had shown it before her mother died. Was it disrespectful of her mother's memory to kiss her now, out of wedlock? Was she being so familiar with him because she trusted him to respect her mother's memory and not kiss her out of wedlock?

She came up on one elbow, leaned over him and smiled. With the sun directly behind her there were beams of light radiating from her hair. Then she laid her head on his chest.

His heart hammered. Yet she didn't move. In spite of the assault to her ear and the significance of it — she must have known what it signified — she kept her head there, resting not entirely with all her weight, he felt, and more than her decision

144

to lie on him and stay lying, this scruple about releasing the whole of her weight showed her awareness of the state of things, and he let his arms fold around her.

She lifted her face, her eyes half closed, and brought her mouth close to his, and all he had to do was close the gap between their faces.

They kissed a long time, and then something else happened that never had before, which was that their lips parted and their tongues touched. They both shivered. His hands stroked her hair down her back. He let himself imagine by the glossy feel and warmth of it that it was her skin.

When she drew away, he said, 'How dear you are.'

She nodded to tell him the same.

'We can do this every day when we are wed,' he said.

She looked back and forth from one of his eyes to the other. 'You never said that before,' she whispered.

'I never *said* it. But we both of ourselves knew we would marry.'

She shook her head, and the motion was perishing. He thought, "She doesn't want to," but she only said, '*I* didn't know.' She sat up and regarded him from the greater distance.

'Sure you knew,' he said, boisterous with relief. He threw an arm around her. 'What about when we kissed at Mary's wedding and you said you hated kissing Ferris.'

She picked a blade of grass and wound it around one finger. 'You love me?' she asked.

'Oh, aye. Do you love me?'

She didn't answer. She wound the blade more tightly, and the tip of her finger turned the colour of beetroot. Her silence entered everything. All his presumptions rattled in it. He thought, "She doesn't, she doesn't love me."

The grass broke and she flicked it away. 'I love you more than anything,' she said.

This time, kissing, their lips parted right off. And he did it at last, he slid his palm down her side and felt her breast, and she let him, she just went on kissing him. He was the one who had to end the kiss.

He jumped up, saying he wanted to talk. They descended the other side of the hill to a stream and sat with their feet in the cold water that rolled over stones. From here they could still

145

hear the fighting at the Pattern, but it was distant enough that it might have been some natural sound. Etain rested against him and he held her from behind and breathed her hair that smelled of tobacco from the tent.

He told her of his plan for their future. Because he had made it years ago he felt that she already knew it and she kept surprising him with her questions.

They would wait two years to marry, he said. If they were to marry before then he would have to end his studies to provide for her and the babies that came along. But if they waited he would be ready in two years to challenge a schoolmaster to a literary contest and to win the contest and the master's job. That was how Master Dolan got his first position.

She asked, couldn't they live with his father and mother while he studied? That wasn't the footing he wanted to start out on, he said, and she said she'd only asked to find out what he would answer because waiting was best for her, too. With her mother only gone these few months and her father still grieving, weeping like a baby at times, and still fixed on tying her to a rich man, she didn't see how she could leave him for a spell anyhow.

'You won't be leaving him ever. He'll be living with ourselves,' Michael said.

'He will?' she said, turning to stare at him.

'We cannot have him living by himself. And I won't be a beggar, either. I'll go on with the contests, winning them all over the country until I am a teacher in demand and can rake in the fees. We'll have a stone house with a proper bedroom for your father, and the school attached to it.'

'That will be grand, indeed,' she said, staring. 'But my father will never give up his holding. He'll never do that.'

'Well,' he said, bothered by this snag in his plan, even though it was scarcely for his own sake that he had decided her father would live with them, 'we'll see about it down the road.'

Whatever happened down the road, she said, they would have to keep their betrothal a secret. Her father would have a terrible fit if he found out, maybe he would die from the shock. She would break the news to him when he wasn't so deeply mourning her mother. She promised that they could still meet like this, in the pine woods or even here, so Michael said, 'A

146

secret from everybody but Corny,' and she agreed, likely
thinking of the great friendship between the three of them, but
he was thinking of how he'd come upon her and Corny alone at
the end of the tents.

The rest of their future she was ravished to hear. They would
travel together to Dublin to buy books. She would teach by his
side when their children were old enough to attend class. She
would have a servant to help in the house. He even had the girl
picked out: one of Annie's young sisters who wouldn't marry
because she was harelipped.

After he had finished telling her everything they kissed again
and he touched her breast again. Their feet touched in the
water, which felt like a consecration. Then he stood to leave,
but she stayed sitting, she didn't want to go.

'You are mine,' he said, and she leaned against his legs,
looking up at him, her eyes dark, almost black instead of blue,
like ways into her ... a sight that she was showing only him.

The fighting was over by the time they got back to the
Pattern. Everyone was dancing again.

Chapter 22

Wales

Olwen would not immerse her vile body (she feared drowning) and if you did not immerse yourself you could not become a member of the Baptist church. In this one matter, although he maintained that there had never been a single baptism drowning, Rosser didn't order her. A person's religion was between that person and God, he said. He told Olwen that she was free to carry on in sin and imbecility.

So she did, which was lucky. As a chapel member she would have been obliged to attend services, and Michael would have been left alone in the house. Now what if the hired man took it into his head to enter the place and go right up the stairs, since there was no one to prevent him? Olwen said, oh, it was likely. She twinkled and said you had to keep your eye on that man, you couldn't leave temptations lying in his path. She bolted the doors on the evenings that Rosser went to prayer meetings.

Then she came upstairs. They had a new game: taking turns drawing words with their fingers on each other's bare backs, and the person being drawn on had to feel out what the word was. One Sunday evening, in the darkness, she was drawing the longest word on him and having trouble with the spelling of it. She wrote five or six letters, stopped, sighed, wiped where she'd written and began over. It was pleasant, the light travelling finger, the brush of her warm rough hand.

The wind rose, and rain started to patter in distinct drops. You could mistake the patter for the scurrying of a small animal on the roof, but Michael lay with his head turned to the front window, so he saw the drops on the pane. He shivered.

Olwen's finger halted. 'You are cold,' she said.

'No. Finish your word.' The shiver was also in his voice, it made him sound lustful.

'Good gracious!' Olwen whispered, and he thought that his voice had dismayed her. But then he heard scraping outside, against the house.

'Hide!' she said, and hid him herself, throwing the quilt over him. 'Don't budge!' She ran across the room.

Michael lifted the quilt to look. She had picked up the spoon from his supper and was shaking it at the pane. A face was there, on the other side. Olwen hit the window ledge with the spoon. She stamped her feet, screamed in Welsh. Never had Michael witnessed such energy in her. And yet the face remained.

What should he do? Stay under the quilt? Help her, reveal himself? Go downstairs for Rosser's gun?

Then he heard, among the words she was screaming, the name of the hired man, and he saw the face right against the pane now, saw that, sure enough, it was the hired man, so he didn't move. He musn't reveal himself to the hired man. He musn't shoot the hired man, must he?

The window rattled again, not loudly, not as if the man were warning that he'd break it. Why? Either the glass was to be broken so the man could get in, or what was he doing?

Taking the window out was what. It just came away, frame and all, and the man lifted it out into the night, turned it and put it through the opening into the loft, leaning inside to lower it to the floor. The entire time Olwen screeched and hit at him with her fist and the spoon.

But when the man let go of the window, in the instant that his hands were holding nothing, she gave his shoulders a shove. Michael saw the oval of his mouth as the ladder tipped away from the wall. There was a thud, a clatter. The man shouted. Olwen stuck her head out of the opening and shouted back. She laughed throatily. She pulled her head into the room, turned to Michael and whispered, '*He* will not be returning in a hurry.' The she proceeded to replace the window.

Chapter 23

Ireland

As Annie had foretold the baby was a boy with a round head and brown hair like a brush for cleaning bottles. When he was laid on her breast she said, 'Nealie,' and so he was named: Nealie (for his father and maternal great-grandfather) Bartholomew (for the saint whose feast day was approaching) Denis (for his paternal grandfather) Malone.

The birth took place in the second outshot because Annie was eating dinner with Kathleen when her labour pains came upon her, and she fell on to the tester bed and didn't get up again. In the following days she and the baby just stayed on in the cabin, and Neal took his meals and slept there also.

It wasn't suggested that they go back to their own place. The reason was Nealie. Neither Kathleen nor Hugh wanted the child to go, not even that short distance. They were both spellbound by him, everyone was. At the christening women thrust their own babies at people and fought to hold him. It was his eyes, how they appeared to stare straight into you with a look of celestial love and gladness. His mouth went almost ear to ear, so he always seemed to be smiling, even when he was crying, which he scarcely ever did and then only for seconds. What's more, he was the biggest baby people had ever seen, and that made them happy to look upon him.

Even Slieve was charmed. This was a christening that Mary insisted he go to, and as soon as he was in the door Kathleen gave Nealie to him. In his massive arms Nealie was tiny. Slieve held the bundle out of reach of all the women bobbing around, Kathleen being the only one tall enough to see Nealie's face, and she said craftily, 'Ah, Slieve, he's smiling.'

Slieve nodded. 'I have a way with the creatures,' he said.

Annie joked that she was going to bear a herd of Nealies and sell them for fortunes at market and live in the lap of luxury. She was in her glory. She invited all of the guests at the christening to call round again whenever they liked, and many of the women did so over the next week. They showed up bearing gifts: knitted bonnets and blankets for Nealie, cakes for the family. Annie said that she felt like the Blessed Virgin. She was generous in turn, letting anyone hold and inspect Nealie who wanted, and the women who were capable of it, she let nurse him.

When there were no visitors she disregarded him altogether except to feed him. Sometimes she went into flurries of dressing and undressing him, fitting him in his gifts and summoning the family to come and see, but mostly she napped on the hob; she had to regain her strength, she said, and Kathleen did the work for both households.

A month passed and then one evening Neal said that he thought it was time for his family to go back to its own cabin.

'It is indeed,' Kathleen said with good grace since it was the right thing to do, after all, but she looked at Nealie sorrowfully.

'Mama, 'tis only going across the field there,' Neal said.

'Just don't be expecting me to slave away,' Annie said to him. 'I am still trembly on my feet.'

The next morning, by the bridge, she was standing steadily enough, shading her eyes with a fern, watching a man and a cart that were receding down the road. Michael saw her as he was leaving to go to school, and he asked her if she was waiting for somebody.

'Not a soul has called round these three days,' she said, lashing the fern at the bridge.

'So what are you up to out here?'

'You own the bloody road, is it?'

'Only wondering after Nealie.'

'Ah, he's sleeping like a drunk,' she said, as if it were an annoyance.

At the end of the day Nealie was back with Kathleen. It seemed that Annie had brought him over in the early afternoon and gone to visit a friend and hadn't returned yet.

She visited another friend the next day, and the day after that she went with her mother to watch a tarring and feathering in a neighbouring town. By the end of the week she wasn't bothering with explanations. She was just depositing Nealie with Kathleen mid-morning and sauntering off somewhere, coming back at midday to feed him, then disappearing until supper. Mary took to coming down from her place every afternoon to lend her mother a hand.

An unspoken bargain had been struck. In exchange for doing Annie's churning, milking, spinning and marketing, collecting her eggs and cooking meals for Neal and her, Kathleen and Mary could take charge of Nealie during the day. It was plain that Kathleen and Mary thought they'd got the better end of the deal. They received Nealie so gratefully and attended to Annie's chores so unobtrusively, for instance filling her yarn basket with skeins while she was out and therefore she might imagine that she had spun them herself, then retrieving them days later to sell in town. And they were as piqued as Annie herself would have been when it struck Neal that maybe it wasn't becoming behaviour for a wife and mother to gad about like that.

'She is a high-spirited girl, you knew that when you took up with her,' Kathleen said.

'I don't see who it is harming at all, I don't see that it is harming yourself,' Mary said, waving at the hob where he was reclining with his noggin and pipe.

They defended Annie to neighbours, too, until there was no longer the need, after the potboy at The Bull and Castle went into the militia and Annie grabbed up his job because her father said he would pay her and she might sing with the fiddler for tips. So it became obvious why she couldn't be at home caring for her baby, and Kathleen could say to people, wasn't Neal on the sunny side of the hedge to have a wife that brought in a steady wage?

152

Chapter 24

Wales

Olwen said that the hired man tried to get in the window because he craved to bundle, to lie naked, behave as husband and wife. Bundle. Didn't they court that way in Ireland? She and the hired man had bundled many times over the year in her bed. This very bed. To keep herself from conceiving she had eaten batches of hart's tongue and recited a charm.

Their nights together had been Rosser's nights at chapel. If her brother had ever caught them — she shook her head at the thought. Rosser said that bundling was the most wicked and evil of sins, the devil himself copulating through the body of the man, but, Olwen said, if that were true then half the women in the country had been the devil's whore, and that simply couldn't be or else a person would be running across mad and fleshly women at every turn.

In case Rosser should ever come back before he was expected, the hired man had built himself a secret way out. One Sunday, when Rosser was at chapel, the hired man took apart the front loft window, piece by piece, glass and frame, and put together a new removable window, using the original wood. When he was done, all he had to do was joggle the frame out of a groove and he had an opening large enough for a man with narrow shoulders to squeeze through backwards, after which he could hang from the ledge to break his fall. It hadn't occurred to Olwen until this night that he might use the window to get *into* the loft.

Of course, the trysts had to end after Michael came. Rosser was getting suspicious was what she told the hired man, and

153

that scared him right off. For many weeks he wouldn't even glance at her. But in the last few days he had been winking at her, and yesterday he came up to her in the yard and said that his squire was lonely. She had had to say that she didn't want to do it anymore, she didn't love him.

'Is that true?' Michael asked. He wasn't embarrassed because she wasn't and because of the darkness.

'Oh, no,' she said. She laughed. Michael couldn't see her features, yet he felt that she looked entirely unlike herself. He asked her why she and the hired man hadn't married.

Rosser would never allow it, she said. The hired man was beneath her, being only a cottager. But the hired man was saving his wages and learning to make gloves as a second occupation so that one day he might rent his own farm, but even then . . . . She sighed. 'Rosser will never take a wife himself,' she said. 'If I leave him he will need a housekeeper, and she will be a woman that he is not accustomed to and that he will have to pay a wage to. Well, I cannot foresee the day, indeed I cannot.'

'Why do you say he will never marry?' Michael asked.

'Oh, he never will.'

'Has he said so.'

'Oh, no.'

'How do you know in that case?'

'I only know that he never will. Nor will he ever have another woman in the house.'

'You ought to marry anyhow, Rosser is not your father,' Michael said, forgetting that his being in the loft made any ceremony, let alone her absence, impossible. 'I am telling you, Olwen,' he said earnestly, 'you ought to marry that man.'

She brushed back a wisp of her hair. She said, 'Have you got a girl back in Ireland?'

He started at the transgression. She had never asked him about home or about his life before he came here. He thought, "She *is* different. Her salacity. Wanting to know if I have a girl that I lie with."

'The loveliest girl in all of Ireland, I'll be bound,' she sang, and to his amazement his eyes filled.

He lay back on the pillow. 'There is no one,' he said.

She leaned over him to stroke his forehead and began to hum a song that he liked about a magic lady who could turn herself into a river. His hurt stirred, then settled.

154

Chapter 25

Ireland

When Michael heard that Mrs Willis and all of her children but Gil had gone back to Donegal, he thought, "All but Gil and the idiot boy," because he couldn't imagine that Gil would part with him. Then he heard that Gil had whores, and he thought, "The idiot boy is dead," because otherwise Gil would have to be hiding the boy from the whores, and that seemed unlikely.

Everyone wondered who the whores were. Passers-by had seen various girls — a tall girl one day, a short girl another — and the reason it had to be that they were whores was that they hid themselves from view, running into the cabin or behind a bush. They were obviously up to no good. Furthermore, why would they go up to that runt's place at all unless he paid them to?

Gil stopped challenging boys to cudgel fights. Sapped of bellicosity by the whores was one theory, but that couldn't be or else he'd not have joined the Peep o' Day Boys. In fact, the rumour was he was made a leader. None of the Irish knew these things for certain, but it was also rumoured that his uncle John Logan joined and was made a leader as well.

There were other rumours.

At a place called the Diamond, which was near Armagh, a party of Defenders attacked a party of Peep o' Day Boys, and the Defenders were lambasted. Thirty of them died on the field.

These same Peep o' Day Boys changed their name to The Orange Society, after William of Orange, and began hounding Catholics by the hundreds out of their cabins, beating the

155

inhabitants and burning the cabins down around them if they didn't leave. Murders occurred.

There was a rumour that the Peep o' Day Boys in the valley had become Orangemen.

All these rumours showed themselves to be true, the last when Gil and John Logan marched near the head of several hundred Protestants up and down the streets in town, in and out of the bigger shops and twice round the green, all the marchers wearing Orange cockades. A day and a night later the Catholic chapel burned down.

It had been the one Irish chapel in the valley. The other altars were just sheds, or even less that that — stones in a field. In the chapel embers Captain Stout called on parishioners to become Defenders. Father Lynn nudged wreckage with his toe and turned a deaf ear. Captain Stout said wasn't the reek of these ashes the reek of penal times when chapels were burned all over Ireland and priests were hunted down like foxes? He said that there would be no justice, that the magistrates were Orangemen.

And right there, out in the open, men took the treasonable Defender oath. The sexton took it. Neal took it. Hugh took it.

Michael did not, although he could have — two other boys his age, seventeen, were sworn, and so was a boy a year, maybe two years younger. But Michael did not take the oath because Master Dolan had said the Peep o' Day Boys and Defenders were like birds pecking each other to death over the few seeds thrown to them by the landed classes. He had told him and Corny a secret, which was that in the valley there would soon be an enlightened society to join: The Society of United Irishmen, it was called. It was spreading throughout Ireland, its members were thinking men, Catholic and Protestants together, and they recognized the true enemy. They wrote this:

We are ruled by Englishmen and the servants of
    Englishmen,
whose object is the interest of another country,
whose instrument is corruption,
whose strength is the weakness of Ireland.

Michael found out that what Mary had said was true. She had

156

said that living with a Defender was like living with an illness that flared up and died down but that never went away, so even on your loveliest days you didn't feel yourself to be entirely well.

He found out what the symptoms were. In the middle of the night two long knocks and then two short knocks, two long two short until the door was opened; that was a mild fever — a Defender meeting that Hugh must attend, or maybe a drill or a patrol. Long knocks alone were a dangerous fever; they were retribution — threats, fires, a beating, Michael could only guess what. He deciphered the knocks by the set of his father's face the next morning and by the tidings he heard at school.

Nothing was said of these tidings at home. Hugh would not speak of the Defenders, he would not talk politics at all and forbade suck talk in his presence. He seemed to have no stance nor to want one. He seemed to have become a Defender in spite of himself. And, since the Defenders took an oath of secrecy, Neal and Slieve were just as closemouthed.

Michael prayed for them. 'They are only dupes,' he told God. 'Don't let them die or be arrested.' His mother also prayed for them and for protection from Orange Society fires even though it was plain that John Logan wasn't letting torches anywhere near the cabins of Catholics who paid him high rentals.

Rentals were paid on the first of November. And just before that date a fragile truce was called.

And two weeks after All Souls' Eve there was a miracle.

The understanding was that Annie would dash home from The Bull and Castle at eight o'clock for Nealie's evening feed and then dash back. But sometimes she didn't turn up until nine or even ten o'clock. To tide Nealie over Kathleen would let him suck on a piece of potato, or she would dip a clean cloth in watered-down milk and he would suck on that.

Finally Kathleen suggested to Annie that she squeeze her milk into a glass before leaving for the tavern. She'd have suggested it sooner except that she feared giving offence. Annie kept her timorous with remarks about how all her aunts and cousins were longing to mind Nealie. As it was, Kathleen said that she was only bringing up the idea to save Annie having to race back and forth.

157

Annie said, 'Well, if *you* feel that it is the right thing,' as though she had motherly qualms. In fact, she snatched at the suggestion. She filled two glasses. 'I have a power of milk,' she said. 'Sometimes I want to get down on my hands and knees and low like a bloody cow.'

The milk was loosely mixed with fine-ground meal and fed to Nealie with a spoon. During the day it was Mary who fed him. She arrived mid-morning, which is when Annie brought Nealie by, and attended to all of his needs such as they were in the hours that she was with him. She sewed a sack that could be tied to her back or front for carrying him in as she went about her work.

Occasionally Mary gave him his meal and milk on the end of her fingers. Fingers would feel more like a teat to him, she said. Then one day she smeared the mixture on one of her own nipples and tried to feed a bit to him that way. It dripped right off her but Nealie persisted in trying to suckle anyway, so she let him go on for a spell and fed him with her fingers afterwards. From then on Nealie turned his mouth to her whenever she held him in her arms, and she said, 'The creature,' pityingly and undid her bodice to give him her breast.

The miracle happened a week or so after Mary smeared the mixture on herself. She was sitting on the hob with Nealie at her breast, singing to him. And then instead of singing she was saying, 'Mama, Mama, Mama,' like a stricken child, and holding Nealie away from her against one hand, holding in her other hand her left breast, which she had extracted from her bodice and which in its huge white entirety jarred Michael into a terrible instant of riot and remorse as though some lust run amok in himself had willed her to this display.

'What is it?' Kathleen cried, rushing over to her and kneeling, shielding her from Michael and Hugh's sight.

'Look,' Mary said. She indicated something on herself.

'Glory be to God,' Kathleen said softly.

'For God's sake, what is it?' Hugh said, standing.

Kathleen dropped sideways on to her haunches so that the breast was once more visible. She actually pointed at it.

'What?' Hugh said, frowning.

'Milk,' Kathleen said as milk appeared, drops spilling out as Mary drew her fingers towards the teat.

'Jesus, Mary and Joseph,' Hugh said.

The three of them stood in front of her and watched the veritable stream of milk. 'Try the other,' Hugh said, and Mary handed Nealie to Kathleen and squeezed the teat of her right breast. Milk dribbled from it as well.

'What does it mean at all?' she whispered.

'That you are chosen,' Hugh said.

'For what?'

'For revealing God's wonders.' He nodded. 'Enough now,' he said, and told her to fasten herself up, she mustn't be wasting it. Then they all prayed together and Hugh went to deliver the news to Father Lynn and to fetch Slieve.

In the following days the cabin filled with women again, come to witness the miracle of the barren girl with milk in her breasts. Except for the clergy and Doctor Rennie, men weren't permitted a showing. Annie greeted everyone at the door. She insisted on doing this, the tavern wouldn't crumble without her, she said. Wearing the sack that Mary had made to carry Nealie in, she told everybody that the truth was, Nealie was conceived while she was still a virgin. She hadn't said a word for fear of being disbelieved. 'Might we hold him?' the women begged, as before, and women with afflictions asked if they might put their ears that were going deaf, their twisted fingers and sore joints to his miraculous lips.

'Surely, surely,' Annie said, taking their offerings of buttons and ribbons and even pennies, just as if she were a saint at a holy well.

Chapter 26

Wales

Rosser must have had a suspicion. He must have chosen his time, lured away the goose from under the doorstep and entered the house like a thief. Otherwise, even though Olwen was singing, they would have heard something and they didn't.

They were lying together on top of the quilt, Michael's head on her breast, and she was singing. This is what they did now when Michael came back to bed from the window. After he'd eaten his breakfast and she'd bathed him, after he'd limped around the room, she watching from the bed and lauding him on, after he'd stopped at the window to look out, they lay down and she sang to him. This was the pattern of their mornings together now.

Olwen was singing a Welsh song that in English was called, 'In Praise of a Woman'. The woman in the song was tall, queenly, fair and proud and she had a gracious granting heart, which made Michael think of his mother.

He saw Rosser before she did. He sat up. He thought that Rosser was having one of his visions because he was standing so stiffly and his eyes were quivering. Olwen knew better. She slipped off the bed, pulling her nightdress down, not looking at the stairs. She picked up the bowl and knife and spoon from Michael's breakfast, then the basin and cloth from his bath, halted, then strode towards the stairs, head lowered, as though she would charge by.

Rosser hit the side of her head with a flat hand. Everything flew from her arms and she fell.

'Jesus, man,' Michael said, dropping his feet to the floor.

160

Rosser pointed at him. 'Shut up, you.' Vicious.

'It is all right,' Olwen said lightly, but she was commanding him to silence too. She started to stand. Rosser hit her across the head again and she fell to her knees. He said a Welsh word, spraying spittle. She smiled up at him and spoke appeasingly. She nodded at Michael and opened her hands.

'Slattern. Jezebel,' Rosser said in English, and Michael thought, "In English for my sake. He will turn me out."

Rosser waved at the curtain, then down the stairs. He spoke in short, sharp sentences. *'Hel dy ddillad gwely. Ae cer i lawr y grisiau.'* Olwen's voice pleaded, her hands prayed to him. Rosser went behind the curtain and reappeared with her bedding. He threw it down the stairs. He snarled at her, shooing her to follow, and she quickly gathered what she had dropped and did so.

Rosser glanced at Michael and away. Below they heard her dragging the bedding across the floor. Rosser walked to the front window, stopping several feet from it so that he did not have to bend to see out.

'You cannot be sending her from the house?' Michael said.

Rosser shook his head.

Michael sat and covered his legs. He felt naked in only a nightshirt, with Rosser in the room. It occurred to him that it would be wiser to wear day clothing, in case he should have to depart all of a sudden, then he thought, "It will be this day that I go. This very minute." He stared at Rosser's right hand, his thick fingers curling and curling.

'She will be sleeping downstairs,' Rosser said. 'No more loitering up here. Bringing up your food and whatever else, taking it away. That is all.'

It was like a fright, Michael's relief, like a surprise stopping his heart. Rosser walked away to the stairwell and looked up at the rafters. He walked to the sack of apples and looked at them, came over to the end of the bed, frowned at it, tapped the bedstead. He said, 'When I told you to shut up now just, what I did mean was it is not your affair, see.'

'She was only singing me a song,' Michael said softly.

'The devil's songs! I will not have her singing them in this house and well she knows that. But she is pleasure-loving. That is being a woman. Any rate, I will not have her lying down with

161

a man. I am not casting blame on you. You are Irish and the Irish have different ways with them.'

He looked at Michael, and Michael knew that what the man wanted was for him to agree that Olwen deserved to be beaten, that the two of them were in agreement regarding the womanly sin in her. Michael looked down. He felt fearful and antagonized. To show defiance he reached for the newspaper that was on the stool and pretended to read, as if Rosser weren't there.

Chapter 27

Ireland

Etain was tormented but Michael understood why. There she was, keeping house for her father, already saddled with all the toils of a wife while doing without a wife's pleasures. And her father still went into fits of weeping over her dead mother, and when they were out together he pressed her upon every rich bachelor who would give him the time of day.

She never talked about these trials. She only said that she longed to be married, she hated being a deceiver, but when Michael suggested they announce their betrothal in that case, she said, appalled, that they mustn't, then in the next breath, 'Let us run away like Judy and Andy.' And Michael asked 'Truly?' recreating the future in the pause before she answered, but she tossed her head like a branch in the wind, saying both aye and nay with her head, saying aloud, no, no, it would kill her father all out, then, 'Hold me, hold me so tight I go through your skin.'

Secretly he revelled in her suffering, in her great pining love for him. He would touch the tears on her face covetously. Every time they were alone he would look for that pain. They weren't alone often, only one evening a week, Thursday, the evening that her father spent at The Bull and Castle. Since she lived so far away they never met by chance, on the road, for instance. They never had those lucky secret encounters.

Then one morning they did. It was a mild day towards the end of November. Such days are called St. Martin's summer days. He was leaving late for school and saw her ahead of him, sauntering, swinging her basket as if she were in no hurry to get

163

home. He called her name and she waved her basket and ran back to him. She wouldn't embrace him. Embracing where people might see made her uneasy.

But there was no harm in their walking together. Hadn't they met innocently, she pointed out, he going to school, she returning from taking her yarn to the weaver's?

She was in high spirits, the way she always used to be. It was the warm air, she said, and the treat of their coming upon each other. She apologized for her impatience these past weeks.

'The one who waits for the fine day will have the fine day,' she said.

And just as she spoke, like a sign, like the eye of the sky opening, the sun came out in a growing circle of light down the road. In the light Michael spied two riders charging toward them. He pulled Etain over to the ditch to make way. Children playing marbles in the road jumped up and did the same. Michael saw a gold-coloured cape whipping behind one of the riders.

'Who is it?' Etain said.

'Arthur and his huntsman.'

The children who were wearing caps took them off, and a man standing on his stoop took off his wig. Michael kept his hat on. The United Irishmen said that the king himself was only a servant of the people.

Where the road went around a thorn bush, Arthur's horse unaccountably reared. He dug in his heels, whipped it, turned it in circles then finally got it to charge on. All he did nowadays was charge around, now that Lady Morrery was dead. She had died of gastric fever on May Eve, and for the funeral Lord Morrery and Arthur came up together from Dublin, where Arthur had been studying at the university. The morning of the funeral the two of them were heard having words in the library over Arthur's terrible scholarship. The day after that The Big Lord went back to Dublin alone, leaving Arthur to stay on, and the day after that Arthur began to ride, dawn to dusk. He and his hunstman claimed the whole valley for themselves, chasing foxes and hares, but mostly just riding, Arthur badly, disabling his blood racers. He wore a long gold-coloured fur-edged cape that he bragged had belonged to an Irish chieftain but that couldn't have done because Irish chieftains never wore capes. Michael saw that the cape was in tatters as the horses pounded by. He saw the whites of Arthur's eyes.

When the horses were out of sight he looked down at Etain. She had moved partly behind him and covered her hair with her shawl. Now she drew the shawl down to her shoulders and glanced at the children, who had gone back to playing marbles. Then she looked up at him as if he had just said something startling.

'Let's kiss,' she said.

'Here?' he said.

She pointed down the road. 'Beyond the last place. Behind the hedge. We can do it there.'

'But the people,' he said because it was what she would have said normally.

'We can lie down. Nobody will see.' She took his hand and tugged him.

'Come along then,' he said, pulling her now.

They passed through a gap in the hedge. She dropped her basket, opened her shawl on the ground and lay down. He spread his coat alongside her. So that his books wouldn't get wet he hung his satchel on the hedge. When he turned around she was lying with her hair fanned out from her head so perfectly that he knew she had arranged it.

They kissed each other's faces, quick kisses, spilling endearments in between. He stroked her hair and her back. Over the autumn their loving had settled into ritual. First this kind of kissing and these chaste strokes, then deep thick kisses and stroking her legs and thighs. Then slipping both of his opened hands up between their bodies to her breasts, and after that it was for her to keep him and herself on that brink. Without her will, he might do anything.

She always prevailed. If he started to roll on top of her or pull up her skirt she would say no. It was all he needed since he was the transgressor, he was waiting for the repulse.

But on this St. Martin's summer's day morning, in the field beside the hedge, one of his hands went under her skirt and she said nothing. His hand usurped the silence. It told him to go on, it slid up her leg to the back of her knee, which was moist, and she said nothing. His hand slid further up, past her knee to her thigh. She said 'Michael' in a moan. She said, 'Pulse of my

165

heart.' She untied his rope belt. She put her hand inside his breeches and touched him with the tips of her fingers. A touch like embers and breath.

'Please,' she said.

He lived in the places where her fingers touched.

The fingers moved. A little brushing movement. So she knew what it was she was touching and yet she kept her fingers there. He was lost entirely.

'Love me like I am your wife,' she whispered.

Somebody screamed. On the other side of the hedge, directly by their heads, it sounded like. Etain's hand fled. It gripped her other hand at her mouth. He yanked his belt into knots, his heart booming in his ears, and she leaned to peek through the hedge.

'Ah!' she cried. 'A sow! An old sow!' She sank to her knees, laughing.

'Jesus,' he said. 'Be off!' he shouted at it. The sow trotted across the road. 'Farther! Go on!' he shouted. He scooped up a clod and threw it and missed.

Etain was laughing into her skirt. He cast about for rocks. He was going to knock that sow's brains in.

Etain fell on to her side, heaving with laughter. ''Tis wicked wicked I am,' she wailed. She was not laughing at all, she was crying.

'No, no,' he said. He dropped down beside her. She shook her head. He pulled her up and held her.

'I am wicked,' she said. She said it again. She said it again because she was speaking of something else altogether, but he didn't know that then.

Maybe she would have confessed but he wouldn't let her speak. He even covered her mouth with his hand. 'If anybody is wicked it is myself,' he said.

He meant it only as he said it. So he said, 'It is myself,' again, firmly in self-reproach and to reach God's ear. On Stone Peak he had promised God that if he could touch her breasts he would never defile her in unwed state. He began to think of penances.

'From this day on I will be the strong one for both ourselves,' he said. The first penance.

She wept into his shirt, and he patted her and told her that he

166

loved her all the more, told her that she was the most virtuous girl in the world, told her that God Himself couldn't blame her for wanting to be loved like a wife when she had been betrothed since the Pattern, told her how their life together would be once they were wed, told her every sweet thing he could think of until she stopped weeping.

She sat up and clasped her knees. Her back was a slender desolate curve. 'The jacksnipe is calling,' she said. 'There will be frost tomorrow.'

There was frost for three weeks. In the mornings the grass and ricks and the cabbages that were still in the garden were white with it, and a lid of ice lay on the furrows and the holes in the road. Miraculously, a man who was buried up to his neck in a bog during the frost did not freeze to death.

Michael and Corny found the man, and they found him only minutes after being told the most spectacular news by Master Dolan. So the abutting of these two events was a sign. But Michael did not appreciate this because his head was too full of visions from what Master Dolan had said.

Which was that he was a United Irishman. After swearing the two of them to secrecy on pain of death he revealed that the week before, he had gone to Belfast not to buy books but to take the United Irish oath. It turned out that he had been carrying on a covert correspondence with the society for months, he had even written an article for the society's newspaper, the *Northern Star*. His job now was to win the Defenders in the valley over to the idea of becoming United Irishmen under his command. Defenders and United Irishmen were allying throughout Ireland, he said. 'And once all the Defenders are United Irishmen ...' He paused and looked from Michael to the Corny. 'There will be a rising,' he said softly.

'A rising!' Michael and Corny said together.

'Against those servants of the English that call themselves our government. Even as I speak, a United Irish agent is on his way to France to negotiate French assistance.'

He poured out three whiskeys and said that the two of them would be his seconds in command in the valley. 'The morning star is shining,' he said, toasting them.

167

'The morning star is shining,' Michael repeated, guessing it was something that United Irishmen said to each other, saying it back as an offering of himself, a plunge into allegiance.

Corny held his whiskey in both hands and looked down at it as if it were an evil elixir. 'But do the Defenders want a rising, sir?' he asked quietly.

'Are you deaf, Cornelius? Have you not heard them bellowing, "Liberty! Equality!"? Do you know what they pledge themselves to when they take their oath? To dethroning all kings, to planting the tree of liberty, to pulling down all English laws.'

'I thought that was only talk.'

'For some of the lower rank and file, sure it is. Ah, but they'll follow orders. And I'll tell you another thing. Captain Stouts across the land are arming. Our own illustrious Captain Stout has every Catholic smith in this valley making pikes.'

'Pikes,' Corny said.

'For a start. The United Irishmen are collecting the guns and ammunition. And you don't think the French will be coming over empty-handed, do you now? But by God, my lads,' he downed his drink, smacked his lips and smiled past them, 'with every last Irishman and every thinking Protestant in the land rising up, seven centuries of English tyranny will lie down at the every sight of those pikes alone.'

Michael had visions. Waves of Irish soldiers, led by French generals, pouring over the countryside, and the big lords fleeing before the waves. Victory. Himself and Corny and Master Dolan being cheered, decorated, issued titles, the grateful peasantry building his school, the United Irish directory consulting him on all the new laws. 'When might Corny and myself be sworn?' he asked.

'I cannot give you the oath by myself. It takes two members for that. An agent will be passing through here in several months' time, and he and myself will swear you in then. In the meantime, I bring round Defenders. Plant little seeds in certain ears.' He pretended to deposit a seed in his own ear. Then he poured himself a second glass and raised it in a toast again. This time he said, 'Ireland! Oh, Ireland!'

Outside the schoolhouse Corny said, 'It will all end in disaster.'

'What do you know?' Michael said.

Corny counted on his fingers the past insurrections, giving the years. 'Fifteen sixty-eight, fifteen seventy-nine, fifteen ninety-five, sixteen forty-one, sixteen eighty-eight. All disasters in the end.'

'*They* didn't have the French behind them.'

'Neither will we.'

'Jesus, you'll make a terrible second-in-command.'

Corny shook his head. 'I don't want to be a second-in-command.'

'If you don't relish the notion of fighting in the field, you'll want to be a leader sure enough,' Michael said, although he wasn't actually contemplating anything so dire as a battle.

'When it is all over, 'tis the heads of the leaders that will roll,' Corny said.

Michael was getting galled, he wouldn't listen. He looked at the hills. Like everything else they were grizzled with the cold. He had another vision. Himself standing at the door of his schoolhouse on a hill, in a new Ireland of tolerance, of citizens equal under heaven, and lines of Protestant mothers and Catholic mothers climbing the hill, bringing their children unto him like the mothers of Salem bringing their children unto Jesus.

Corny said, 'The rivers will run red with blood.'

'Shut up, you coward!' It was out of Michael's mouth before he knew it. A lance out of his mouth.

Corny stopped walking. He hung his head.

'Ah,' Michael said.

Corny began running down the road.

'You're not a coward!' Michael yelled.

But Corny kept running. Michael started after him. They were at the place on the road where it was black bog on the south side, beyond a thick overgrown hedge, and Corny ran to an opening in the hedge, peered through, lifting his spectacles, then ran through.

'Where are you going?' Michael called. He thought, scornfully, "Thin-skinned." He thought, "He's crying and doesn't want me to see," and in the next moment he knew this to be so — he could hear Corny's shameless loud whimpering.

When he reached the opening in the hedge he called,

169

'Corny!' and in the same instant he saw Corny fall on to his hands and knees.

Corny yelled, 'Michael!' and he thought, idiotically since there was nobody else in all the black flatness, that Corny had been shot.

He ran on to the bog. Each footfall squished out icy water. Corny was clawing at the earth in derangement, whimpering. But it wasn't him who was whimpering, it was a man. A man's head. Blood on it, blood on the ground.

'Come on! Dig!' Corny screamed, whirling a panicky face, ripping slabs off a long mound of packed peat in front of the head. And though the head whimpered, Michael only now realized that it had a body, that the man was buried on his back under the mound.

He dropped to his knees. Then he saw the ear. It was gore, dangling from a thread of skin. He turned away.

He vomited, vomited, and Corny was screaming at him. When he turned back, Corny had the man's arms and chest uncovered.

The entire way to the nearest cabin Michael carried the man slung over one shoulder. Corny had said that it would be easier all round if one of them took the man's feet and the other held him under his arms, but Michael wanted the whole burden for himself to atone for having vomited and to keep the man's mangled ear out of his sight. The man babbled. Corny walked behind and spoke into the hole above the ear. Corny, who balked at the idea of bloodshed, could nevertheless look upon the bloody ear.

Over and over he asked, 'Who did it?' first in English in case the man was Protestant and then in Irish in case the man was Catholic. All that was needed for an answer was one comprehensible word in either language because if he was Irish-speaking they would know that the Orangemen had done it and if he was English-speaking they would know that it had been the Defenders. Both societies had buried people in bogs before.

But the man only said, 'Naaah, naaah, naaah.' Finally Michael told Corny to leave him be, and just as he did the man said clearly and with horror and in English, 'Pig!'

'Pig?' Michael said, stopping.

170

'Pig! Pig!' the man said.

'Oh, good heavens,' Corny said. 'The Defenders set a pig on him, that's what happened. A pig chewed his ear. They undoubtedly salted it. Did a pig chew your ear?' he asked the man.

'Pig!' the man said.

The wife in the first cabin they came to poured poteen down the man's throat until he closed his eyes. Corny said that he and Michael would fetch Doctor Rennie. 'No trouble, mind,' the husband warned, meaning that they had better not be fetching a magistrate, meaning that he was either a Defender himself or a sympathizer.

'No trouble, I assure you,' Corny said.

When they were outside, Michael said, ''Twas a mercy you heard him crying out. I didn't hear a thing.'

Corny grasped his arm and said furiously, 'You see!'

Thinking that he was pointing out who had vomited and who had borne the sight of the ear, Michael looked down at the thin fingers on his sleeve and said, 'I am that sorry I called you a coward.' He looked up.

Unexpectedly, Corny's eyes were beseeching. He said, 'That was nothing, Michael. A man with a chewed ear, that is nothing to what there'll be in a rising.'

Master Dolan had meetings with Captain Stout but wouldn't reveal what transpired. 'When the apple is ripe it will fall,' he said. He disappeared for days, and while he was gone Michael read United Irish pamphlets and articles, placed inside books to conceal them, and he and Corny taught the younger scholars. One morning the two of them went to Doctor Rennie's cabin after hearing that the man they had dug out of the bog was still there. They found him mute and under a heap of blankets in Doctor Rennie's bed. He was bodily recovered, Doctor Rennie said, he could speak and move if he wanted to, only he never did. 'What am I going to do with the wretch?' he asked. Winter passed.

On St Brighid's Eve, Kathleen baked a big cake and invited the neighbours in to eat it. Afterwards she and Mary made five rush crosses in honour of the saint and to gain her protection. Three of the crosses were for hanging in each of the family

171

cabins, one was for the byre and one for the sty. St. Brighid's Day also happened to be Rose's birthday, and when she was alive she'd made upward of a dozen crosses every year in the belief that she was an especial favourite of the saint's, crosses so tremendous and elaborate that even hanging from the rafters they had hit your head, and visitors hadn't even know what they were.

She would have been twenty-one years old this St. Brighid's Day. In the morning Kathleen cut wintergreen sprigs and put them in the pitcher that Rose had used for her bouquets. Hugh said that she was with them in the cabin, he could smell her nature the way that dogs smell fear and command. That's why when the man who claimed to be a fiddler (although he had no fiddle) arrived at the door and said, 'If this be the household of Hugh Malone I bear tidings from his daughter,' Hugh and Kathleen and Michael all went speechless. They thought that he meant tidings from Rose.

He took a letter from his coat and held it out to Hugh. 'From the great republic of France itself,' he said.

'Judy?' Kathleen cried in revelation.

Hugh accepted the letter and turned it slowly in his hands. He touched the blue wax seal.

'A gentleman of my acquaintance brought it over,' the fiddler said. 'To Belfast, from where I've come, and seeing as how I was passing this way he entrusted it to my safekeeping.'

Hugh opened the letter, and Michael came to look over his shoulder. There was a page of large wobbly writing. ''Tis in the French,' Michael said.

'You've got French,' Hugh said, passing it to him.

Michael went to the door for the light.

'To my dear father and my mother and to my brothers and sisters,' he read, translating slowly because the spelling was odd and the pronouns wrong. For "my" she had written "her".

'I am writing this letter myself. My friend that lives in Dublin but that is French now, like me, learned me to read and write in the three languages. In hours only I learned. I live in Paris. I have plenty of ... to know ...' He stopped. 'Acquaintances,' he said, realizing what she meant. 'I have acquaintances of influence. I know the ambassadors and a writer that is ... a

172

celebration . . . that is famous. I have plenty of money because I have friends that are bankers and I live in a beautiful house like a castle. I eat meat at all meals. I drink wine also. I have a damask bed. I have plenty of servants. Andy Coogan that was my husband is dead. He was in the French navy and he drowned courageously in battle on the first day of June in the year seventeen hundred and ninety-four in the . . . in the manner of English reckoning. I have plenty of suitors since he died. There are plenty of Irishmen here that detest the English. We are friends. We go to the theatre. I will not send you any of my money because you do not need my money and where was my dowry? I met a Frenchman that thinks Ireland was a town where the English go to be infamous. Your daughter and your sister. Judith Coogan.'

Michael looked up.

'Is that all?' Kathleen said.

'Aye.'

'By God, I don't believe my ears,' Hugh said.

Kathleen took the letter from Michael and studied it as if she could read. 'No blessing, no prayer that we are all alive and thriving. And her husband dead, God rest his soul, and not a bit of sorrow over it.'

'Meat at all meals. And writing in the French,' Hugh said. ''Tis beyond belief clean out.' He uncorked the poteen bottle, took a swig and handed it the fiddler.

'Ah, may God spare your life,' the fiddler said. It was then that he said he was a fiddler and if he had only had his fiddle with him he would have played a French tune for the occasion.

'I suppose she can have no children or she'd have put a word in,' Kathleen said. 'However, with Judy there's no telling. Indeed, there's no telling if any of it is even truth at all.'

'The part concerning acquaintances of influence must be truth anyhow,' Hugh said. 'Sure one of them went to the trouble of bringing the letter across the sea for her.' He turned to the fiddler. 'Who did you say that gentleman of yours was?'

'His name, now I don't know that. I never met him face to face.'

'Is he a Frenchman?'

'Oh, no, Irish, but as I understand it he goes back and forth across the sea.'

173

'Can we be sending a letter back to our girl through himself and yourself?'

'No, indeed, sorry to say. I am off to Derry from here.'

'There's no place to send it to,' Michael said. 'No street, only Paris.'

'All them evil doings over there,' Kathleen said. 'I cannot think of her being over there at all.'

'Ach, Mother, our Judy can mind her neck, she's proved that. By God, from the sounds of it she has the place by the tail.'

'So she tells it.' Kathleen gave the letter back to Michael. 'Read it out again,' she said.

He did. Then Neal came by and he read it for him. Then he lit a candle and sat at the table under the window and read it to himself.

Who were these Irishmen that detested the English? Soldiers in the Irish Brigade? Was Tom Paine, who wrote *The Rights of Man*, the famous writer that she knew? Tom Paine was in France. Who were the important visitors? Who would Judy consider important?

Michael wondered. He read and reread every sentence and wondered about it. And he wondered how it could be that Judy, who had lived every moment at the peril of the next, was now living this splendrous life.

He sniffed the paper and the wax to smell the Frenchness of them, but they smelled of tobacco from the fiddler's pocket.

'Holy Virgin, speak of the devil,' Annie said. She covered her bosom with her serving tray.

The devil was Master Arthur. He was standing crookedly in the tavern doorway, favouring his good leg, craning his neck this way and that as if searching for someone in particular. He was wearing his gold fur-edged cape.

Who had been speaking of him was Annie, sitting on the edge of the table, and Michael and Corny and a thatcher's son named Pat, who were sitting around it. They had been speaking of how, lately, Arthur had been amusing himself by stopping men at their plough and planting, and with his huntsman doing the translating asking them their names and what sports they preferred and did they own a horse? How he

174

had been showing up at markets, crashing his racer into stalls, inquiring about the trading. How this behaviour was queer and unlordly. And Michael had said that if Arthur should ever ask him any of these idle questions he would spit in his eye, and Corny had said, 'I'd give a guinea to see that.'

In a wave, starting at the door, men were taking off their hats and pushing back their stools to stand.

'Pray, remain seated,' Arthur said in a girlish voice, smiling, patting the air with one gloved hand. 'Carry on with your conversations.' His eyes fluttered around the room, landed on Michael, passed, returned. Michael looked at the table. He told himself it wasn't possible that Arthur could recognize him after ten years.

'Michael, he's staring straight at yourself,' Annie whispered. 'Jesus, Jesus, he's coming over.'

'Pardon me, I beg your pardon,' Arthur said. Conversation hadn't carried on. There was only his voice and the stools scraping out of his way and his lame foot scuffing and his good foot clumping.

'Michael. Michael Malone, is it not?' Michael raised his eyes. Arthur was smiling so widely that he looked as if he were about to scream with laughter. 'Is it not?'

'It is,' Michael said. A thrill went through him because of daring to say only that, of not adding, 'Your lordship', or 'Master Arthur'. Pat jumped up and silently offered Arthur his stool.

'How kind,' Arthur said, sitting. He pointed his crop at Annie. 'Claret, I think. No. No, a glass of the native brew, why not?'

Annie jabbed her tray into Michael's back. 'Poteen,' Michael said to her.

'Michael Malone,' Arthur said, cocking his head. 'I have been wondering when our paths would cross. How have you been keeping yourself? How is your honest father, Hugh the mason? Didn't we have a time of it, the three of us, putting up that infernal wall?'

Now he did laugh. A laugh that turned into a cough, and he coughed and coughed, tapping at his throat. Annie rushed over with his poteen. He grabbed it from her, glugged half of it and began coughing again.

175

None of them slapped him on the back. 'Shall I fetch water?' Annie asked.

Michael nodded. Anyone else would have been turning red, but Arthur was going whiter. His skin was white and smooth, like an innard that has been bled. There was no bristle on his chin or upper lip. That is an indication of madness in a man, a hairless face. And it was mad, his talk — talking about the incident that lamed him at all, let alone splitting his sides over it.

When Annie brought the water he brushed her away and coughed himself out, ending with several loud engrossed clearings of his throat. He pawed a handkerchief out of his trouser pocket and dabbed his eyes. 'A hearty concoction,' he said.

Michael smirked at Corny.

Corny was already looking at him. Michael glanced back at Arthur, who was draining his glass, fanning his opened mouth between swallows, then glanced at Corny again, and it struck him that Corny was defying him to spit. He got a plug of tobacco out of his coat pocket and yanked off a chew. Obviously he couldn't really spit, he hadn't meant it as a vow. What would the good of such a provocation be now, with the insurrection still months away?

'Rode a coursing today,' Arthur was saying fuzzily. He held his glass up and Annie filled it. 'Perhaps you espied me, Michael.' He took a swig of his drink. 'Haaa!' he breathed, his eyes bulging. He leaned across the table. 'My dear fellow,' he said, 'do you own a horse?'

Michael shook his head, looking deliberately at Corny.

'Oh,' Arthur said, crestfallen. He finished his drink, and Annie tendered the jug.

'By all means!' Arthur said. 'Pour away. A glass for Michael. And for this capital fellow.' He waved at Corny. He waved around the room. 'A glass for the entire throng. Pour! Pour!' He motioned pouring.

Annie understood. She began splashing out measures fast. Arthur nodded, smiling exultantly, crying, 'Pour!' until every man in the room had been attended to. Then he lifted his glass and his burning eyes and toasted Michael, 'My dear friend,' drank, dropped his glass to the ground and dropped his forehead to the table. Thud.

'He's out,' Corny said. He touched Arthur's arm. 'Your lordship?'

'He cannot be, he hasn't paid,' Annie said.

'Out on two and a half glasses,' Michael said. He spit tobacco juice on the floor.

'Missed your mark,' Corny said. Annie cried that her father would murder her.

Men got up and came over. They stood across the table and at a distance on either side of Arthur's stool. 'He's not his father's son,' one said. Another said, pointing, 'A neck on him like a swan.'

Annie punched Michael's shoulder. 'Search him for his purse,' she said. 'You're the one that got him up to treating every last spalpeen in the place.'

'Very well, I will,' Michael said, thrilling again at the irreverence.

'Why not, now that he's out?' Corny said. Michael lashed him a look.

'Do you think you should at all, lad?' an old man asked. 'Sure they'll pay Annie at The Big House.'

'Who will pay?' Annie said. 'That thief Logan?' She nudged Michael. 'Go on.'

First he investigated the inside of the cape for a pouch or a pocket. Nothing. And no pouch hanging from the waistband of the trousers, either. Nothing in the waistcoat pocket. He would have to try the trouser pockets. He slid his hand inside one of them and felt the smooth lining, and the hard thin thigh, which made him swallow with revulsion, then he felt something cold and hard.

It was a door hinge. Also in that pocket was a length of fishing line, three coloured stones and a silver-handled knife. In the other pocket were only more stones.

'Christ's sake, where's his money?' Annie cried. She seized the knife and his handkerchief. 'I'll take these anyhow,' she said.

To her horror Corny suggested that Arthur lie where he was to sleep the liquor off. 'He cannot bide, what if he wakes up?' she cried. Pat said that Arthur's stallion was outside, he could take him to The Big House on it, and Annie said, 'Fine,' and helped him lift Arthur off the stool.

177

'There you go, your lordship,' Pat said, balancing him gently on one shoulder.

Arthur's arms and head hung down Pat's back. 'Dead to the world,' a man said.

'The look of the future?' Corny said to Michael, smiling, making amends.

Michael hated having to wait to become a United Irishman, having to wait months beyond the several that Master Dolan had forecast. He wondered why life should ever be uncertain and irregular when God had created a world where the sun always rises and sets and the seasons come and go.

Master Dolan dispensed reassurances of imminency: 'The water is starting to simmer', 'The fire is almost lit', but February, March and April passed and nothing happened. Nothing whatsoever happened in the valley. There were only births and christenings and the customary batch of marriages on Shrove Tuesday (these would all be unhappy as portended by a storm in the morning), and there was an unremarkable number of deaths, since the truce between the Orangemen and Defenders still held.

Then, early in May, in the week before Whitsunday and also Michael's eighteenth birthday, the waiting ended. Master Dolan told him and Corny that the agent was arriving from Dungannon tomorrow. After dismiss, in the schoolhouse, there would be a secret meeting.

'Until then, tight lips,' he warned.

Corny seeemd to take him at his word. On the way home he wouldn't even speak. When Michael asked him if he was going to be sworn, he shook his head.

The following morning the sky was a watery blue with pink scratches of cloud on the horizon, and white daisies tossed in a warm breeze along the banks of the river, and the dewy air dripped the scent of hawthorn. As Michael went down his path, feeling the good solid earth, the long length of his stride, hundreds of birds sang so that it sounded as though the day itself were shrieking its glory.

Before he got to the River Road he saw Corny. He only knew him by his spectacles, for he was dressed in somebody else's wide-brimmed hat and long trusty. He had on dazzling white stockings that flashed in and out of the coat.

Michael walked out to the road and watched him approach. Corny waved. Michael decided that Corny must have changed his mind about taking the United Irish oath and dressed up for the occasion.

When he got to Michael he took off his book satchel and dropped it heavily on the ground between them. It was so full that the straps wouldn't go round it and it was secured with rope instead. 'I am going away,' he said.

'Going away? Where to?'

'Dublin.'

'Dublin. When? This day?'

Corny pulled out a watch from his waistcoat pocket. 'Thirty minutes,' he said. He closed his fingers smartly over the watch face.

'Where did you get that?' Michael frowned at Corny's hand.

'The old rip. A parting gift.'

'The old rip?'

'My father,' Corny said sighing, putting the watch back in his pocket.

'What are you going to Dublin for?' Michael asked belligerently. He felt that Corny was trying to provoke him with 'old rip' and Dublin and the watch, the white stockings.

'To work in my uncle's brewery,' Corny said quietly, pushing his spectacles up on his nose and looking at the ground, and then Michael understood.

'When he was here last,' Corny said, 'he told me that there will always be a place for me.'

'But you wouldn't have had to take the oath,' Michael said. 'Master Dolan would never force you to.'

''Tis not only that. I have been considering going for a year.'

'But are you certain?'

Corny tapped his foot against the satchel.

'Sure you can come back at any time,' Michael said.

'I won't be coming back.' He looked up, suddenly earnest and preoccupied. 'The mail coach departs on the dot,' he said, holding out his hand.

Michael took it and they shook over the satchel. 'The blessing of God keep you,' he said insensibly, not feeling at all that this was a real leave-taking.

179

Corny's eyes swung away from him. He picked up the satchel. 'And may God bless and prosper you and yours, Michael,' he said, passing a starchy smile over the house and the byre.

As Corny walked off, Michael stood there looking at him, thinking that he should call out something apt and fond and extraordinary. Then Corny was out of sight, and so he carried on to school thinking, "Corny is gone," and waiting for the sadness. But it didn't come until he told Master Dolan who said brutally, 'Well good luck to him,' and then he felt wounded himself by that and hollow with loneliness.

And yet, as he had known it would be, the day was still a peak in his life. An hour after dismiss the United Irish agent showed up. He was more heroic than Michael had ever let himself imagine. He was bigger even than Slieve, and he had a beautiful godly face with a scar down his right cheek, and clever kind eyes, and although he was a Protestant he spoke perfect Irish, which, for the sake of Captain Stout who was also at the meeting, was what was spoken.

He said that there would be an insurrection within the year. That it would succeed. Catholics in droves all over Ireland were pledging themselves to the United Irishmen, he said. Cotters, bankers, militiamen, all of the Defenders.

The oaths were given separately, first to Captain Stout and then to Michael, in the empty schoolroom. 'Repeat what I say,' the agent instructed, and at the part, 'I will persevere in endeavouring to form a brotherhood of affection among Irishmen of every religious persuasion,' Michael's voice caught, he was so overcome.

After the oaths, the agent told them what their duties would be. Captain Stout was to go on organizing drills and collecting arms, not just pikes but guns and ammunition as well, and he was to order all Defenders to take the United Irish oath. Michael and Master Dolan were to set up committees throughout the valley, and Michael was also to copy out mottoes on to banners and papers for plastering everywhere once the rising was underway.

The mottoes were: "The people are awake — they are up!" and "The diffusion of light!" and "Unite and be free!" and "Ireland! O! Ireland!"

And "The morning star is shining!" Before he left, the agent said this one to each of the three of them in turn. So it was a benediction. It inspired and softened them, even Captain Stout was softened, and far into the night they drank porter and dreamed aloud and swore everlasting allegiance to each other and all Irishmen.

Everything was happening at once. The morning after Michael went to bed a United Man, and Corny left the valley, Annie flew in the door with news that there had been a big battle in the next parish between Orange and Defender patrols. Two men were dead, one from each side.

'Damned fools!' Kathleen said, and Annie cried, 'What?' in delight, never having heard Kathleen curse before. In her next breath Kathleen prayed to the Blessed Virgin to spare her men, because such a battle was surely the end of the truce and the beginning of more killings, of arrests and maimings.

Before supper Michael gathered his courage and told his father that he was a founding member of the valley's United Irish Society. Seeing as how he would be giving the oath to the Defenders, it was not a thing that he could keep secret.

'You steer clear of them,' Hugh said. 'Any man that tells you that Protestants and Catholics can bury what's gone on between themselves is a black deceiver.'

'But, Dada, I have taken my oath. You cannot be telling me to go against my oath.'

'In that case, you are as good as gaoled and gibbeted.'

'Master Dolan and Captain Stout are sworn,' Michael said. 'Defenders everywhere are being sworn.'

'Another child lost, four out of six,' Hugh said to Kathleen, including Judy and the miscarried baby in his totals. He pointed at Michael and said there would be no United Irish speechifying under his roof. Then he really became incensed and thumped his chest and swore an oath that he himself would never take those deceivers' oath, although he must have known that he would have to because Defenders were sworn to obey Captain Stout unto death.

Michael was so maddened by his father that he slept that night in the byre. Hugh didn't sleep at all, he went walking, and therefore he saw the flames of the cabin that was burning a mile down the River Road.

It turned out to be a Defender's cabin. The next night an Orangeman's cabin was set on fire. The night after that another Defender's cabin, back and forth through a week of dry weather.

Master Dolan charged Captain Stout to break this cycle before the magistrates brought in the infantry. But Captain Stout maintained, and it couldn't be proved otherwise, that the fires were the work of renegades, and so they went on. People climbed on to their roofs and drenched them with water and filled all their buckets and pails. Defender wives kept watch while their husbands trooped to the schoolhouse to take the United Irish oath.

On the evening that Hugh and Neal were to be sworn, Michael asked Master Dolan to be excused from the administering. He feared that if he were there his father would shout at him to cut the shenanigans and go home. Master Dolan was sympathetic. He promised to have a private chat with Hugh.

'I'll bring him round,' he said.

He didn't. When Hugh returned and there was Michael on the stoop waiting for him, he said, 'Not a word.'

Michael came to his feet.

'Not a bloody word,' Hugh said, shouldering past him into the house.

Michael kicked the door. The latch broke and the door flung open. Hugh, standing just inside, spun round, and Michael turned and ran around to the back of the house and over the garden. He didn't hear pursuit so he stopped there, in the cabbages. His throat hurt. The red hills blurred and blazed before his eyes.

He didn't know what to do. He looked towards Neal and Annie's place and saw Neal sitting on a stool outside the door, bent over some occupation. He wiped his eyes and walked over.

Neal was whittling. As Michael came up to him, he said, ''Tis not yourself he's mad at, 'tis your United Irishmen.'

'They're not mine,' Michael said crossly.

'Well ...' Neal held up his carving and studied it from various angles.

182

'Did you take the oath?' Michael asked.

'Oh, aye,'

'Did he?'

Neal nodded.

'Why is he mad at them at all?'

'Ach, this talk of a rising, for one thing.'

'Defenders have been talking of a rising all along.'

''Tis bull, that.'

'Don't you want a rising yourself?'

Neal dipped his head.

'Don't you want to be free?'

Neal looked up at him. 'Free of what?'

'Free! Free!' Michael swung his arms around, indicated everything.

'How can you call yourself your own man at all when you cannot even hold a seat in the parliament that governs you?'

'Is that what you're bent on, Little Scholar?' Neal asked with interest. 'Holding a seat in the parliament?'

'*I* don't want it. I want it for others who want it.'

Neal brushed away shavings from his lap. ''Tis only that in a rising we stand to lose what we have already.' He waved his carving at the fields.

'But we won't lose. We cannot. There are too many of us. And think what we stand to gain, man alive!'

'What?'

'No tithes. No rentals so high you cannot reach them. No more of these battles and burnings over property.'

'Now, Dada says there's where you'll find Defenders parting company with you lot. Ourselves and Protestants, we'll be battling each other so long as the world is a world, Dada says. 'Tis in the blood.'

'No, Neal, no. The United Irishmen are proof that that isn't so. The United Irishmen are Catholics and Protestants together. United.' He laced his fingers and brought them down in front of Neal's eyes.

Neal resumed his carving. 'Dada says some queer business is going on when Protestants talk of giving the country back to Catholics.'

'Not giving! Sharing!'

Neal nodded. His round face was as benign as a pancake. He

183

said,"Tis only that speaking for myself, I am not altogether unhappy with the way things are now.'

Kathleen was down on her knees among the turnips, weeding. When she looked up, Michael waved at her. She waved back and took off one of the old stockings that she wore on her hands to protect herself from thistles and wiped her forehead. It was early morning but it was already a rare warm day.

Instead of going to school Michael was going to visit Etain, and he waved so that his mother would see the book satchel on his back and be deceived. He and Etain had arranged the visit after mass. Her father was selling a ewe over the hills, she had whispered, so she would be alone in the cabin the entire day. Owing to his work with the United Irishmen, they had not spent a moment alone together in weeks.

The sun lavished gold on the fields and he whistled and sang as he walked. He passed a cabin that had been burned down but it did not sober him because there was a new truce between Orangemen and Defenders and it would probably hold through the harvest work.

He thought about how Etain's mouth got swollen and red from their long kisses, and he thought of her breasts under his hands. Then he thought of what he thought of too much — the time that her fingers touched him — and he grew hot and lightheaded. To recover himself he sang: 'Man after man, day after day, Eire's noblest princes pass away.'

Mr McCaffery was supposed to have left before sunrise. But just to be safe, Etain would signal with the door whether or not he was still there. Half-closed meant he was at home, completely closed that he was gone.

The door was closed. Michael knocked. But it didn't open. He knocked again, calling her name and saying it was himself. It stayed shut. He opened it and stepped inside. Nobody in the gloom, the fire low. He went out and into the byre and called. He went around to the back of the cabin and cupped his hands to his mouth and called.

Nonplussed, he surveyed the fields and summoned up what she had said after mass. *This* Wednesday, she had said, he was certain because he had repeated it and then so had she. Her father must have made her go with him, that's what must have happened.

The old bugger. Michael regarded the place vindictively. He thought of uprooting some potatoes except that they were hers as well. He tramped back to the road and stood there, wondering whether or not he wanted to go to school.

Far down the road somebody was coming. A dark-haired woman. She was bustling along, running and walking. He jumped over the embankment and crouched, swiping off his hat. If she were to see him she might mention it to Mr McCaffery. Her head was lowered so she hadn't seen him already.

It was Annie. He stayed down. She would wring it out of him what he was up to, skulking at the foot of Etain's property. She would tell the whole world. And her hurrying and the oddity of their crossing paths at this distance from home, these kept him down, too. Maybe in the back of his mind he perceived that she had her own secret, but in the front of his mind he was casting around for who she knew that lived up here. She passed him by. She looked fussed.

He didn't decide to follow her, he just began dashing from bush to bush as when he had stalked Gil to the river. This was easier than stalking Gil. Annie kept to the road and she didn't glance around.

At every cabin that she approached he expected her to turn up the boreen. She went by the last cabin, a Protestant's place, and the road ascended and narrowed and the land grew wilder, and he expected her to go off on to a path. Presently he expected nothing, he considered nothing. His heart, though, it beat hard. It had a presentiment. In his right ear he heard a cuckoo, a sign of luck.

She stopped at an old sheep track. He had been willing her to go past it but there she stopped. He was familiar with this track and he felt that in defiance of his will he had directed her, had tempted fate by calling Gil to mind.

She plucked a bit of cloth out of her bodice and rubbed it over her face and throat. She spat on it and cleaned her hands, then stuck it back in her bodice. She plumped her breasts up. She took something out of her pocket. A comb. Holding her hair in a tail she yanked the comb through, and when she had

185

done that she gnawed on her lips, then pinched them. Then she started up the track.

There was no reason to follow any farther, there was only the one place that she could be headed for. Yet he did follow because now he wanted to behold her expedition into sin. He was beside himself with incredulity and suspense and a strange elation.

He waited until he judged that she would be at the top before he began to climb. The track was steep and devious, skirting every rock and thorn. It opened on to flat land that had once been summer grazing and then became the O'Neills' farm and then Gil's. But you couldn't call it a farm any longer, with the dock and nettles and furze that had annexed the two fields. Where Annie had made her passage there was a fissure. She was midway between him and the cabin, still hurrying. Michael wanted to witness her actually going through the door.

Somebody shouted. 'Here!' or 'Heigh!'

Michael ducked. He ran, bent low, to the wall and along it to a big hawthorn. He peered around the trunk.

It was Gil, of course. He was in the second field. He had been hidden by his cow and had come around it and was standing with his arms crossed. He was bare chested.

Annie altered her course and her walk. She traipsed towards him, swishing her skirt. The stone wall between the fields had fallen to rubble and she stepped over it daintily, lifting limp hands. Several feet from Gil she stopped.

Michael could hear their voices but not what they were saying. Annie was whining in her little girl voice. She swivelled and swung her arms. Gil's voice was low and even, and it was a queer spectacle, him being so small, the top of his head not even reaching her shoulders, standing with his arms crossed like a stern child, and she swivelling and whining like a petulant mother.

Suddenly she started running. Gil chased her. She shrieked and laughed and lifted her skirt, her white knees capered out of the weeds. Twice round the field she galloped, Gil right behind, making snatches at her skirt. Then back to the cow, circling it, she shrieking, both of them pawing the cow in their darting until it lowed at the sky, which made her stop and throw back her head with laughter. She had a raucous man's

186

laugh. Gil flung his arms around her hips. Laughing, she tried to disengage him. In vain. He clung like a winkle.

When at last he let go they started shoving at each other. They seemed to be trying to push each other over. She looked to be by far the stronger one, but Gil was possessed of the preternatural strength that won him cudgel matches, and he won this match. He executed one of his famous fighting leaps, snapped his hands at her chest while he was in the air and knocked her flat on her back.

Like a shot she was up again and scrambling away. There was a mound in the middle of the field and she raced over and jumped on it.

'I am the queen of the castle!' she sang, waving over her head.

Gil seized her ankles and dropped her on to her hind quarters. She surrendered. Slowly, with a swooning 'Ahh,' she lay on her back, the mound arching her.

Gil stood straddled over her. He wiped his forearm across his brow and planted one foot on her stomach. He contemplated the horizon and unfastened his belt and took off his breeches.

Naked, he stayed straddled. He must have felt safe from observation since the field was not visible from the road. With his foot he drew up her skirt above her waist. Michael was transfixed, he wasn't breathing. He was living a dream he had where he was dead or prostrate and all around him babies were in midair, houses on fire, people drowning, and he could do nothing.

Gil sank to his knees on top of her, sitting back on his haunches. He took her hands and made her slap her own face. She tossed her head, said, 'Aye, aye.' Oh, her sin. Gil's hips began an easy rock. She cried out.

Michael bolted. Down the sheep track. It was as if he were reliving the night he saw the idiot limbless boy. He was bolting down the same track, he was running until he was breathless, he was falling on the ground.

'The whore! The whore!' he yelled, pitching himself about on the ground, ramming his palms into his eyes to rub out the sight. Neal would murder her, murder Gil, get murdered by the Orangemen. Michael would avenge, get murdered, be avenged. There would be slaughter.

That was why he never told Neal — that and the thought that Annie would deny it or claim she was forced. Then Michael would have to describe her venery, and how could he to his brother's face?

He went home that day and slept, pretending he was unwell. Thereafter he spoke to Annie only when he had to. He knew her for what she was. He knew now that she *had* touched his groin at the Pattern.

He kept furious. He would stare at her with hatred, saying silently 'whore, harlot, slut' until he discomposed her.

'What are you gawking at?' she'd say? Her agitation gladdened him.

But he was furious with Neal, too. Less so, and the fury was mixed with pity, but he was still furious because Neal had married her, because Neal hadn't known better.

Chapter 28

Wales

It wasn't so bad as Michael had thought it would be, because Olwen disobeyed Rosser. She said that if she had done everything Rosser had ever ordered her to do, she would have died long since from the sorrow and strain.

She was resolved to carry on coming up to the loft. But now she was cautious. When Rosser was in one of the fields and she was upstairs she would go to the window every few minutes to watch out for him. Only when he took the horse anywhere and she could be warned of his return by the hoofs on the cobbles would she lie on Michael's bed. Michael said that what she needed was the second sight, and she said that you could get it by killing a cat, taking out its gall, mixing that with hen's fat and smearing the mixture over your eyes, but she could never bring herself to kill a cat.

The days passed. Rosser spoke again about building a false wall for Michael to hide behind. He was there at the foot of the bed every morning when Michael awoke. His questions and talk of politics bothered Michael less than they had two months ago. Michael hardly listened, though he had to pretend that he did. He nodded, agreed with whatever Rosser said, and so Rosser seemed to feel that the two of them were like-minded, declaring once that they were brothers.

In his solitude Michael read the newspapers. He expected to come upon a story about himself but he never did. With a detachment that he hadn't the spirit to wonder about he read that the Irish government had captured most of the United Irishmen's guns and that United Irishmen were being purged from the militia.

189

When he wasn't reading he looked out of the window and walked up and down the loft to strengthen his foot, which nevertheless stayed feeble. He lay on his bed and listened to sounds and gazed at light and dust particles, his mind vacant. He played with the cats. One morning the orange cat had kittens under his bed, and he lay on his stomach, hanging over the edge, to see them being born. As their heads emerged he gave them names.

In sleep he dreamed of Etain. He had one recurring dream where they were at the top of a hill, walking down. The walk was effortless because the hill curved so gently, as the edge of the world appears to curve when you look out to sea, and in his dream Michael wondered if he and Etain were not indeed at the edge of the world. Another reason the walk was effortless was that the grass underfoot was as springy and smooth as The Big House lawn. It was a shimmery shade of green that he had never seen in life. At the bottom of the hill there was a brilliant blue body of water, and to the left and right on the shore there were white Grecian columns. Everything was refulgent, the incarnation of goodness and what he yearned for.

Chapter 29

Ireland

On the twelfth of July the Orangemen marched from the town to the River Road and back. Gil marched at the head, which meant that he was the big leader. He was one of the youngest and he was surely the smallest, but somehow he had got himself made leader of them all.

His uncle John Logan and two other men marched in a line directly behind him, and the rest marched in twos behind them. The rumour was that Logan was seething over not having been made the big leader himself. And plodding behind Gil, he did look fit to kill somebody.

But he was the one who was killed. Three days later his corpse was found by a bog pool. And the most extraordinary thing was that just a day before, the corpse of a little boy with no limbs had been found at the same pool. It wasn't that the boy's limbs had been cut off — the man and woman who found the body said that it looked as though there had never been limbs in the first place. No one claimed the boy, of course, as he was obviously a fairy child. He was left by the pool for the fairies to deal with, and the next day, when a crowd of people went on an outing to see him, he wasn't there. But John Logan was, lying on the ground with his face in the pool, as if he had drowned whole looking into it.

So that's what the doctors and magistrates said: 'Drowned while looking in a bog pool.' There were bonfires and dances. There was no inquest. Since everyone, high-ranking and low, Protestant and Catholic, despised him, no one was concerned that he might have been murdered. Not even the Orangemen cared. They might have slandered the Defenders, insisted on arrests, but they couldn't seem to muster the outrage. Especially when his only relation in the valley was so evidently *not* outraged. Gil didn't even show up for the wake, and at the funeral he spit on the coffin as it was being lowered into the ground. 'Holy water,' he said to the scandalized gathering.

'No love lost between the two of themselves,' people said. They prophesied, 'Logan, won't have left that boy a brass farthing.' Well, Logan had. Heaven only knows why but he left him everything — house, furnishings, farm, stock, monies, leases and, by prior arrangement with his lordship, the job as agent. So now Gil was not only leader of the Orangemen, he was agent to Lord Morrery and middleman of most of the north shore as well.

Catholics were in terror. But Gil didn't persecute them, nor did he favour Protestants in land auctions. Like his uncle before him he favoured whoever offered to pay the highest rental. In auctions where men were obviously bidding crazily, he had the two top contenders battle it out with cudgels, winner take the lease.

People didn't know what to make of him. Here he was, leader of the Orange Order, sworn to banish Catholics to hell or Connaught, and yet he was letting his Catholic tenants live in peace and, furthermore, he always had sweets in his pockets for children and cripples, be they Catholic or Protestant. And here he had Logan's grand house to live in and yet he went on living in the godforsaken O'Neill place. And the way he treated Master Arthur, who might have stripped him of all his lands and leases if he'd had the gumption, was shocking. He shouted to him across markets and field to be off, let people alone, fraternize with his own class, why didn't he? Arthur would ride away all in a dither.

Certain of his women, his slatterns, crawled out of the woodwork now that he was rich and powerful. They trotted out babies that they called "Gil", and "Gilda", and "Willis". It seemed that Gil examined these babies scrupulously, once or twice summoning a doctor for a medical opinion, and if he concluded that they bore enough of a resemblance to himself he would give the mothers money. It was joked about that every pregnant woman in the valley was praying to deliver a pygmy.

Annie was pregnant, and all Michael could think was, "Is it Gil's?" Everyone else was in ecstasy. Kathleen and Mary wept with it. Neal cupped and gazed at Annie's belly as if he were seeing paradise in a crystal ball. Michael gazed, too, imagining the child of an Orange leader corporifying in that bulge, imagining a little Gil leaping out, prowling, laying claims, hectoring. He was so disturbed that he could scarcely forbear commiserating with Neal. Finally he unburdened himself to Etain.

He hadn't spoken to her before about Annie and Gil because he was too ashamed. It was such a blemish on his family, the family that he was asking her to marry into. If the truth about Rose and Judy were faced, then Etain already had to reckon with a suicide and a horse thief's accomplice, and now here was a cuckold, a slut and maybe a bastard to boot.

As he told her, she paled. Perversely he found himself wanting to repulse her further. He described Gil making Annie slap her own face.

'He forced her,' she whispered.

'She was saying aye,' he repeated, thinking that she meant he forced her to slap herself.

'He threatened her with some terrible consequence if she did not go to his place.'

'Not on your life. You should have seen her preening on the road there. Jesus, the slut.'

Etain jumped down from the bed and fell on to one of the stools at the fire. They were in her cabin, they had been lounging on her settle bed. Her father was slipping hay across the river, so they were safe.

''Tis only calling a spade a spade,' Michael said.

'You hate her,' she said, as if there were no reason to.

'And why wouldn't I?'

She shook her head.

'She may well be bringing Gil's baby into my family, and I'll tell you, it will be my mother and sister that rear it, not herself!' He was yelling. He couldn't believe that she was speaking up for Annie, whom she didn't even care for. He couldn't bear it. Certain things were either right or wrong. There were unassailable truths, such as, Thou shalt not commit adultery. 'The girl betrayed my brother,' he yelled. 'Neal that is kindness and devotion itself!'

Etain let out a sob, catching it in her apron.

'Ah, what?' he said. He went over to her and dropped on his knees. 'What is it?' he said, tugging her arm.

She held herself rigid. Her sobs pulsed out. 'What is it?' he asked with more concern.

'My mama,' she said into her apron.

'Your mama?'

'I miss my mama.'

'You miss your mama?'

She nodded.

He stroked her hair and rifled the last moments for whatever had brought this on. In a while her sobs quieted and he tried again to pull her hands from her face. She jerked away and he lost his balance and fell back, knocking over her knitting basket. A ball of wool rolled into the fire.

'My wool!' she cried.

'I have it here,' he said, plucking it out of the sods.

She bent down to righten the basket. 'Where ... where are my needles?' She patted the hearthstone.

They were by her hands. 'Here,' he said, picking them up and giving them to her. 'Couldn't you see them?' he asked gently.

'I could so,' she said, keeping his head bowed. She tapped the needles together.

'Are you recovered?' he asked.

She nodded. 'You had best be going,' she said.

He went because it struck him that her time of month must be upon her. He didn't try to reason out any further than that what the matter was. He was reassured by thinking of how Rose, before her time of month, had cried at almost anything, at a dead lark in the yard, for instance.

Captain Stout had stripped most of the valley's gentry houses of arms. He had stolen kegs of powder from a military stores in the next barony. He had drilled the United Irish membership into a crack corps. He had chopped his hair short at the back of his head and grown a moustache, believing this to be the French fashion, and had dyed his jacket United-Irish green.

He was ready for the rising but the rising was still months down the road.

The waiting made him peevish. In the evenings that Michael stayed at the schoolhouse to copy out mottoes and other United Irish writings, Captain Stout would turn up and sprawl on a bench and needle him. He had taken to calling him "Scholar Boy".

'You know what for they have you doing that, don't you, Scholar Boy?' he said. 'On account of you're no good for anything else. 'Tis the Defender boys that will be winning this country, by God, while you scholar boys are sitting on your arses writing out pretty verses.'

If Master Dolan was there he would try to draw Captain Stout away from Michael by asking him to regale them with stories of his exploits, and Captain Stout would do so, telling obvious, stupid lies. If Master Dolan wasn't there Michael kept his mouth shut. Master Dolan had said that as long as Stout had Michael for a whipping boy he might not feel inclined to take his restiveness out on the Orangemen. So Michael kept silent for the peace of the valley. He missed Corny terribly.

He didn't say anything to Master Dolan, but the truth was he was as impatient as Captain Stout. Copying out the same slogans and articles, over and over, for people who wouldn't be able to read them anyway, became more of a chore each night. He was raring for something exciting to happen. And just before corn harvest something did.

Dolan ordered Captain Stout to rob Bridun Castle. Dolan himself had orders from the United Irish county committee, which had learned that Bridun Castle's gunroom held the largest collection of weapons in the north.

'The Big House, is it?' Captain Stout said, twirling his new moustache. Eyes popping with challenge, he left the schoolhouse to scheme.

Two nights later he had his plan. From one of The Big House coachmen he had found out that Arthur and his huntsman would be going to a cockfight near Dungannon in three weeks' time, departing on the morning of the fight and returning the following morning. The robbery would occur during their absence. The servants who were United men would be warned to spend the entire night in a crowded tavern for the sake of having alibis. The old gatekeeper would be bound and gagged, and a mastiff belonging to the huntsman and let loose on the grounds at night would have its throat cut. Captain Stout would get the guns himself, working with just one other man. The fewer the thieves the quicker and quieter the theft.

'Who will the other man be?' Master Dolan asked.

Captain Stout looked at Michael.

'This is no laughing matter,' Master Dolan said.

'Am I laughing at all?'

'Speak sense. Michael has no experience of this kind of thing.'

'Then it is full time he was getting a bit.'

'Nay, 'tis too important a job, this one. Use a man that knows what he's about.'

Captain Stout spat into the fire. 'I'll use Scholar Boy or by God there'll by no robbery. Look at himself there. Shitting with fear. I can smell it. Coward shit.'

Michael picked up his quill, dipped it into the ink and bent over his page. 'I'll do it,' he said, making his voice sound easy. He wasn't even aware that instead of writing, 'Unite and be free,' he was starting to write what he'd said — 'I'll do it' — in shaky blobbed letters.

He didn't sleep that night. Envisaging the robbery, he couldn't get himself safely out of the gunroom. He imagined himself and Captain Stout throwing guns out of a window into a cart. He imagined the door opening and a man standing on the threshold, holding a candle. In the candle's light the man's face was strange and fiendish. The man raised the hand that was not holding the candle and pointed a pistol at Michael's head.

And Michael thought, both in his waking dream and out of it, "I will die."

The possibility had never entered his mind before. He felt it now as a profane, preposterous, foregone event. He began to gasp, and his mother woke up.

'Are you unwell, Michael?' she called.

'A bad dream,' he answered.

All night he thrashed and sweated. The dog whined in its sleep. His father snored, 'drove the hogs to market', as his mother would say. His father got up twice to relieve himself at the stoop. The wind rustled the bush outside the door. Michael flung his thoughts everywhere, but they snapped back, all enthralled by the one thought that he would die in The Big House gunroom and that, fearing death, he must be the coward Captain Stout had said he was.

The next two days and nights he was in agony. On the third day, instead of going to school, he got himself hired as a reaper on Neal and Slieve's team. His hands bled, his arms lost feeling, his back felt like it had a cleaver in it. Neal, who was setting the pace, inquired at every halt how he was holding up, and Michael answered, 'Grand, grand.' He mustn't stop. Filling his head was the chant: 'Grasp the straw, slice the straw, step. Grasp the straw, slice the straw, lay the straw, step.' If he did not obey the chant it would leave his head and death dread would come back.

This was the case. When the sun set and the moon rose and work ceased, Michael raised his eyes to the hills, and what did he see but that the highest hill, the one that was the final and most glorious peak in his life, was lost in cloud. It often was. But Michael, being in dread again, and being bloody and bodily sore like some holy man, said to himself, 'And this shall be a sign unto you.'

Before going to his cabin he let Neal swab and bandage his hands, since if Hugh was to see how lacerated they were he wouldn't give him a sickle tomorrow.

Neal said, 'I wouldn't go on cutting with them hands.'

'I need the books.' He had told Neal that he wanted the wage for buying books. He was under oath not to say a word to a soul about the robbery, and anyhow he would never speak of his fear.

That night, as he'd hoped, he slept, his first sleep in four nights. He awoke, however, from a nightmare that not himself but Etain was dead. It troubled him all day, his sore hands were nothing beside it. He had to see her. At the end of work, though it was not Thursday and her father would probably be home, he borrowed Neal's horse and rode up to her place.

She answered the door. There she was. Alive. She stepped back into the cabin, looking alarmed. 'What is it?' she said.

'Your father's not within?' he asked, peering past her.

197

'He will be in no time. I thought it was his horse.'

Michael picked at his bandages. 'Well, I was riding by,' he said. Now that he was there he didn't know what to say that would justify the risk. Saying aloud, for fate to hear, that he had dreamed of her death would be to court the event.

'What in God's name have you done to yourself?' She seized his wrists.

'I've been cutting.'

They both gazed at his dirty, torn bandages. 'I'd make you new ones but there's no time,' she said.

''Tis nothing at all,' he said. Her hair was combed and tied back with a white ribbon. He felt unworthy of her. 'Might I hold you?' he asked. Normally he would just have done it.

She let go of his wrists and leaned into him. He put his arms around her, bending low to press her into his chest.

'Darling,' she whispered. He whispered, 'Darling.' He thought, "If I could only hold her until the robbery."

She drew away. 'My father will be back any minute.'

'I'll go,' he said, but he held her hands, loosely because of the pain of closing his fingers. Her small white fingers lay like captured things in his palms. He thought, "If only I could hold her hands until the robbery." He wasn't afraid now. He said to himself, "Perfect love casteth out fear."

But the next morning he was in dread again. He awoke with his hands clenched, his nails digging through the bandages. Blood was smeared on his shirt and on his bedclothes. He thought, meaninglessly, "Whoso sheddeth man's blood, by man shall his blood be shed." It occurred to him that the reason these biblical fragments were coursing through his head was that his death was nigh.

His mother unwound the bandages to change them. As his palms were revealed she exclaimed, and his father came over to investigate. 'Go to school,' he said.

'They look worse than they are,' Michael said, not to grouse but to reassure his mother. He didn't intend to reap today anyway. Before rising from his bed he had decided that the answer to his fear was to consult Tyrrell the Fairy Man.

Tyrrell's place was humble, notwithstanding the wealth that the fairies had conferred on him. The cabin walls were mud,

198

the roof sagged like a saddle. He had no byre or outbuildings, so his fowl roosted in the boor-tree bushes and his pig and cow lived with him in the cabin. For furnishings he had only a potato bin, some wooden bowls and a deal bed that he shared with the pig. He had no chairs or stools, there wasn't the space, it was all taken up by the tools of his trade, floor to ceiling. When the cow was in her nook by the door you couldn't see her from the fire.

Not even he knew what he had, he had so many things. You could surprise him by pulling out some odd relic — a twisted stick or a ball of feathers — from one of the stacks. 'God bless us, will you look at that,' he'd say.

He had hundreds of jars of herbs and potions, all of them benign for his intention was good. He had a firkin full of sea shells and a purse full of fairy stones. He had many ordinary-seeming things such as halters, chains, rags and ribbons, which were in fact magical. He had the dried bodies of animals and birds, and floating in bottles he had their organs. He had the dried foot of a dead person.

Michael found him sitting on the bed with his pig, eating porridge out of one of his ancient magical bowls. Michael got straight to the point. 'I want to know if am going to die within the month,' he said.

Tyrrell cleaned the inside of his mouth with his finger. 'Them Orange boys been threatening you?'

'Nothing like that. I've been having a nightmare.'

'Ach, nightmares. Nightmares and dreams don't signify. 'Tis only the quacks and hags that will tell you different.'

'I'd like to know all the same.'

'You would, would you? In that case let us see what there is to see.' He put the bowl under the pig's snout and hopped off the bed. He was a small dapper man with a coronet of white hair. Meeting him for the first time you'd have taken him for a linen merchant.

'Now then, would you kindly remove your hat and sit yourself down on the floor,' he said.

Michael did so. Tyrrell stepped behind him and began to rub and press his hands all over Michael's head. 'Hummm,' he said.

'What is it?' Michael said, his insides griping.

'Easy now,' Tyrrell remonstrated.

Next he uncorked a purple potion and had Michael swill a mouthful. It tasted of mint. Tyrrell folded a white cloth, held it under Michael's mouth and told him to spit out. When Michael had, he unfolded the cloth and took it to the door to examine the purple stains in the light. He hummed again.

'What?' Michael said.

'*Easy* now, lad. All in good time.'

He laid the cloth aside and rummaged through one of the stacks. What he pulled out was his purse of fairy stones. He lined seven of them up along the stoop and then said, 'If you would kindly pick them all up, one at a time in any order.' Michael selected in order of size, biggest to smallest.

'Well, will you look at that now?' Tyrrell murmured, taking them back. He cogitated. Michael pulled threads out of his bandages and thought how Master Dolan and Corny would scorn him for this. But he had faith in signs, he couldn't reason himself out of it.

Tyrrell wasn't done. He stood up, tugging down his vest. 'Now then, Michael, lad, would you kindly go to the river and pluck nine rushes and bring them to me.'

Michael balked. From the river his mother or Mary might spot him. 'Could you not pluck them yourself?' he asked. 'The truth is, I should be at school.'

'Nay, nay, nay. The choice must be your own.'

Michael slunk down to the bank, twisted off nine stalks, gasping at the pain it caused his cut hands, and raced back up to the cabin. Tyrrell had him throw the stalks high into the air, the augury being in how they landed. Then he tiptoed around them, studying them from every vantage. Then he stood for a long while pinching the bridge of his nose.

'Well, well, well, well, well,' he said at last, coming to sit next to Michael on the stoop. 'Giving it to you plain because you are a scholar and the son of your good father, you might die within the month and you might have another eighty years in you.'

'Well, which?'

'One or the other or somewheres in between.'

'But what did everything say? My head and everything?'

'Your head said long life. Your spit said your days are few

before you. The stones said you will outlive your children. The rushes said you should have been dead these many years.' He looked at Michael. 'And your living self, sitting here sturdy and blooming, says you will go on to be a hundred and three.'

'But which one of the omens is the most powerful?'

'They're all about the same in that regard.'

Michael dropped his head to his knees. 'For the love of Jesus,' he said.

'I'm giving it to you plain.'

'You know when other people are going to die. You know things like who the girls will marry.'

'Not for sure and certain I don't, and there's the truth. Which I'm trusting you to keep under your hat. I read the omens, I use my eyes and ears and what's in here,' he tapped his head, 'and then I make a guess worth wagering on. Now I'm not giving you a guess, what I'm giving you is the truth.'

'Which is that you don't know a thing at all,' Michael said wretchedly. What right did Tyrrell have to confess like this?

'Concerning what lies down the road, I know only one thing,' Tyrrell said. 'That we are all going to die one day.'

'I bloody well knew that before coming over,' Michael shouted. 'Which is why I came over in the first place.'

Tyrrell looked at him sternly. 'Would you prefer that I'd given you a fabrication?'

'No,' Michael said, defeated. 'No.' He picked up stones and threw them at the bushes. After a minute he said. 'If all a person can know about what lies down the road is that he is going to die, then how is he meant to live his life?'

Tyrrell stood up and frowned down at him. 'You know what you love, don't you? Eh? Cleave to that.' Then he sang a song:

'There was a melody in the throat of the lark,
And in the bud there was a sweet blushing flower,
And a roaring flame was in the heart of the girl,
And in the boy that I was, there were dreams.
In the murky beyond there were mystifications.
Through the green valley I walked, to its end, to the
    keening,
To the day of the dazzling light.'

201

That evening Michael found himself saying breezily to Master Dolan, 'The robbery will forge a bond of fellowship between myself and Stout.' He pretended to be nonchalant, a born thief. But he was still terrified. Every time there was a pause in his activities, every time he was alone and every time he closed his eyes, he saw the man in the gunroom pointing a pistol at his head. The image was so clear and consistent that it was starting to assume the authority of a memory and he had to tell himself no, it wasn't foregone, it was the apparition of his dread, and then he hated himself for being a coward.

But one night, as he lay awake in his bed, he remembered Master Dolan saying 'Michael has no experience of this kind of thing,' and it struck him that maybe he wasn't so much cowardly as inexperienced; he was captivated by the vision of his own death because, having spent most of his life bent over books, he had never risked death.

So in the morning, going to school, he aggravated a bull in a field and just escaped over the stile. At midday, when Master Dolan asked him to deliver a message to Father Lynn, he took the master's horse and jumped her over every wall and ditch on the way. Then, coming back, he galloped past a man who was notorious for his brutal temper and shouted at him, 'Clear off the road, vagabond!'

With each incident he grew increasingly reckless, aroused and fearless. After supper that night, as he was setting off to do more perilous things, an opportunity for what seemed like true danger presented itself. He had his hand on the latch when he heard his father outside say, 'Let's get it over with,' and Neal say, ''Tis not dark enough.' He stopped to listen.

The two of them were standing by the byre door. 'Dark or light, what's the difference?' Hugh said. 'Jesus, I hate this kind of thing.'

'What I wonder is, where does Captain Stout keep all the pikes he has already?' Neal said.

Michael opened the door and stepped out.

'And where are you bound for this fine evening?' his father asked in a lively voice that Michael was meant to be fooled by.

'Dada, I know you have some business to do for Captain Stout,' he said. 'I want to go with you.'

Hugh bit off a chew of tobacco. 'Eavesdropping, is it?'

'I couldn't help hearing, I was at the door.'

Hugh glanced at Neal.

'I'll do whatever you say, Dada. I won't get in your way.'

'We're not off to see the king, Michael.'

'Ah, let him come, why not?' Neal said. He made a joke. 'He might even help out with a slogan or two.'

'Over my dead body, by God,' Hugh said, and Michael said quickly, 'I won't say a word.'

Hugh looked at him and ruminated. 'All right,' he said. He spat. ''Twill be a family occasion,' he said bitterly, making his own joke.

All they were going to do, it turned out, was call on Darby Fennel next door and try to persuade him to fashion pikes for the rising. Yesterday Captain Stout himself had been to the forge but had been run off by Norah, plying her pizzle and screaming that she was no stinking Papist, if the Defenders wanted pikes they could bloody well shell out the hard gold. Hugh and Neal had been charged to employ neighbourly persuasion yet insinuate menace by showing up in the pitch dark.

It was hardly the hair-raising mission — the robbery of someone's forge, the practice for The Big House robbery — that Michael had imagined. He couldn't back out now, though, not after his pleading. He shared a pipe with his father and Neal while they waited until it was dark as it would get under a full moon.

'I never hoped to find myself caught between a rock and a hard place like Captain Stout and Norah Fennel,' Hugh said as they walked across the bog.

'The three worst things to have in the house,' Michael said. 'A smoky chimney, a leaky roof and a wife that shaves her face.'

They halted when they entered Darby's yard. No light came from the forge or cabin, no smoke rose from the chimneys. This was unexpected. Hugh had said that Norah and Darby were bound to know something was afoot, that you didn't cross Captain Stout and hope to sleep nights.

'They've gone off somewhere,' Michael whispered.

Hugh shook his head. Neal began to whistle, to make himself easy or maybe to let Norah and Darby know, if they were home after all, that they had visitors, and Hugh lifted his hand to signal silence, and just then, as if his raised hand were really the signal for this, the double doors of the forge flew open.

There were three flashes, three reports, and a single report a second later. Hugh fell. Neal staggered, made a gurgling sound and fell. Michael threw himself to the ground behind them.

Three men moved slowly out of the forge into the yard, their pistols still aimed. Michael smelled the gunpowder. A smaller man slipped around and ahead of them. From the cabin, somebody in a high hat and white nightshirt came running. Darby.

He gaped at them on the ground. 'Mother of God,' he said. Hugh rose to his elbows and dragged himself towards Neal.

The man who had slipped ahead of the three men with the pistols, who was not a man at all but a woman in a man's coat, smacked Darby on the back. 'Didn't I warn you so?' she shrieked. 'Didn't I?'

Hugh was shot in the knee. Neal was shot through the body. He died at dawn. Norah was arrested in her cabin. The three men were her brothers from over the hills. They fled but were apprehended, still carrying the horse pistols, by Colonel Crosbie's corps of yeoman cavalry. Norah had fetched her brothers to guard the forge against Defender attackers. Darby claimed that he had thought "guard" only meant keeping an eye out. He claimed that he had been sound asleep when she slipped out of bed to go to the forge. He wasn't arrested.

The Defenders were all set to cut his throat and burn his place down, but when Captain Stout told Kathleen this at the wake, she cried, 'No more!' with such a berserk look on her face that he backed away from her, hands up in submission. A little later he stood beside Michael and muttered, 'You're out of it, I'll get another man.' It was some minutes before Michael understood that "it" was The Big House robbery.

For most of two days Annie lay on the corpse bed, clasping Neal with her legs, holding his face in her hands and blubbering to it. When she started screaming, people thought that it was the summit of her anguish and they keened in chorus until the blood was noticed. Then her father and Slieve carried her across to her own cabin.

204

A baby girl was born dead. She was washed, anointed, wrapped in a white cloth and nestled against Neal. She was perfectly formed, only too tiny. One of the women said that she should be tucked under the sheet, Annie would perish of sorrow altogether to behold the wee creature in the crook of Neal's arm, but Kathleen shook her head. 'Let the babe come unto its father,' she said, quoting something. It seemed to make no difference to Annie. She returned to the wake house before the coffin was closed, and though she placed her hands over Neal's eyes for a moment, she didn't even appear to see her daughter. To those who said that they were sorry for her now loss, she said back, ''Tis no loss.' It could have been that she had no grief left in her, or maybe losing both her husband and baby had unfixed her mind. In body, she was quite recovered. She drank two glasses of poteen and said she fancied a stroll.

Two of Slieve's cousins carried Hugh in a chair that had a pole under it, which the boys supported on their shoulders. Michael, Slieve, Annie's father and a friend of Neal's carried the coffin. They led the procession down to the River Road and started to turn west, but Hugh shouted, 'The other way! The other way! I'll mourn my son where they murdered him!' so they did as he ordered and went across the bog to the Fennels'. The place looked the same as on the night of the shooting — the doors shut, the fires out. They lowered the coffin on to the biggest patch of blood in the yard, and at once the keen rose. It lasted many minutes. When it began to die down they bent to pick up the coffin again, and as they did the upper half of the cabin door opened and a head peeked out.

Darby's head, but you had to gather your wits to realize this for his face was so stricken. Also he was hatless, which, publicly, he hadn't been in years. The pallbearers set the coffin back down.

Darby clung to the lower door and swallowed. He plainly wanted to say something but couldn't.

It was Hugh who spoke. 'Lift us up,' he muttered to his carriers. They hoisted the pole and he motioned to be conveyed to the door.

Darby found his voice. 'Hugh. My friend,' he said.

'What? What?' Hugh shouted. His carriers lowered the chair.

Darby blinked at him.

'You call me *friend*?' Hugh shouted.

Darby dropped his head. Tears dripped off his chin and dashed on his hands. 'I would be obliged if you would take my Lightning,' he said. 'For your loss.'

'Your nag?' Hugh said at last. He sounded interested.

Darby nodded. He swiped at his tears.

'In exchange for my son?'

'I paid ten guineas for him.'

Somebody started to laugh. It was Annie. Her mother hushed her but she kept laughing, so her mother embraced her tightly to smother the noise, and to drown it out the women around raised the keen.

Hugh came to his feet, supported by one of his carriers. 'God damn your black soul to hell!' he thundered at Darby. All the keening in the world couldn't have drowned that out. 'Conniver!' he thundered. 'Villain! Murderer!'

Darby shut the door. 'Murderer!' Hugh roared, pointing at the door. 'Murderer!' In the field beside the forge Lightning became agitated and began to trot in circles.

Chapter 30

Wales

All the way from the hills you could hear the ewes bleating for their lambs that had been taken away and sold at market. Michael stood at the front loft window, listening. Olwen had just walked out of his range of vision, carrying a basket of clean laundry over to the hedge where she would spread the things out to dry. Brown, black and grey strewn on the green hedge because Rosser wouldn't permit the wearing of colours.

Tears stood in Michael's eyes, he didn't know why. But once they fell he thought of why they should and he wept aloud. He limped back to the bed and dropped on to it. He wept for Rose and Neal. For the dead baby. He wanted to feel the way he had a year ago. A year ago he'd been elated and furious all of the time, he'd been master of his fate, of Ireland's fate, that's what he'd believed. But everything was blasted now and he could never go home. He could never go home.

Something touched the back of his head. He started. 'Husht' — a whisper. Olwen. She stroked his hair and he let out a breath and went on crying but not so loudly. She sat on the bed.

After a while he turned his head on the pillow and saw a man's arm, not a woman's, not Olwen's. He sat up, backing into the wall.

Rosser said softly, 'Your suffering is a test, it is not a punishment.' He rubbed on his own knee the hand that had been stroking Michael's hair.

Michael could feel his face burning. 'I am not myself,' he said.

'Within our suffering there is God,' Rosser said distantly. He looked down at the wound on Michael's ankle, and Michael looked at it too, and it seemed hideously garish and indecent to him. He leaned forward to cover it with the quilt, then stopped because Rosser's hand moved in front of him and he thought that Rosser was going to pull the quilt up.

But it was his nightshirt that Rosser was reaching for. He held the hem of it and and rubbed the cloth between his fingers. His hand shook.

Michael glanced up at him and went still to see his eyes, which were quivering yet intent — the same look he'd had the day he'd made Olwen sleep downstairs, just before he'd hit her across the head.

'A linen cloth,' Rosser whispered, drawing the shirt up over Michael's knees, 'about his naked body.' He drew the shirt higher, slowly, up to Michael's thighs, and Michael shivered, but looking at Rosser's eyes he could not move or speak.

'And the young men laid hold on him,' Rosser said, lifting the shirt up to Michael's waist.

Chapter 31

Ireland

This death was different. Hugh took his crutch and hopped out to the byre to cry alone. They could hear his sobs through the connecting wall. For Michael there were no days of grace from grief as there had been after Rose died. The grief came the instant Neal's life left, and it stayed. Sometimes he had to lie down and curl up in himself wherever he was, on the road, in a field, his heart was so sore.

He was doing most of the work on both farms, his father's and Neal's. With his bad leg Hugh could do next to nothing. He hobbled about the property, stopping to frown at a stook, at a section of wall. Every afternoon he sent Michael to the tavern to buy whiskey. Michael had to ask his mother for the money and it made him feel sheepish and a traitor to her but she gave him the coins saying, 'There's a good lad,' as if they were all conspiring together to squander the rental.

She spun and baked and fed the visitors who came by to pay their respects. One of these visitors pointed out that her lovely hair was now all grey, and called it her veil of sorrow. Everyone asked after little Nealie, for there was his cradle in the corner, filled with the toys that Neal had made. The child would be such a comfort to the household, everyone said, when Annie brought him home.

Annie and Nealie had gone to stay with an aunt of hers who lived out of the valley. They were away ten days. As soon as Kathleen heard that they had returned to The Bull and Castle she started to bake a ginger cake, Annie's favourite, to bring over to them. But they came by before the cake had cooled —

Annie's hair had dust and straw in it and looked tangled beyond recovery. Her eyes were bloodshot. Nealie, though, was clean and combed and wearing new green stockings.

'I cannot mind him any longer,' Annie said, 'you can have him.' She dropped a sack on the floor. 'Them's the rest of his things.'

'You'll be working for your father again, is it?' Kathleen said.

'I'm telling you, you can *have* him. For good and all.' She pushed Nealie. 'Go to Grandmama.'

Kathleen picked him up. 'Oh, Annie, 'tis your misery speaking.'

'I don't want him. I don't want any of it. The cabin, the land. You can have it all back.'

'Surely not.'

'And what would I be doing with the place?' Annie snapped.

Kathleen turned to Hugh. 'If the girl doesn't want it, she doesn't want it,' he muttered.

Annie said, 'My father says you are welcome to the hens and the cow he bequeathed to the marriage, but might he have the mare back?'

When Mary and Slieve called round that afternoon, Kathleen told them what Annie had said. 'Do the two of you want the place?' she said.

Slieve's big jaw dropped. Neal's holding was twice the size of his and Mary's in the hills, and who didn't covet a riverside property?

'The sooner you're in the better,' Kathleen said. 'You can re-let your own land after harvest.' She looked at Hugh.

'They might as well have the stock to boot,' he said thickly. He assembled his jug and pipe and crutch and hopped out to the byre.

Mary and Slieve settled into the cabin the next day. Nealie, as well. 'This is his home,' Kathleen said, bringing him and his cradle and clothing over. She said, 'You be his mama and dada.'

Slieve would be attending to the farms, which meant that Michael could return to school. But he didn't. Early in the morning he went up to Stone Peak and sat between two graves, out of the wind. It was a fitting place to be.

210

Now that he might resume his life, he was swathed in death thoughts again. Not a particular death, not just his own, or Neal's, but all death, everyone dying on a day that only God knew of. He thought about the rising and couldn't see the waves of marching Irish soldiers. He saw instead what Corny had said: the rivers running red with blood. He thought of Neal whistling a tune one second and having his heart smashed the next. He thought of fatal illnesses.

He couldn't understand why he and Etain hadn't married yet. What could be more important? His schooling? Her father's dreams of rich graziers? These vanities? What if he or she died while they were waiting? He'd had nightmares of their deaths. Tyrrell had said that nightmares didn't signify, but Tyrrell had also confessed to not knowing anything.

They must marry right away. He would go to her place this evening. He would announce his intention to her father, divulge their betrothal. If her father refused to give consent, and he likely would, they would run off to a couple beggar. Tonight. He had a bit of money put by. Really it was fated because they even had a house to come back to afterwards — Mary and Slieve's old place. Etain said her father wept like a baby for her mother. Well, everybody was weeping for somebody, her father would survive this.

He raced home and curried the mare. He brushed his Sunday coat, shaved, pared his nails. Whatever happened he would be presentable. Hugh and Kathleen watched his preparations but didn't inquire. They would presume that he had some United Irish business to do and they'd prefer not to know. He would astonish and cheer them. Bring them back a daughter-in-law, a generator of grandchildren.

The sun dropped before his eyes as he rode northwest on the River Road. The hills beckoned, and halfway there the wind rose and whipped a misty rain. It felt apocalyptical to be galloping at sunset in a high wet wind to red hills.

About a quarter of a mile from her cabin he saw her. Even in the dusk and with her yellow hair covered he knew that it was her. He was surprised and yet not — circumstances were in league with him. She was scurrying along but she stopped and went over to the ditch as he approached.

He rode up to her and leaped to the ground. "Tis me,' he said.

211

'Oh, Mother of God,' she said, as if she'd been frightened. 'Michael.'

He pulled her to him. 'Where are you rushing off to?'

'To your house.'

This gladdened and excited him, this concurrence of their thoughts. 'Your father allowed you out after dark?'

'He is gone 'til tomorrow. To the Dungannon cockfight.'

So her father was not at home. Very well, very well, fate was manoeuvring. They would run away together. Her father would have forced them to it anyway. She could go back and write a note, pack some things.

She looked down. 'I had to see you,' she said. 'I have something to tell you, Michael, and — ' she drew in a quavering breath — 'if you do not forgive me, I am lost.'

The horse snorted and threw its head. He led it across the road to tie it to a dead tree. 'What is it?' he asked. He was expecting nothing because she was always worrying over nothing. To himself he was laughing with the anticipation of what she had to say.

'I was forced to be a whore,' she said. 'God help me.'

He knotted the rein, which wasn't necessary. He said 'whore' to himself, weighing it like a word he didn't know.

'With Master Arthur.'

He turned to face her.

'I was forced to let Master Arthur love me, Michael.'

He nodded as if this were understandable. His arms seem to fold by themselves over his chest. They felt as if they weren't attached to him.

'Hear me out,' she said. 'If you love me, hear me out.'

She said that one day, the summer before last, a humble carriage came to a halt beside her on the road. The door opened and to her amazement Arthur leaned out. He bade her enter, he wanted to ask her a question, he said, and since he also offered to take her wherever she was going and he was, after all, the young master, she obeyed. But when she was inside he grasped her hand and kissed it. He said that he adored her, that for months he had been watching her at markets and fairs, he had asked people about her. He said that if he had not been promised these ten years to a cousin of his he would marry her tomorrow. She said he certainly would not because she herself

212

was promised to another, so would he kindly stop the coach and let her out. He tried to take her in his arms. She struggled. He grew cross. It was his right to kiss her, he insisted. She hit at him, though he was The Big Lord's son and she might be gaoled for it, and though the carriage was going at a clip she opened the door and jumped out. She was lucky not to have broken her legs.

The next day Arthur and his huntsman arrived at her door. Her father was delirious with joy. He went on and on about the honour. She hid in the corner behind the dresser. Arthur spotted her anyway, he saw her feet — the whole time he stared at them. The huntsman did the talking, in Irish even though her father spoke good English. What he said was that Master Arthur was contemplating having this cabin levelled and the land appropriated in order that a road might be built through it. A road? her father said. But there was nowhere for a road to go up here. The hunstman said the matter was still being considered, Master Arthur might yet be persuaded against it by a certain party. Then he asked that Master Arthur's respects be paid to the daughter of the household, and the two of them left.

Her father got an attack of the tremors. He said he would prefer to die a thousand deaths than to lose everything he had in the world. She reminded him that Master Arthur might yet be persuaded against the road. She fixed her father's dinner told him she was going to vist a neighbour's and set out for The Big House.

She didn't have to go that far. Arthur was riding up and down the road in the same humble carriage, expecting her. It struck her that he used this carriage to travel unnoticed, that it was his place of assignation. She climbed inside and begged him not to persist in his evil bargaining. He smiled. He tickled and pecked at her. He would have his way, he said, or else. Or else.

It did not hurt. She prayed that none of his seed be sown in her womb. When it was over he gave her a purse full of shillings and said that the mating of landlords and tenants' daughters was an ancient and noble Hibernian custom. He said that his huntsman would fetch her for their next liaison.

Over the following months she was fetched to the carriage fifteen times. Oh, she kept track. Did Michael recall that day in

May when he came to her cabin? The day they'd planned to spend together because her father was selling a ewe, but she wasn't at home? Well, that was a day she had to go to the carriage. The huntsman always appeared when she was by herself — he must have spied on the house.

She pleaded with the huntsman. He said she was muck and to count her blessings. She pretended to Arthur that she was suffering from a contagious fever. He said he never caught fevers. She hid in the byre. Hours later a note was delivered advising that the matter of the road was not yet settled. 'What does this mean?' her father asked wretchedly. He had no inkling of her connection with Arthur.

Leaving Arthur's carriage, walking home smelling of him, she would think of ways to kill herself. But if she died, her father really would lose everything. And Michael would lose his wife, and she would lose all her years ahead in the stone house with the school attached. She must hold to her plan, she told herself, for she did have a plan to spurn Arthur before she and Michael were married. Arthur was continuing to give her money and eventually, by spring or summer, she reckoned, she would have enough so that her father might rent another farm under another landlord. In another barony, if need be. She would invent a story for her father about how she'd come by the money, maybe say that the huntsman had delivered it to pay for the appropriation.

Then, a fortnight ago, she met with Arthur and he gave her a purse containing not shillings but guineas, ten of them. Perhaps he was finished with her and this fortune was his parting gift. Or perhaps he was just feeling generous. In any case she was finished with him. She had her spurn money and then some. She got out of the carriage and went to a priest in the next parish. She could not bring herself to confess to a priest whom she knew, such was her shame. The priest said she must tell all to her betrothed. And she realized that. Hadn't she wanted to tell him every day? But how could she have? How could she have told him when she was not free to end it? And even when it ended she had to wait because on the same morning that Arthur gave her the guineas Neal died.

'Neal died,' she said. She closed her eyes and pressed her fingers at her mouth.

Michael bit off a wedge of tobacco from his quid. While she had been speaking he had been two people. The first person had attended to her story closely and had pictured everything, had even felt a dispassionate interest in some corrupt link, some inevitable corruption joining the two families: The Big Lord taking his sister; The Big Lord's son taking his bethrothed. The second person had only heard this and that phrase, the worst: 'it did not hurt', 'fetched to his carriage fifteen times'. This person was on some dangerous verge.

'You should have told your father, that first day they showed up at your house,' he said quietly. 'And if they'd gone through with their threat, your father could have borrowed whatever money —'

She shook her head.

'— whatever money he needed to get another place. There are people who would have helped him. My father would have.'

'He never would have borrowed money. He is too proud.'

'Too proud, is it?' He spat. His separate selves leaned into each other like burning trees. He shouted, 'So his daughter whores for him, is it? You sacrifice yourself for your father's pride?'

'He'd not have borrowed. He'd have lost our home. It would have killed him.' She started to cry. 'My mama was not in the ground seven months when they showed up.'

Michael looked at the gloomy clumps of hedgerow. His heart was clenched. 'For no man or woman on this earth would I have betrayed you,' he said.

'I did not betray you!'

'You said yourself you are a whore.'

She sobbed into her hands.

'For the love of Jesus,' he shouted, 'that is betraying me.'

'No!'

'Fifteen times! Jesus Christ!' He gripped her arm. 'What did he do to you, eh?' He rubbed her breasts. 'Did he do this to you?'

'Stop it!' she screamed.

He let her go and she ran from him. Her shawl fell off but she didn't pick it up. She ran down the road, crying, slipping in the mud. Her eyes were poor, he remembered that. His heart opened, then spasmed shut, a bigger fist.

He had knotted the mare's rope wrong, it wouldn't pull loose.

215

He took out his pocket knife and cut it. The rain turned into a downpour. He rode through spears of rain flung down on him. The spears were what she had said, he heard her voice in them, he heard everything, a riot of utterances. He heard her saying that her father had gone to the Dungannon cockfight.

He had been flying to nowhere, riding over fields. Now he turned back to the road.

Captain Stout's lodgings were in a Catholic inn two miles beyond the town. By the time Michael got there the mare was heaving. He strode inside and ordered a boy to tend to her. A girl in a white cap and apron came into the hallway, and he asked her, 'Where is Devlin?' using Captain Stout's real name.

Without answering she went back through the door. He followed her up a flight of stairs. She ran ahead of him, shaking out her candle flame to slow him down, but he stayed close enough to hear her rap softly at one of the landing doors that she passed.

It opened as he was feeling for the latch. A man he didn't recognize lifted a candle to see who it was. Michael thought that he'd made a mistake. Then Captain Stout's voice said from within the room, 'Who the hell is it?'

'Michael Malone,' Michael said. A pause, during which the man and Michael looked at each other.

'Let him in,' Captain Stout said. The man pulled the door wider and Michael entered.

'Well, Michael,' Stout said. Not "Scholar Boy". This would be out of respect for Neal. He was sitting in the middle of the room at a table that had a candle and a bottle on it.

Michael said, 'I would speak with yourself alone.'

Stout nodded at the door. The man left. 'Sit,' Stout commanded, kicking the other chair.

Michael swivelled it around and straddled the seat. 'Is tonight still the night you're going to The Big House?'

'Why?'

'Count me with you.'

Stout looked blankly ahead, then back at him. 'What for?'

'Just count me with you.' He lied: 'I never wanted out of it.'

'I have my man.'

'Get rid of him. Or bring him along. Because I am going there tonight one way or another.' He picked up the bottle and swallowed two big slugs. It was like swallowing live coals.

'Don't be getting screwed,' Stout said. He stood. 'Wait here,' he said and went out.

Michael held the candle up to the walls. A narrow bed along one, a pot and trunk against another. Nothing else. A soldier's place, he thought. He thought that he should be living in such a place himself. It could be cannonaded to rubble by the English and what was there to lose?

When Stout returned he said, 'Just the two of ourselves.' He sounded unsure but intrigued, game. He said he trusted that Michael had himself an alibi.

'Four men, United men, Protestants, they'll swear I was with them,' Michael said. Lies tripping easily out of his mouth. Later he would think of things like alibis.

Over the next hours Stout emptied the bottle, consulted his watch and reviewed the plan. He said that as there had been no word to the contrary, they could assume by now that the mastiff was dead and the gatekeeper taken care of. He and Michael would ride round to the laundry house where they would leave the horse and cart. The door to one of the kitchens would be unlocked, a housemaid was seeing to that. The same housemaid would leave the key to the gunroom on the ledge above the door and would be standing guard on the stairs that climbed to the servants' rooms. If she perceived trouble from that quarter she would pull the bell cord and then, to delay discovery of them downstairs, she would pretend to have some kind of fit.

He made Michael repeat the plan. He asked if Michael was scared, if he had qualms, if he was in two minds, and Michael answered, truthfully, no, no, no. 'I just want to get on with it,' he said.

At half-past ten Stout announced that this was it. They went out separately, Michael first and Stout two minutes later, both of them by a rear corridor. In the cowshed they met. No cows were there, only Stout's horse, already harnessed to the cart. Sacks for carrying and a tarpaulin for covering the stolen guns were on the cart floor. Next to the cowshed door, beneath a burning lantern, a pot hung on a nail. Stout slid the pot off the nail. 'Start rubbing,' he said.

The pot contained soot. They smeared their faces with it.

The rain had stopped outside, so they wouldn't be washed clean on the way there, and in any case another pot was hidden in the laundry.

When they were done they regarded each other. Michael saw no face he knew, only big white-rimmed eyes and a fat wide mouth. He would look the same. He felt a rank kinship. Stout patted the pistol in his waistband and told Michael to open the cowshed doors.

Everything was as Stout had said it would be. The Big House gates were open, the park was quiet, the laundry house was open. Everything as easy as a trick that you've figured out.

They tied the horse to a post in the laundry house and crossed the courtyard to the kitchens. The door there was not only open it was ajar. Stout shut it softly after them, then they tiptoed across the flagstones to one of the doors on the far wall. Stout had been given a map, so he knew the lie of the place.

They went down a long corridor. In the light of Stout's torch the tile floor glinted like a river. Portraits paraded down the walls. Huge pale heads.

The key was there, on the ledge above the gunroom door. When they were inside, Stout closed the door behind them and turned and pocketed the key. He stuck his torch in a holder at the fireplace. The entire wall opposite the fireplace was glass cases, locked and holding the guns. The glass would have to be broken. All the servants slept on the third floor, over the wing where the kitchens were, and Stout had said you could fire half the guns off in here and they'd not awaken, but all the same he made a muffler. There were brass animal figurines arrayed in niches between each row of cases, and he took an elephant and wrapped it in his jacket. He and Michael moved a carpet over to catch the falling glass.

In spite of the muffler and the carpet, the glass clattered violently. Michael had a first tremor of fear. He hesitated, listening for somebody. Stout glanced round at him with raging eyes. 'Start filling!' he said.

Michael didn't choose. Fowling pieces, blunderbusses, duelling pistols, he plucked them all out and put them in the sacks. Stout didn't want the powder flasks and bullet moulds but Michael snatched these, too. He couldn't make decisions.

'Whisht!' Stout said.

He froze, muffler raised to strike, eyes on the door. Now Michael heard something. He lowered his sack to the carpet. Footsteps. Uneven, scuffing. Getting louder. Louder. Outside the door.

The door handle rattled. Keys jingled. They clanged to the floor.

Stout ran to the draperies. He swiped at them, parted a pair. He was going to escape. But the windows were small and high, up at the ceiling. He parted the next and next pairs. More high windows. He ran to the fireplace, threw the torch into the grate and smothered it with his jacket. He ran to the door, waving his gun for Michael to follow.

On the other side of the door a man was muttering. He had picked up the keys and was jingling them again. From the corner beside the door Stout beckoned Michael to get over there.

Michael stayed where he was, at the second row of cases. He was calm because, unlike Stout, he was not surprised.

A key was inserted. The door opened. It was like a dream of his dream. In his dream the man had held the candle in his left hand and the pistol in his right, and he had brought the pistol up to Michael's head in a slow certain action. This man's right hand had a candelabrum in it, with two of the candles lit. The pistol, in his left hand, was pointed at the ground. He was swaying. He was Arthur.

'Halt!' he said.

He lifted the pistol. The muzzle looped in Michael's direction. 'Halt!' he said again. Michael hadn't moved.

Arthur took a couple of steps towards him. 'What is the meaning of this?' he said. He took another step. Glass crunched under his foot and he stopped and looked down. 'Aha!' he said.

Keeping his eyes on the pistol, Michael reached out to the wall. He touched something cold and smooth, a brass animal. His fingers closed around it.

Arthur straightened and pointed the pistal. 'Villain! Declare yourself!' he shouted. He staggered closer. Behind him, Captain Stout moved out of the corner, holding his gun high.

Arthur peered at Michael. He brought the candelabrum nearer to Michael's face. Then he rocked away from him. His

219

left hand dropped. 'Michael Malone,' he said quietly and with astonishment. He swayed forward, inches from Michael, gawking at him.

Michael's arm swung from the wall. There was a crack as the figurine met Arthur's temple. Arthur folded in on himself and sank noiselessly to the floor. Michael caught the candelabrum before the candles fell out of it.

He put the figurine back in its niche. Captain Stout whispered, 'You've killed him.'

Michael lowered the candelabrum. 'I don't know,' he said.

Stout stuck his gun in his waistband and came over and knelt. He touched Arthur's temple. He rolled him on to his back, and blood drooled out of one corner of Arthur's mouth. His eyes were open but seemed not to see anything.

'What the hell did you hit him so hard for?' Stout said.

'He recognized me,' Michael said, not in answer but because looking at Stout's sooty strange face he couldn't believe it.

Stout rose, 'You bloody let him. Why the hell wouldn't you budge at all?'

A drip of wax fell on Michael's hand. He set the candelabrum on a table. Stout stepped in front of him and clamped a hand at his throat. 'Do you know what you've done, Scholar Boy? Do you bloody *know*?'

Michael shook him off. He knew. But minutes ago he'd felt that he was in the instant before his death. Now he felt as if a disease were leaking out of him.

They both looked down at Arthur. Stout touched him with his toe. There was a stench of human waste. Stout knelt beside him again. 'This man is dead,' he said.

He got up and ran to the fireplace. He fished his jacket out of the grate.

'Are we still taking the guns?' Michael asked, moving away from the body.

'To hell with the guns,' Stout said. He cast his eyes about the room. 'To hell with the whole bloody thing. I'm getting out. They'll be turning the valley upside down on this one.' A three-barrelled pistol was lying on the carpet, and he crossed to pick it up. It was too big to tuck into his waistband so he kept it in his hand.

The room seemed very hot. 'Where will you go?' Michael

220

asked. He was beginning to feel queer, anxious.

Stout didn't answer. He ran past him as if Michael weren't there, or as if he were another corpse. Michael followed. The corridor was also hot. Michael thought, "The fires of hell. I have killed Master Arthur." Sweat poured down his face.

In the laundry house Stout sliced the harness from the cart. He pulled the horse into the yard and climbed on to her. 'I'll take you to the gates,' he said. 'No farther.'

They rode through another downpour. A hundred yards or so past the gates Stout stopped and Michael jumped down. Stout pointed the pistol at him. He said, 'You did it. There was only yourself alone taking the guns, see? You give the law boys my name and I'll be back for your guts.' He galloped off, throwing up mud.

Michael stood there on the path. The gate creaked in the wind. Arthur's soft amazed voice had said, 'Michael Malone.' He had fallen like a girl in a faint.

'God in heaven!' Michael cried. He covered his mouth. The gatekeeper might have heard, might know the voice. Michael had an urge to untie the old man. Which was mad.

"Get ahold, get ahold," he commanded himself. He said to himself, "You have felled an enemy of the people, he would have died in the rising anyway, you have done the bravest thing."

He wanted back the moment before he had swung the brass animal. He wanted back the moment when Etain's shawl fell off and he had not called after her.

No! Whore! She said, 'I have been a whore.' Fifteen times she went to him.

He veered off the path into the stone wall. He punched it. He hurled himself into it and punched and kicked it. Then he thought he heard a horse and he ran into the woods, so completely frightened that he thought he was running down the sheep path from Gil's place.

Chapter 32

Wales

It wasn't that Rosser was having a vision, because his eyes never went up into his skull. And yet he didn't seem to know what he was about. When Michael hit his arm away and pulled the nightshirt back down, Rosser stayed sitting on the bed for a moment, hunched over, gazing at Michael's covered legs, and then he repeated the passage about the linen cloth. Then he got up wearily and went downstairs.

Michael thought, "It is not safe any longer. That man is a lunatic. I have to get out of this place." But the prospect of leaving was even more daunting than that of staying, and he knew that he wouldn't go.

That night he couldn't sleep. He paced. He went to the front window, and for something to do he jiggled it to see if he could take it out.

He heard a noise down below in the house. He stepped softly back to the bed. The stairs creaked and he thought, alarmed, that it was Rosser. It was Olwen, though, it really was her.

She set her light on the stool. 'Is it troubled you are?' she whispered.

'Oh, aye.'

She leaned over him and kissed his forehead in little pecks, down his cheek to his chin. She kissed his lips.

He kissed her in return. It felt like something that was good for him. He put his arms around her neck and she lay down next to him and they kissed and held each other, her breasts big and soft against him, her whole body along the length of his warm and soft and enfolding like a place to die in.

What he thought of, incredibly, was being in bed with Neal alseep beside him. Why didn't he feel lust for her when she was kissing him, then tugging up her gown and his shirt and they were lying skin to skin and then he was on top of her, entering her, and she was gasping and rolling her hips?

No, it wasn't lust he felt. It was almost serenity, but suddenly it was anguish, and he wanted to pull away from her yet hadn't the will. He said, 'Etain,' and dropped on to her and she clasped him.

Their hearts pounded, his faster than hers. Their skin was wet. 'Oh, Jesus, Etain,' he said to himself, and he trembled. Olwen kissed the top of his head. He lifted up to look at her. She was smiling.

'I murdered a man,' he said.

'In the legion, my little one?'

'Before I was a soldier. I murdered a man in Ireland. The son of a big lord. A nobleman. That's why I can never go back there.'

'Oh,' she said mildly. She ran her fingers through his hair.

'I did it to save my life,' he said. But that was a lie and he wanted to speak the truth, so he said, 'But I didn't have to kill him, I did it to avenge a girl's honour,' but even that wasn't the truth, and he shook his head and said, 'I was in a fury. I was in terror.'

He told it as if it were another man's story — a parable — and obscurely he hoped that in the telling it would become a parable so at the end he would perceive an explanation of events. But how could he? The end was the murder, and then there was only running away.

Where he ran to that night, the night he killed Arthur, was the schoolhouse. Even though it was well past midnight, Father Lynn was there with Master Dolan. Michael fell at the priest's feet in frenzy and contrition. When he told them what had happened they wouldn't accept it. 'But are you sure he was dead entirely?' they kept asking. 'He is dead! He is dead!' Michael finally shouted, incensed at them, and then Father Lynn prayed for the valley and Master Dolan cursed Captain Stout and forecast martial law. Michael cried, 'Am I damned?' and Father Lynn said no, a man might kill to overcome evil and drive out invaders. Master Dolan uncorked a jug. They all drank. Master Dolan hatched a plan. To preclude searches, and investigations and arrests of United Irishmen, he had Michael compose a confession, in which he claimed that he had acted alone in the robbery, he had no affiliations, he had killed Arthur in self-defence and he was leaving the province. Father Lynn would deliver the confession, sealed, to Colonel Crosbie the next morning and say that Michael had just delivered it to him an hour gone. 'The sacred word of a priest,' Father Lynn said wryly.

Master Dolan then gave Michael his horse, fifty guineas and the name of a man in Belfast who, for the gold and the horse, would get him across to France. Michael rode all during what was left of the night and through the next morning, entering Belfast at midday. The man, being the publican of a big tavern, was easily found. He hid Michael in a cart for that day and night and another day, and at dusk on the second night took him to a beach where there was a smuggler's boat anchored offshore. The smugglers took him to Brest.

'Where would Brest be?' Olwen whispered. She was twining his hair around her fingers.

'France. On the coast, on the tip there.'

'I will cut your hair in the morning.'

'They imprisoned me.'

'The French did?'

'Aye.'

'For killing the nobleman?'

'No, that would have won me a medal of honour, had they believed it. They thought I was a spy.'

'Your poor little Etain, she must be longing day and night for you to come home to her.'

'She must despise me.' The terrible things he said that night, just standing there, letting her go.

'No, no, she will love you forever. You must write her a letter and tell her that you are well with you and someday you will send for her so she must keep a brave heart.'

This was so inconceivable that he said nothing. He rolled off Olwen. Even if a letter were to get through to Etain, unintercepted, and she were to forgive him and leave her father to come to him, where would she come to? Here? London? And how could they live as fugitives? How could he ask her to live like that? No, he would never see her again. It suddenly and finally struck him as the truth. He would never see her again, Jesus God. He knew it now. But his heart didn't know it, his heart was fighting it, beating as if to shatter him who would think such a thing.

It began to rain. 'You had better go back down,' he said to Olwen.

'Right you.' She sat up. 'Rosser would beat us black and blue,' she whispered cheerfully, as if it were not a fact. She swung her feet off the bed and hit the stool. The glass that was there fell to the floor with a loud knock then rolled thunderously before she could stop it.

They both went still, he half-sitting on the bed, she standing at the foot of it. The rain fell hard on the thatch. There was a high wind. But not a sound from below.

She tiptoed back to the stool and put down the glass. She sat by his head. 'Did that give you a fright?' she whispered.

'Sure enough.'

'Sometimes the cats bat things, he knows that.' She pressed her finger to his lips.

'You'd better be going down,' he said.

'You are dear, dear,' she whispered, and touched her lips to his.

And despite wanting her to go he kissed her back because he was suddenly grateful, and chastened that he had said nothing fond to her.

Her breasts lowered on to his chest. His blood sank and he kissed her thinking of no one else, only of her, of her breasts, thinking angrily and greedily, why not?

A cat could make the stairs creak, yet Rosser could walk up without making a sound, he could be so lightfooted. What with the rain beating and the wind soughing and Olwen gasping, there was no hope that they would hear him, and they didn't.

Olwen's head yanked back. She screamed and reached up to grasp her hair as her weight was dragged off him and she was pulled to the floor.

'Ah, Jesus,' Michael said.

'Speak not His name!' Rosser shouted, turning on him.

Olwen got to her feet. 'Rosser,' she said. '*Cysgur yr oedden. Cysgur yr oedden.*'

225

'*Dos on hol, Satan.*' He shoved her from him.

He hulked above the bed, his hands balled in fists. Michael stood to face him. They both had to stoop in the low space.

'She came up at my biding,' Michael said. 'I bade her come.'

Rosser was so close to him that Michael could see his eyes quivering. His whole body was quivering.

'You know yourself the girl does what is bid of her,' Michael said. 'Strike me if you must strike at all.'

'No!' Olwen cried. She came between them and hit Rosser on the chest, inviting the brunt of his wrath. Both of them, Michael and Rosser, pushed her away.

Rosser gripped Michael's shoulders. 'You have betrayed me.' His voice was a whisper.

''Tis not betraying you, man.'

'Betrayer, betrayer, betrayer,' Rosser whispered savagely, shaking him, and the sickly dizziness that Michael hadn't felt in weeks came back and he had to hold Rosser's arms to brace himself.

Rosser stopping shaking him but still squeezed his shoulders. He grimaced and Michael flinched, anticipating the onslaught now.

'We were brothers,' Rosser said in a high voice, so different from his normal voice that Michael thought it was some awful height of rage.

He and Rosser were standing there, in their nightshirts, gripping each other, and Rosser was grimacing at him. Michael said, 'We are brothers still,' hearing how spurious and inadequate that sounded.

Rosser lowered his head, shook it. 'Nay. Brothers we were. We were the same, you and me.'

'I will marry her,' Michael said madly.

Rosser looked at him, horrified. He bellowed and hurled him towards the wall. Right on his temple where his injury was, Michael smashed into the end of a beam. He bounced from the impact and fell.

'Michael!' Olwen screamed, dropping down beside him. She tried to prize away his hands from where he was clasping his head.

Rosser hauled her off. Michael felt blood under his hands.

'Up you,' Rosser said to him. Malignant.

Michael got to a crouch, but had to stay like that, head down, because he thought he would lose consciousness. Rosser pulled him to his feet. He pushed him to the stairs. 'Go from my house,' he said.

Michael swayed. He held out his hands. 'I am bleeding,' he said. On her knees between him and Rosser, Olwen entreated. '*Ni sedr fyned. Mae n gwaedu.*' She kissed Rosser's feet.

'Go.' Rosser ordered Michael, pointing at the stairs.

There was something Michael must say, something Rosser was daring him to say and if he said it he was saved. But he didn't know what it was. He was stupid with pain. Lamely, knowing it wasn't this, he said, 'But we are brothers.'

'And the Lord said, the brother shall betray the brother to death!' Rosser shouted. He kicked Olwen, strode to the stairs and pushed Michael.

All the way down he pushed him, but Michael stayed upright by holding the railing. Olwen screamed behind Rosser. At the bottom she managed to edge past him and attached herself to Michael's back. She clung to him with arms and legs, bringing him to his knees. Rosser roared and tugged at her. She screamed. Michael went down on his hands. Above him, on his back, their battle raged.

Then Rosser said, in English, 'I will shoot him dead,' and she cried out and fell to the floor, and when Michael got up and looked at Rosser he saw the gleam of a pistol in Rosser's hand.

'Go from here!' Rosser shouted, pointing the pistol at him.

'Might I have my clothing?' Michael said. He had the wit to realize that the pistol would not be primed.

'Naked ye came and naked shall ye return,' Rosser shouted.

'You cannot leave!' Olwen cried at Michael. She reached the door before he did and planted her back against it.

Rosser charged at her, poking her with the pistol. They blared at each other in Welsh, Rosser jabbing her harder, then raising the pistol to strike her across the head.

Michael lunged at Rosser's arm and caught it raised. 'Clear off!' he yelled at Olwen, and she did, bolting to the corner, obeying him as if she thought he had a strategy.

He hadn't, except to get out of the place. Rosser was punching him in the stomach with his free hand, feebly because he had to reach across himself. Michael let go of Rosser's arm and grasped the door latch. Lifted it. Ran out into the rain. Behind him Olwen screamed. The door thudded shut.

His right foot wouldn't take his weight, his leg buckled when he went down on the ankle. The pounding in his head was so violent that he could hear it outside himself, like a stamping, but he wasn't stamping, he was sinking in mud, splashing, slopping, then there was firmer ground. Flat stones, mud, ruts. The road.

From the loft he hadn't been able to see the road. He didn't see it now. The rain gauzed all the landscape into one blackness and the sky into another. "I am dying," he thought.

When he fell he didn't know it. He imagined that he was still running. What told him otherwise was swallowing water from the puddle his face was in. He coughed and rolled on to his back.

Time passed. It must have, since all at once the night wasn't so dark. The rain had stopped. Was it possible that he had slept? Dusky clouds, like smoke from a bonfire, tumbled across the sky. There was a perfect, whole, yellow moon sliding through the clouds. There was the sound of the sea.

He wasn't dead. He was soaking, trembling, aching head to foot, surely on the brink of death. He would pass from this life as Rose had. Unpurified, unwept for.

He began to cry because the moon was cold and profound. 'Forgive me, Etain,' he said aloud. 'Pulse of my heart.' She had called him that before the pig had screamed, before untying his belt.

He heard his name. 'Michael!' Somebody calling him. He held his breath.

'Michael!' It was Rosser. He sat up, surprised that he had the strength. He crawled to the ditch. Could he climb over it? Did he want to, did he want to be found? He didn't want to be found on his knees. Pushing against the ditch he got himself up. He saw the dark glitter of the sea not a hundred yards away, down a cliff. He heard the horse, and looking up the road saw the lantern.

Rosser jumped to the ground and ran to him. He extinguished the flame, put the lantern down and gripped him by the shoulders. 'Thank God,' he said. 'I have been searching for you and up and down this road. How is it you got so far?'

Michael thought, "I ran." Once he had run past everyone, past the boy with the webbed toes, past Reagan Lunney. The most thrilling race people had ever seen in their lives.

Rosser dropped his hands. He touched his hat. 'I went mad. All along I did know it was Olwen. I went mad.'

'I bade her come to me, Rosser.' It was not altruism, since he didn't think he had a fate left to sacrifice.

Rosser went on as if Michael hadn't spoken. 'So please to come back with me now. Before it is light. You must come back.'

Waves splashed to shore. Michael listened to them, feeling and thinking nothing. It was how he had learned to listen in the loft. He was in a pocket of peace.

'Take my coat,' Rosser said. He started to remove it, then stopped because there were voices. Michael heard them in the same instant. Rosser crouched, pulling him down. The voices had come from the sea side of the ditch and from down the road. They were men's voices, approaching.

'The horse,' Michael whispered. Rosser squeezed his arm for silence.

Very close to where Michael and Rosser crouched, the men halted. '*Là-bas,*' one said. It so startled Michael that he rose to look.

He'd thought that they'd spotted the horse. But they stood at the cliff's edge, facing the sea. Two men. One was gesturing at the water. The other said, '*Le petit*?' The first hit him on the shoulder. '*Non,*' he said, stabbing his finger downward. '*Le grand, le voilier.*'

Rosser tugged Michael's shirt and Michael ducked back down. They heard scrabbling, stones falling. The men were going down the cliff.

Escaped prisoners, *Légion Noire* men they must be. Half a dozen ailing *Légion Noire* were still being held in the district. But these two didn't seem to be ailing.

Michael looked over the ditch again, then straightened. The men were out of sight.

'Get down,' Rosser whispered.

Michael was about to, but suddenly he was vaulting over the ditch.

'Come back!' Rosser whispered, standing.

But it was as if the world had torn in two and Michael was in one half and Rosser in the other. Michael ran to the cliff edge. Below two sailboats lay anchored. The Frenchmen were wading out to the bigger one. Gulls circled and the tops of the waves were silver. It was almost dawn.

'Come back!' Rosser said, as loudly as he dared. 'They will kill you!' Michael turned. Rosser was beckoning him over with his hat. His long white hair blew out to one side of his head, indicating another direction, down the road towards the house.

'Do not go down,' Rosser said. He extended his hat and his other hand. 'Begging you I am, Michael. Begging you now.'

Michael slid down the stones on his bare feet, snatching at grass. Miraculously he didn't feel any pain, not in his head or his foot or his leg.

He was at the bottom of the cliff and running across the sand before the Frenchmen noticed him. One was in the boat, one was still in the water. The one in the boat shouted and the one in the water looked over his shoulder then began running and paddling with his arms to reach the boat faster.

Michael dashed over pebbles and through the rushes at the shore, waving his arms. '*Attendez*!' he called.

The man in the boat pointed at him. His hand glinted. He had a pistol.

'*Ne tirez pas*!' Michael yelled. '*Camarade*!' He galloped into the water. '*Je suis l'un de vous*!'

The gun stayed aimed.

When he was up to his waist he swam. He thought, "This is what will happen — there will be a shot, a pain like a kick. Now." And never in his life had he been so strong, so fleet. It was his body foretelling the end, wasn't it?

His knuckles scraped wood. A hand seized his, pulled him up.

Epilogue

Brest, France 1797
His window was larger than the loft window had been, but the view was all bleakness. An alley of grey stone. A few stranded weeds in the fissures. Some of the stones were splashed with brown stains. Was that blood? The jailer said that during the reign of terror the alley was where the condemned were herded together for the guillotine.

Once a day the French prisoners were allowed out in the alley. Those who could, paced. The others sat against the wall of the next building and turned faces white as a row of lights up to the sun. The intrusion of these faces, trained, so it appeared to Michael, on his window, seemed to give the men a liveliness and authority that they, even less than himself, didn't have.

They were invalides. This place was L'Hôpital des Invalides, the same military hospital that Michael was held in after his first landing. The arrest on the wharf, the allegation: that of spying (Michael was blamed for the entire fiasco of the Fishguard invasion, the captain who questioned him referring to the incident as '*votre petite escapade*') and then the imprisonment here ... all of it was a reprise of the first landing.

Except that, having been a lieutenant and in spite of his status as spy, he was given a room of his own this time, and better rations — broth thick with pork, fresh bread, large helpings of beans and potatoes, wine, tobacco. He was given a pen, ink and as much paper as he desired and was encouraged to write letters.

He wrote to every ministry, every director he could think of.

231

"I am being held unjustly," he wrote. "My circumstances are extraordinary."

Then he waited. Days, weeks, the hardest yet. In Wales he had often believed himself to be in the decrepit place between suffering and death. Waking up from dreams of Etain, he had thought, "This is how dying of a broken heart feels."

But it was when his heart opened to her, when lying on the body of another woman he forgave her, that it broke. He didn't die. He entered another place of suffering, austere and infinite. In the weeks of waiting for replies to his letters, he remembered Wales as an oasis. He remembered the soothing hours of feeling nothing, the recesses of peace. Where was the peace to be found here? He waved his arms to brush against it, he thrashed in his bed as if peace were a position he could fall into, he pawed the walls for it.

Sometimes, believing that he must write to her whatever the cost, he composed long, fevered letters. Letters he didn't send. What if she loved somebody else? What if she was married? What if his letter was intercepted and she was implicated in his crime?

Sometimes he saw her face like a glare wherever he looked and he was mad to be rid of it. As soon as it was gone he was mad to recapture it. He drew pictures of her and kissed the paper and spoke to it. He burned the paper to ashes. He scrutinized the prisoners who brought him his meals, gazed at men in the alley, at scurvied dying men, for some likeness to her, some like feature.

Weeks passed without one response to his letters. He began to suspect they had never gone beyond the gaoler.

A physician visited him once a week to examine the wounds on his foot and temple, and unlike the wretches who brought him his food as if he wasn't there, this man smiled and talked, mostly of his own complaints, exhibiting scars and malformations. He would not surmise about the fate of Michael's letters — he obviously felt himself dangerously compromised when the subject was not his health — but he did advise him to keep writing.

'Write the same letters over again,' he said. 'Write to ambassadors, generals, other Irishmen in France. Make a nuisance of yourself.'

So Michael did. Not knowing anyone's whereabouts, he addressed the letters: "Thomas Paine, France", "The American Ambassador, Paris".

There were days when he was wild to escape, when he kicked his door until his foot bled and he shook the rails of his window like any lunatic in the place. On these days he had a presentiment that he must go home at once and claim Etain before it was too late. He had a presentiment of peril, a final hour. Other days, convinced she couldn't love him, he felt that if he were released the next minute he wouldn't have the spirit to cross the room. He pictured himself growing old and dying in this room. Then he craved for nothing more than to be buried in the valley, next to his sister and brother and baby niece. That graveyard, where they were, produced the brightest green grass in the barony, a springtime growth in every season, as if the treasure within all the souls beneath were at last unleashed. Corpse-fed green, mists dancing into lady shapes, fairy rings, miracle wells, prayers, hopes, grand designs. That was Ireland. 'Ireland! O! Ireland!' Even the recollection of copying out that slogan over and over figured in the breviary of his anguish.

If only he had word of her.

He wrote to Master Dolan. He hadn't before, not only out of fear of implicating him but out of shame that in killing Arthur he had hurt the valley's United Irishmen. From reading the newspapers in Wales he knew that the district had been put under curfew and that meetings had been suppressed. And he recalled how easily the master could dismiss people — 'Good luck to him,' he said savagely when Corny went to Dublin.

He hadn't any expectation that his letter would leave the building. None of his letters so far seemed to have done. It was this hopelessness that gave him the courage to write at all. He described his adventures and circumstances and asked about the state of things in Ireland. He asked about his family. About Etain. The master hadn't known of their betrothal, and Michael didn't mention it. As a postscript, he wrote only, "Is Etain McCaffery well?"

On his meal tray there was a letter. His whole body shook as he reached for it, so that when he picked it up it slipped from his

233

fingers, dropping into the tureen of soup. He snatched it out and wiped it on his shirt, threw it on the bed. He paced. He washed his face and looked out of the window at the alley until something happened down there — a starling fell with the speed of a rock from the eaves above him, landed soundlessly on the stones and lay still.

He sat on his bed and with steady fingers now took the letter out of the envelope. The seal had already been broken.

He knew the hand. Holding the letter in a shaft of light, he read:

12 October, 1797.

My dear Michael

You can have no idea of the joy which the arrival of your letter occasioned. For a year we had been fearing the worst. Six weeks after you left the valley, we received intelligence that the wherry which was to take you to France was discovered wrecked upon a reef near Donaghadee. Your poor mother was fairly heartbroken, coming as this terrible news did upon the heels of yet another grievous loss in your family.

Michael, my lad, it rests with me to tell you that your father is dead. On All Souls' Day a year ago your sister Mary came upon him in his oat field, reclining there in an attitude which, inasmuch as he was smiling, resembled a sound and blissful sleep. I implore you to dwell upon his final countenance and be consoled. You will recollect that following the murder of your brother he was in a state of the utmost desolation. Your deed and disappearance did not, I believe, augment his sorrow, for by that time he was beyond all cure and care. I speak as the one who informed him of your misadventure, and for all he seemed to listen to me his spirit might even then have commenced its bodily departure.

As for your mother, she was a marvel of fortitude throughout the wake. It will comfort you to know that no member of your family was made to suffer, either at the hands of the authorities or the Orangemen, for Arthur's

234

death. Remarkably, it was that queer leader of the Orangemen himself, wee Gil Willis, who protected them, arranging for patrols to guard the property. As expected, there were arrests, myself included in the assemblage, but we were soon released to a man, the only evidence being your confession.

You should know that amongst the Irish you are a hero. A song entitled 'The Scholar From the Vale' has been composed about the fateful night in The Big House, and whilst it has little connexion with the truth it is nevertheless tuneful and exceedingly popular. I imagine that in regard of your fantastic exploits of the past year, other songs will be forthcoming. Despite the discretion with which I relayed the tidings contained in your letter (you may be out of reach of British law, but I am not persuaded that you are as yet out of reach of Lord Morrery) they have been broadcast throughout the valley, and I am daily accosted by veritable swarms who urge me to send you their prayers.

Your mother's prayers counting for the most, I mention them in particular. At one and the same time she is overjoyed to discover that you are alive, and greatly alarmed to learn of your imprisonment. I endeavour to calm her with reassurances of your imminent release, of which I have every confidence. Thank God your letter reached me. No sooner had I read it than I rode to Belfast to inform a certain party there of your situation, and by day's end a plan was underway to secure your liberty. Courage, my lad! France is rife with our comrades. Perhaps you will be free by the time this letter arrives, if it does at all, in which case you will undoubtedly never read it. You will not of course be entirely free, so long as you are exiled from hearth and home, and in all truthfulness I cannot forsee the day when you might return unless a miracle be wrought in our favour. You will appreciate that it would be imprudent of me to elaborate. Let it only be said that the prospects for Ireland are as gloomy as possible.

In answer to your inquiry about her, Etain was not at all well throughout the early part of the year, but she is now

fully recovered. She, too, lost her father. Indeed, her loss
occurred but three weeks before your own, and within
days of your leaving us. For many months her grief was
such that she could scarcely speak, and so pale and sickly
did she grow that there were fears for her life, the more so
as she would sequester herself. In the spring, however, she
abandoned her father's cabin for rooms above the
draper's shop on Castle Street, and there she started a
school for young girls.

Simultaneously, our own Corny returned to the valley,
having found himself unequal to the high life in Dublin.
He brought Etain a gift of spectacles, which she wears
constantly and to far prettier effect than does her sorry
benefactor. From what I have observed I would venture to
say that he is courting her. Unfortunate girl! I took the
liberty of telling her that you had inquired after her health,
and she was utterly dumbfounded by this information, as
if the two of you had never been great friends. At all
events, she joins the multitudes who have begged me to
present their ardent wishes for your immediate release. As
I have said, I am certain that there is little question of it. I
have lost hope for Ireland, but not for yourself, my lad.

God bless and preserve you.

Patrick Dolan

Two days later, Michael had a visitor.

He was Irish — Colonel Healy, a round red-faced man of
about fifty years. 'I have come to release you,' he declared.

He apologized on behalf of the Directory for the
imprisonment. He seemed mortified that Michael had been
held for so long, but blamed his story about being hidden in a
loft for three months by a Welsh farmer. 'Could you not have
fabricated something better than that?' he asked.

While they waited in Michael's room for the gaoler to draw
up papers, the colonel asked, 'What will you be doing with
yourself now?' and Michael understood that he was dis-
charged from the army.

236

But he answered, 'Going home, if there is any hope that General Hoche will be sending another expedition there.'

The colonel looked surprised. 'Have you not heard? Hoche is dead. So there's no hope at all. Not a thread of it, that's the chat.'

Michael went to the window. Through fog, the grey stones below were like sea swells. 'In that case,' he said, 'I'll be going to America.'

The colonel brought him to his own house in the neighbourhood of Brest. The place was packed with the colonel's close and distant Irish relations, and Michael shared a bed with nephew. Since this boy was the same size, Michael borrowed a jacket and trousers from him while he waited for his own clothes to be made. In the meantime the colonel got him a year's discharge pay and secured him a berth on a ship bound for Baltimore in three months' time.

'Before you sail off,' the colonel said, 'sure you've got to see Paris. I have a sister there that you can live with.'

Michael stared at him '*I* have a sister there,' he said.

'What?' the colonel cried. 'A sister? In Paris?'

'I clean forgot.'

In all those months in prison, all those hours spent scouring his mind for names of people in France who might help him, he hadn't once thought of Judy.

'*Forgot!*' the colonel cried.

'In the hospital I was mad.'

'What? Mad?'

'I was.' He thought that he was recovered because he hadn't raved or wept when he'd read about Corny and Etain. The stupefaction he was still feeling had felt then, in the first minutes after reading Dolan's letter, like deliverance.

There were people in every street. From his carriage window Paris was a line of people as long as his journey through it. Yet nobody seemed actual to him, even when the coach stopped and a soldier's roaring face lifted to his ... when a little girl threw a stone at the glass and the woman beside her, mistaking him for someone, raised a gloved hand like a raven.

Everyone seemed insubstantial, shapes that would turn into other shapes. He watched faces as he had watched a strange

237

landscape clarifying at the edge of the sea, when he'd been aware of the deceptions of vantage and light.

What was actual was the piece of paper folded in his hand.

Judy's address was on it, written out by Colonel Healy — from memory. It turned out that not only did the colonel know her, he knew her well enough to say wistfully, 'Ah, Judy Coogan.' Michael said what an astonishing coincidence, but the colonel protested that it wasn't a coincidence at all, that every Irishman in Paris knew Judy.

'Go to her this very day,' he cried, the prospect of a reunion between brother and sister sending him into raptures.

Michael did leave that day, but when he arrived, instead of going straight to her, he took a room in the L'Hôtel des Etrangers and wrote a note to send ahead to her house.

The note became a letter of five pages. Everything that had happened to him since and including Arthur's death he reported, because no part of his story struck him as credible without the other parts and because, believing that she was the last member of his family he would ever see, he wanted her to understand, or at least to have a record.

A full day passed before she sent her reply. "I will be at home this morning," she wrote in French. "Eleven o'clock."

He might easily have gone on foot: the map that Colonel Healy had drawn beneath the address showed that her place wasn't far; also the day was fine for December, and despite his limp he had no pain walking. But he hired a coach, feeling that she would expect him to. He felt that she must be devoted to what was fashionable, since she was famous, and judging from the formality of her note. No signature! But that was Judy.

A clear image of her — the memory of her face — should have risen to his mind as he thought this. When it didn't, he let the void be. The face of another might rise with any effort to recollect faces. He let his thoughts become languorous.

The coach had been forced to stop by a street dance. Soldiers were dancing with children. A fiddle was being played, and a drum. Michael leaned out of his window to see ahead, but something, not a voice or a glimpse but a sense, made him look back instead.

Before she turned he saw her profile. He saw yellow hair, a shaking of it — *her* gesture — that cut right through him.

238

'Etain!' he shouted. He opened the carriage door and jumped down. 'Etain!'

Faces swung round. Not hers. She moved away, into the thick of the dancers. She was so small . . . he would lose her among children.

He pushed a path towards her. A man who wouldn't budge he lifted by the shoulders and threw aside. She hurried away, the only one not to stop and look up at him, charging after her and bellowing her name.

And then she did stop. And turn.

She was nobody.

A man, maybe the man he had thrown, came up to him, windmilling his right arm, and punched him in the stomach. Michael swayed and was caught by the crowd. Behind him his driver was calling for payment, so he threaded back to the coach and tossed a gold coin. The driver gaped at it.

He had no idea where he was going. Once he was through the throng he mindlessly followed a soldier who seemed to have a pressing destination. It was a tavern, the name *"L'Epée Rouge"* painted above a picture of a sword through a bottle; Michael stood at the door for a minute, then went around the side of the building into a narrow empty alley. He sat in a doorway, covered his face with his hands and cried like a child. And when an old man asked him what was the matter, he answered like a child, *'Je suis perdu.'*

The old man led him all the way to Judy's house. He, too, was lame and favoured his left leg, and the two of them limped along like father and son, the old man indicating this and that — a statue, a building — with his stick: *'Voilà, voilà,'* but not expounding. In his left hand he clutched the paper with the address. *'Ah, la Rue de Cléry,'* he had said, reading it. *'Très élégante.'* Which is just how Colonel Healy had described both the street and Judy. He had also called Judy 'A great beauty', so that Michael had been sure that there was a mistake until the colonel, revealing an adulterer's knowledge of her, convinced him that there wasn't.

In spite of his bad leg, the old man moved quickly. 'Come along! Hurry up!' he called back to Michael in gravelly French, and Michael stopped and asked where they were going.

'To the Rue de Cléry!' the old man answered. To Judy's place, Michael remembered, then forgot in the next instant and yet kept walking. What stunned him wasn't that the woman hadn't been Etain but that he'd thought it was her, that he'd been so frenzied by the sight of a small woman with yellow hair he would have killed to reach her. How could Etain still be raging through him when she was Corny's now? His blood and breath were hers, and this trembling from head to foot as he walked, this was his body's awareness, his body resonating its need and protest.

'Here it is!' the old man said, pointing his stick across the street at the last house.

'There?' Michael said. 'That house?'

'That's number eighteen,' the old man said in a proud voice as if he'd lived there.

Michael looked up and down the street with no recollection of having just come down it. All the houses were three or four stories high, grand and quiet as cliffs. Number eighteen was built of rose-coloured brick, the same as Bridun Castle back home. It was so unlike Judy, so perfect and calm, that Michael couldn't believe she lived in it and asked again, 'That house?'

'As it says on this paper,' the old man answered, beginning to sound doubtful himself.

'Should I knock on the door?' Michael asked, looking at the old man's face that was like tree bark. He would do whatever this man told him to do.

'If you want it to open,' the old man answered.

Michael began to cross the street, and just then the door swung wide and a woman in a draped white gown stepped out.

'Are you coming in or not?' she called in Irish.

'My God, Judy,' Michael said. He started towards her. His bad foot slipped on the cobbles and he stumbled, falling to his knees.

'Jesus,' Judy said, walking over. 'Straight out of the bog.' The old man reached him first and helped him up. 'Who is *he*?' she asked, frowning.

Michael pulled his eyes from her to the old man, who was giving her an appraising look. 'He helped me. I couldn't find the way.'

'Pay him and get him out of the street,' she said.

240

Michael took a franc from his jacket pocket. 'Not that,' she said. She felt in his pocket and brought out two centimes. '*Voici*,' she said to the old man, snatching his left hand and slapping in the coins. '*Maintenant, allez-vous-en.*'

She pulled Michael across to her door and up her steps. He saw that she was wearing sandals. When she was on the top step and he one below, she turned and said, 'You have got to mind the company you keep over here.'

He gazed at her. Though he knew the face, no single feature was hers. Her eyes were Mary's, her full mouth was Rose's. The shape of her face and her high brow, these belonged to their mother. Even her hair wasn't hers — it was black and curly, cut short as a boy's.

'How you have altered,' he said, seeing her smooth arm now, her plump pale hand on the balustrade.

'I m told that I am the image of the goddess Diana,' she said, and there for a moment, as she challenged him, were her own narrow spearing eyes.

'So you are,' he said sincerely.

She lifted her chin in a reconciled, arrogant gesture that he remembered and that struck him as very dear because he saw it now as frailty. He would have embraced her but she turned and went through the door, telling him to shut it after him.

They entered a white hall that had pillars at the doorways. She said, 'I have servants galore but I was looking out for you.'

'Do you own this place?' he asked. Before them was a wide staircase with a statue of a naked woman on the first landing.

'I have it on a long lease, but I don't pay a sou. I leave that to my tenants.' She walked over to the stairs and looked up. 'Men come begging to rent my rooms. Noblemen, officers. They'll pay anything.' Her laugh was private and slighting. 'For the love of Jesus, are you coming?' she called, continuing down the hall.

'*Le petit salon*,' she announced as he followed her through double doors into a room all green and white — the walls papered in a pattern of exotic trees and emerald castellated towers, the chairs covered in a pattern of shamrocks. There were vases of roses everywhere, although they should have fallen by this time of year.

She lay back on a settee by the far wall, where light from a

241

window moulded one side of her body like God's arm resting there. It was all staggering to him, the sight of her, the furnishings ... the degree to which she had devised and achieved her queenly effects. It made him shy, especially with the expanse of the room between them now. He took a chair by the door.

'So why have you come?' she said. 'Is it money you're after?'

He forced a laugh.

'Is it?' She wasn't joking.

'Christ save us,' he said, 'what do you *think* I've come for? Are you not my sister?'

She looked at him as if that weren't established.

'Sure I've come to see how you're doing after all these years,' he said.

'You knew that before you came,' she said. 'I'll wager Colonel Healy had a story or two to tell.' She sat up, alert. 'Did you ever read the letter I wrote home? Did it arrive at all?'

'It did.'

'Did it cause a stir? Did you all marvel?'

He nodded.

She smiled and lay back. 'So then, you *knew* I was thriving. You knew before you came.' On the table next to her was one of the vases of roses. Extending a languid arm she drew out a flower and with her eyes closed inhaled the scent.

It was her doing that — she who hated flowers, who had tormented their sister for her bouquets and rapture (did she imagine *he* forgot?) — it was the lie, the parody of all the flowers, that suddenly enraged him past fury to a dull calmness he had felt only once before. He stood, took a step, knocking over a table. Something smashed on the floor.

'Ach, you dolt!' she said. She came to her feet.

'Rose is dead,' he said, his voice sounding both loud and distant in his own ears. 'Do *you* know that? Rose drowned herself. And Neal, he's dead. Murdered. And maybe it will interest you to know that our father is dead. Our father walked into a field and lay down and there he died because his son was shot before his living eyes.'

What a quiet room it was. There was no noise of servants, no street noises. She stood facing the window. She was so still and straight standing there, while he trembled like a receding storm. He had meant to tell her in a chosen moment.

'Forgive me,' he said.

She didn't move.

It was a vase that had smashed. After righting the table he picked up the strewn flowers and green glass, putting them in a corner, out of the way. Then he fell into a chair.

Our father walked into a field and lay down and there he died.

Once, when Michael was eleven or twelve years old and they were going to mass, the family together, their father cuffed him in front of other people and said that a thieving son was to the heart what wind was to the candle. What Michael had stolen was some tobacco from the dresser, and it occurred to him now that Rose must have told their father about it because she was the one (Michael could see her there on that path, in her red petticoat with the flower-shaped patch, carrying her shoes and stockings to keep them clean) their father was walking with when all at once he strode back to Michael and hit him. Even though Michael stole the tobacco for Neal, at his urging, he kept silent and waited for Neal to speak up. But his brother swung his shoulders and walked ahead, saying nothing.

Neal, Rose and their father. All dead seven years later.

But how was it that he couldn't feel they were gone entirely? How did you ever feel that about a sister who had your mother's eyes and a brother who you'd slept beside most of your life and who was the image of your father and your father's father, and back and back through all those shadowy reassuring lives you were bound to, back to the very first father?

Judy turned around. She wasn't crying and hadn't been. 'I suppose you'll be wanting to bide here 'til your boat sails,' she said. 'Lucky for yourself I happen to have a room you can rent. Ten *louis d'or* a month, payment in advance.'

The room was at the top of the house. It was small immaculate and outlandish. Like Judy. The upholstery, the wallpaper, the canopied *papier-mâché* bed, the draperies and carpet were in a pattern of deep red, so that walking into the room he felt as though he were entering a heart.

It was good for him, the enfolding heat of red surroundings, which could also be the opposite — an insistent materiality, nudging him to life.

He would have slept to death.

Etain. His madness for her exhausted him. He felt like a consumptive. His brutal longing for the past half year amazed him for all the vigour it had involved. It struck him now as the more healthful state. Now nothing aroused him.

Except for the sight of a woman resembling her, and then he must see the woman's face. At these times what drove him wasn't his own need but a beckoning, as if Etain were calling him in a despairing, waning voice. He saw her in the most unlikely women. Why did he? Why did he expect to see her at all? He wondered if she was dead, if it was her spirit, hovering before his eyes, that was blinding him. Sometimes, sooner than think of her married, he wished her dead.

The first night at Judy's, hearing from a tenant about a man who would be returning to Belfast in a week's time and who would carry anyone's letter, he wrote to Master Dolan to tell him of his release. He asked the master to present Etain with this message: 'Forgive me. God keep you.' At the end of the letter he wrote out Judy's street and number, he even gave directions to the place — he had no idea why.

The second night, he went to the Grand Opera. He went with Judy and her friends, who talked and laughed throughout the performance, but more distracting was the woman Judy ordered him to sit beside, an Irish officer's wife with large moist hands that grasped and stroked and kneaded his hand in a dedicated way. Afterwards at dinner the woman presented him to somebody as 'my current scandal'. When he told her he would go to his bed alone, she threw a fried carp at him.

Judy was delighted. She pronounced him a charmer, a heartbreaker. She invited him to dinners, luncheons, to the ballet, and he went thinking he had to because he was her brother and a visitor.

'Meet the hero of Tyrone!' she introduced him to people, then made him tell how he had killed Arthur. She bragged that he was Ireland's finest scholar. She bid women to rub his head. 'Have you ever felt hair so silky and thick as that?' she asked.

He had everyone's attention. But he could scarcely bring himself to finish sentences.

'Will there be a rising?' all the Irish asked, and he had no answer. Talking about Ireland made him feel low and tired past caring — he yawned in people's faces. After several weeks Judy let him be.

He read. She had a library that nobody, certainly not her, used. He made himself walk. Every afternoon he went to the Louvre. He walked past Notre Dame one day, past the Tuileries another, past the Pantheon and the Sorbonne. He hoped to be inspired and if not, never again to be inspired. Some days, in a stupor of weariness, he would think, "I have no feeling left in me, not even for her." A day or two later he would see a woman walking away from him, a profile in a carriage window, or only a hand, and he would be running to see more of her. It was as though he knew Etain was somewhere near but lost.

He was in the Louvre, gazing at Le Brun's *Magdalen* — he was, just then, longing neither for narcosis nor inspiration but for simple wholeheartedness, to be good and brave as the lamb of God — when a fire seemed to consume him, flaring up from his feet. That was how quickly the fever came.

The next instant he was drenched with sweat. He felt drunk. He reeled outside into icy rain and hailed a carriage. By the time he reached Judy's place he was only half-conscious, and another passenger and the driver had to bring him to her door.

In his moments of wakefulness, all his senses were poignant. More than hours passed between these moments — days passed, he knew by the change in the odour and density of the air, by how, each time he looked, there seemed to be as much as a season's difference in the line of light where the draperies met.

There was candlelight and no light. A calloused hand was on his forehead, and sometimes a smooth hand was there.

An old French woman attended him. She had pity and love in her voice. Whispering, she told him not to worry, she was with him. To calm him she said that she was Etain — *'Je suis Etain. Je suis ici. Je t'aime.'* — which didn't fool him but sent him into a sleep he would have died in. Her tired kind whispers seemed to be bidding him to die.

But always another voice pulled him back. Judy's voice,

reaching like claws into that place of light.

'Michael,' she said sharply, over and over, and she would even shake and slap him. 'You give me the puke,' she said. 'Flat on your back over a bit of a fever. Ach, dirty hen-hearted spalpeen. Wasn't it myself that ever said so? Open your eyes! Open them or I'll thrash you 'til you're black and blue!'

So he opened them. And she would look at him hard, then order the old woman to feed or wash him.

When the fever broke, after ten days, both the old woman and Judy were at his bedside. Judy was wearing street clothes and fixing her hat on with long pins. The old woman, praising God, was wiping his skin all over with a cold cloth.

'Jesus, look at yourself,' Judy said to him. 'White as a slug.'

He closed his eyes. He felt the cloth as unmerciful life reclaiming his body. He wondered how long he would live. How many years did he have left to live without harbouring the thought he'd had before: that there was always death. How long without Etain?

He had come to Judy's empty-handed. He left with a valise containing five of her books — 'Help yourself,' she'd said, as if the library were her bane — and the clothes he'd had made in Brest, which were too large for him since his illness.

When he was ready to go, a servant told him that Judy would see him in the *petit salon*. As on the morning he'd arrived she was reclining on the settee, in the same attitude and wearing the same white dress. This was how she intended for him to remember her: idle and elegant.

'One more Paddy off to the the new world,' she said.

'Baltimore,' he said, smiling.

She presented him with her profile: high forehead, straight nose, fearless jaw. She turned her face away and held it in the light as if to give him another aspect for his later wonder and self-reproach — the lovely profile of the sister who was loved the least.

She said, 'I was thinking I would lower your rental if you want to stay.'

'No,' he said. 'I want to go. All the events of this past year seem like a sign to go.'

He no longer felt as though he were running away. Having

survived his fever, having heeded her summons back to life, it now occurred to him that he must live with some trust in what was ahead. Since he didn't want to die he felt obliged to be resolute. Through the green valley I walked, to its end, to the keening, to the day of the dazzling light. That part of Tyrrell the Fairy Man's verse was in his mind all the time now, like a paean. Also something else Tyrrell had said: Cleave to what you love. As if there were any help for it. Ireland and Etain — *they* cleaved to *him* ... inextricable, graven.

'What class of name is Baltimore anyhow?' Judy said scornfully.

He bent to embrace her.

'No,' she said, pushing him away. 'Don't start now what we never did.'

The *York* was meant to sail from le Havre de Notre Dame de Grâce in six days' time, but when he got to the town he learned that the ship was delayed in Brest and not expected for another fortnight.

He took a room in a lodging house and read *The Vindication of the Rights of Women*, one of the books he'd brought to read at sea. Upon finishing it he was driven to write a letter to Judy. *"You are the most valorous person, man or woman, that I have known in my life,"* he wrote.

He walked up and down the gloomy town, still looking for Etain, even here. At the shore he called to her. He had stopped caring that she was another's; until his last day on earth he would crave her, he accepted this and he left it to fate whether the craving would ravage or guide him. But what deliverance, in any case, to shout her name. What sadness.

What sadness to leave. He hadn't anticipated it. As the *York* came into harbour, a man said, 'Look how dark her sails are — there's a ship that's seen long service,' and Michael thought, "If I should die on board, who will tell them back home?" They didn't even know that he was leaving France. He hadn't said, out of fear. In France, Morrery was powerless, but he might not be in America, despite all the miles.

He went to a tavern. While the ship unloaded its cargo he drank. He met a man who made him laugh, and he and the man drank and laughed all day and into the night.

When he woke the next day the sun was high. Running to the docks he could see the *York* out in the harbour and yet her sails were furled so she must be anchored.

'Is everyone on board that ship?' he asked a sailor on the quay. He surprised himself by hoping that everyone was, that it was too late.

'No parlez,' the sailor answered.

An American, Michael realized. He asked the question in English.

Everyone *had* been on board, the sailor said, but then the captain forgot something in town, and the sailor had rowed him back to shore.

Michael showed his papers. 'Then I can still get out to her,' he said.

The sailor nodded. 'You are lucky, you are,' he said.

Michael sat in the stern of the ship's boat, the sailor sat in the centre, the captain in the bow. As the sailor rowed them out of the dock, a man carrying a monkey came on to the pier. The man lifted the monkey, which was dressed in a purple turban and pantaloons, on top of a pyramid of barrels, and the monkey proceeded to juggle two red balls. A crowd immediately gathered around. The captain, also wanting to watch, ordered the sailor to stop rowing.

Simultaneously, a light rain began to fall, although overhead the sun shone, so that a rainbow appeared, beginning at one end of the town and ending at the other, and then a low ringing of bells started from some church, or maybe all the brilliance of the sun that was gathered below the rainbow's arc and above the sorrowful streets and roofs of the town broke the air in a thunder of chiming. A small white-haired boy walked to the end of the quay and held up both arms as if inviting them out of the ship's boat to behold the wonder.

Now the monkey was doing a frantic dance that featured somersaults. His keeper played a fife. The captain and the sailor laughed, the sailor clapping to the rhythm of the music, as the people on the quay were doing. The small boy ran back to the crowd, into it and out the other side, down to the shore, and then he was gone behind a carriage that had just drawn up and stopped on the road.

248

The carriage door opened. A woman stepped out. A small woman. She had a blue petticoat on, and a red plaid shawl covered her hair. She lifted her face to look around. She was wearing spectacles.

Michael stood.

'Easy there,' the sailor said.

The woman walked quickly over to a man who was mending nets. Michael knew that walk. The woman pointed at the ship, and in lifting her arm, her shawl slipped partway off her head.

'Etain!' Michael's shout was so violent that the monkey stopped its dance. The music stopped.

The woman looked in the direction of the boat. Her face seemed to magnify and shine with a diamond, dream-like clarity.

It was her, he was sure of it. In spectacles. He had forgotten that she wore them. He couldn't be imagining what he had forgotten. He shouted, 'Etain! Etain!'

The woman craned her neck. She began hurrying down the pier to where all the people were turned to watch her approach. For a moment she was hidden by them.

Michael roared at the sailor, 'Take me back!'

The sailor looked at the captain. The captain stood, tipping the boat. 'Is that girl a passenger?' he asked.

But Michael was calling to her again. He would swim back. He threw off his hat and began to remove his boots. The woman passed through the crowd and ran to the end of the quay. Her shawl was down around her shoulders. With his free hand he waved at her.

The fife started to play again. Michael jumped on to his seat and looked at her there on the end of the quay, shining and discrete as an angel. The sun beat down. In a long reach of his body he dived over the side of the boat, hearing the fife, the people clapping, a gull cry and then his own name cried before he was submerged.

BARBARA GOWDY is the daughter of an Irishman and the wife of a Welshman. A resident of Toronto, she was Managing Editor of Lester & Orpen Dennys, Publishers, before becoming a full-time writer and reviewer. In 1982 her collection *The Rabbit & the Hare* was published in England, Canada and the United States, and her short story, 'Mare Serenitatis', was selected to appear in the *North American Review's* anniversary issue.

It was while travelling in Britain that she decided to write *Through the Green Valley*. She spent the summer of 1983 doing research in Cardiff and in Pembrokeshire, Wales, and the following year went on to Ireland, to Dublin and County Tyrone.

What her experience confirmed for her, and what is at the core of her novel, is that the story of a country is in its people, together but also individually, that the heart of a place may be contained within a single life.

You have been reading a novel published by Piatkus Books. We hope you have enjoyed it and that you would like to read more of our titles. Please ask for them in your local library or bookshop.

If you would like to be put on our mailing list to receive details of new publications, please send a large stamped addressed envelope (UK only) to:

Piatkus Books, 5 Windmill Street
London W1P 1HF

PIATKUS

The sign of a good book